our ride to forever

JULIE OLIVIA

Author's Note

Our Ride To Forever is the third book in the *Honeywood Fun Park* Series. This book is a standalone and does not need to be read with the series. However, there will be spoilers for previous books.

Please be advised that this book is an **open-door** romance, meaning there is **on-page** sexual content. Mature readers only.

Also, while this rom-com is 95% exciting, heart-warming theme park moments, there is also about 5% angst, including an on-page anxiety attack. Be kind to your heart when you read, friends.

To my husband.
Thank you for being my everyday friend.

Playlist

"Can I Call You Tonight?" - Dayglow
"Gimme! Gimme! Gimme!" - ABBA
"Electric Love" - BØRNS
"Dreams" - Fleetwood Mac
"Memories" - Conan Gray
"Call My Name - Acoustic" - I'm With Her
"Lover" - Taylor Swift
"i'm yours" - Isabel LaRosa
"Halley's Comet" - Billie Eilish
"Nothing" - Bruno Major

Honeywood
FUN PARK

1. The Bee-fast Stop
2. The Beesting
3. Bumblebee Greenhouse
4. Bumblebee's Flight
5. Buzzard of Death
6. Canoodler
7. The Grizzly
8. Little Pecker's Joyride
9. The Romping Meadow
10. Honey Pleasure Stage
11. Security Office
12. Main Office
13. The Great Forest Journey

1

Theo

I t must be a mistake that DO NOT CALL is calling me. Nobody outside of my circle of close friends calls me. Not even my sister. And especially not the only person in my phone who is listed as a command.

DO. NOT. CALL.

First, middle, and last name.

Warning one, two, and three.

Don't. You. Dare.

But the sinking feeling in my stomach—something that must be nothing more than the alcohol seeping through my system—instead asks, *But what if he needs you?*

Laughable. Totally laughable. *Snort alcohol-spiked honey iced tea out of my nose* laughable.

I tuck my phone closer to my waist as I watch DO NOT CALL get sent to voice mail and disappear. But the lingering weight of it—causing the tug in the back of my gut, the racing in my chest—does not.

I glance up from my phone to see Ruby smiling over at me.

"Theo," she says, eyeing my phone. She probably saw

who called, but true to form, quiet Ruby says nothing about it. "Please tell Bennett roses are a bad idea."

Our best friend, Bennett, leans against the opposite side of the roped-off queue line with his hands in his pockets, looking down at Ruby with a smile.

"They are, aren't they?" she asks.

I put my phone in my pocket. Thankfully, only Ruby noticed the call, so I shake it from my mind. I smile and laugh.

"Roses, Bennett?" I ask, sipping from my Styrofoam cup. "Really?"

Simple conversation. I can do this. I am the queen of this.

In fact, I am determined to have a fun, perfect night at Honeywood Fun Park surrounded by my favorite, most perfect people in the world.

The fabulous flashing lights of the roller coasters as they soar down their tracks through the pitch-black sky are perfect. The warm blanket of a humid summer night is perfect. The sweet bite of bottomless honey iced tea—with some additional fun juice added for good measure—is perfect. It is close to midnight, and I'm nowhere near close to having an *imperfect* night.

My yoga side business had its most profitable month so far—that was also perfect—and we're celebrating under a starry evening at Honeywood's Employee Night.

Except my mind snags on my phone once more as it buzzes in my pocket.

I wonder if DO NOT CALL left a voice mail.

"Theo, do you have some more ... y'know?" My other friend, Quinn, raises her eyebrows with a smile after tugging off her cup lid.

Yes. Perfect. More alcohol will shake him from my mind.

"Absolutely, I do," I say, pulling out the purple floral flask out of my pocket and emptying some into her cup.

"Y'all. Come on," Lorelei says, pulling her eyebrows in.

"Just because you don't like fun," Quinn says with a laugh, "doesn't mean we don't."

Lorelei, one of our closest friends and the general manager in training at Honeywood Fun Park, doesn't want us drinking at the park. And since we're in line at said park with her and considering that I'm Honeywood's Rides supervisor, Quinn is the stage manager, and even Bennett is the head of maintenance, we should probably be a better example of professionalism. But instead, I drop a wee bit more into my cup.

Lorelei snorts in disapproval.

Oops.

I pocket the flask, and it hits the dormant phone next to it. My thoughts reel.

DO NOT CALL called. He called.

I take a long slurp of my drink, the dregs of it dragging through the straw between the bits of ice.

Him. Him. Him.

"I don't see what the big deal is about roses," Bennett says.

"Too cliché," Ruby says with a scrunched nose.

"Well, do you have any better suggestions, Rubes?" he asks, leaning toward Ruby with a grin.

She crosses her arms and gives a sweetly defiant smile. At least, as defiant as she is capable of. Compared to Bennett's tattooed arms and long black hair, she looks like a tiny redheaded fairy, out to tame the big bad monster.

3

"I just don't think Jolene would appreciate them," she says.

"Why your fiancée put you in charge of flowers anyway baffles me," Quinn says.

Lorelei smiles. "Maybe she thinks he has good taste."

"Have you *seen* Bennett? He hasn't cut his hair since the 2000s."

"Hey!"

"I've seen Bennett," I say, reaching out as if to touch his hair. "And I quite like his beautiful locks. They're Viking vogue."

"Mountain man modern," Lorelei says.

"All the rage, rock and roll rebel."

"Nice one," Bennett says, giving Ruby a high five.

"But no roses," Ruby says with a pointed finger.

"Seriously," Quinn says, her arms crossed. "Don't."

Bennett sighs. "Then what?"

"Just get tulips," I say.

"Why tulips?"

I shrug. "If I were getting married, I'd want those."

The second the words leave my mouth, Bennett's head swivels to me.

"What?" I ask innocently, but I can't help the sly smile that tugs at my lips. The secret that flows between us.

It gets weirdly quiet among our little fivesome, so I pull in an obnoxious slurp from my drink like a kid at a movie theater. I make the awkward moment more awkward. It's my only defense mechanism.

"Yeah, do Theo a solid," Quinn says, tossing her finished drink in a nearby trash can. "She'll never walk down the aisle."

"Exactly," I say, lifting my chin with a laugh. The words

aren't meant to burn. And they don't. Because they're true. "Over my dead body will I be called *wife*."

Bennett scoffs, and the subject is dropped. And thankfully, he doesn't keep giving me that weird look.

The queue line nudges forward, and the five of us finally reach the roller coaster's loading station. The train pulls in, the last group of riders flows out, and the seats instantly fill. My friends file in the last two rows in their usual pairings—Lorelei and Quinn, best friends since high school; and Ruby and Bennett, best friends since … well, they were probably born connected somehow, then ripped apart with how much they share a brain.

I take a step back into the loading line right when they all look around and realize I'm the odd woman out.

"We could …"

"If we just …"

"I'm okay if we …"

I shake my head through their protests, laughing and waving my cup in the air. I try to ignore the tug in my chest.

"I've gotta finish my drink anyway," I say. "I'll catch the next one!"

I give a plastered-on smile as my friends disappear around the corner, their hands already sprang in the air, preparing for the lift hill ahead.

It's fine. It's all fine.

But my hand twitches over my phone in my pocket, like it's a siren song and I'm the lonely sailor.

What if DO NOT CALL needs me?

Just the thought has laughter bubbling up in my chest again.

Ridiculous. Of course he doesn't need *me.*

But before I can stop myself, before I can cement these perfectly rational thoughts in my head, I'm hopping over the queue line railing, tossing my half-full cup into the trash can, and taking the narrow dirt trail away from Bumblebee's Flight.

I find the small alley behind The Bee-fast Stop and pace with my phone clutched in my fist. I take a deep breath. And then I press DO NOT CALL's contact number.

I plug my other ear with my finger, trying to block out the sounds of roller coasters and laughter and excitement and everything that is the opposite of how I feel right now.

The ringing on the other side continues.

Breathe in three, breathe out three. In three, out three.

Maybe he won't pick up. Maybe he butt-dialed me. Maybe he already forgot he'd called me.

Why would DO NOT CALL ring me at midnight on a Friday night anyway? Doesn't he know I'm not anyone's emergency anything—not even for the hospital?

I am the friend who brings the party to the theme park. I am the friend who goes on various dates a couple of nights a week, never remembering their names, but providing hilarious stories to my relationship-involved friends. I'm the friend who, over coffee the next morning, gets you thinking, *Dang, I can't believe Theo convinced me to dance on the bar top!* I'm the one who reminds you it's okay to feel *alive* before you go back to—

The ringing stops. He's picked up.

It's quiet on the line. Just the sound of my own breaths echoing back to me before I finally exhale out a small, simple, "Hi."

And when he responds, it's exactly how it should sound. It's the same Southern drawl. It's the same low tone that used to whisper sweet nothings to me in the privacy of his home. It's the same beautiful voice of a man who is always smiling, an expression I can hear interwoven in the two words that follow.

"Hi, sweetheart," he says.

It's him. And he's exactly the same.

I could never mistake the sound of my husband's voice.

2
Theo

Seven Months Ago

I love a man who is unwilling to commit. I just didn't know Orson Mackenzie was a *never* kind of man. The fact that he is has me more rabid than I should be—practically foaming at the mouth at the idea of *him*.

Meghan told me through frustrated yoga poses that she tried to have a *define the relationship* conversation with Orson. And that man—the very same bar owner I expected to be waiting for some magical meet-cute with the perfect Southern lady—admitted he never wanted to get married.

Never.

Score.

Meghan said she was done with him. He wasn't worth the good lay. But a good lay without commitment is my particular brand of fun. I asked her if I could disrupt girl code just this once, and she laughed.

"Go for it," she said. "Nobody will break that man."

Good. I don't want to.

I watch him from across the bar, lit under the glow of The Honeycomb's hanging Edison lights.

Orson's baseball cap is turned backward, like it is every day, but somehow, it looks better tonight. His jaw has always been square, but now, I'm noticing the slight manly stubble. He's also always been short—an inch or so less than me, I imagine—but has he ever been this muscular and stocky? He looks like a man who could crack a watermelon with his thighs or biceps alone.

I would say I'm watching in a totally non-creepy way, but I might as well be behind a bush with binoculars.

As if Orson could hear my loud, horny thoughts, his head swivels to our table. I don't look away. Instead, I give him a slow smile. He returns it with a gorgeous, crooked grin of his own. The endearing look of a man who smiles all day long and likely doesn't mind it.

Intoxicating.

I know him as well as anyone knows their local bar owner. I know his smile, his laugh, his speech. I know that he volunteers at nearly every place in town, and I know that, if we need mass amounts of alcohol for any event, he's our guy. And finally, most importantly, I know what Meghan has told me, which is that he's a people pleaser—no, a pussy pleaser—in all the best ways. And I'm desperate to know if that's true.

He grabs the two beers our table ordered and walks over. I straighten my spine. Heck, I push my chest out for good measure.

If you got them, flaunt them, am I right?

"Orson, is the air-conditioning even on in here?" Quinn asks him.

She's across the table from me, looking heated with her blonde hair slightly disheveled even though the cool autumn air is wafting through the bar's propped-open door. Something is ruffling her feathers, and my money is on the fact that Lorelei's twin brother is in town. Not that she'd ever admit it.

Orson laughs.

Has his laugh always been this cute?

"What?" he asks. "Is the air-conditioning—whoa, hey!"

I take my chance, grabbing one of the beers from him. I think it's technically Bennett's order, but he took mine earlier, so it's fine. I need to get Orson's attention on me somehow.

"Claiming this one," I say. "Thaaank you."

Orson's eyes catch mine, a slow smile dancing on his face.

"Was it even yours?" he asks with a chuckle.

"You'll never know," I answer. And then, not breaking eye contact again, I run my tongue along the rim of my glass. "But I've already claimed it."

I made my tongue as sexy as possible. I practically tossed lingerie on the thing.

Orson stiffens on the spot, taking in a sharp inhale. I faintly see his cheeks start to burn red, making my own blood boil beneath the surface.

Bennett says something to Orson that I don't hear, but Orson's hazel eyes stay stuck on me the whole time. There's a beat or two of us just existing together, breathing in the same air, letting our thoughts drift across the table to each other like open doors.

He knows what I'm thinking.

I know he knows what I'm thinking.

He knows I know he knows what I'm thinking.

"Well, if y'all need anything else," Orson finally says,

not breaking eye contact with me, even as he addresses the table, "let me know."

Oh, I will.

He walks back behind the bar and settles his forearms on the counter. He continues to stare over at me. A smile tips at the edge of his lips, and I give him a smile right back.

When I glance at my friends to see if anyone's noticed our little stare-off, it's only Ruby who smiles back. That girl doesn't miss a thing.

Oh well.

It wouldn't be the first time I've flirted with Orson or even expressed interest. If one person knows I'm making a move, it's not a big deal.

Life is short. Work less. Take that once-in-a-lifetime trip. And, for goodness' sake, sleep with the tempting bar owner.

I say good-bye to my friends at the end of the night, making some excuse about catching up with the other local regulars, Mrs. Stanley or Frank or Bill—I don't even remember who I specifically said, nor do I care. I'm a woman on a mission.

I pop a squat at the bar and wait. Orson's attention is immediately split between Frank and me. I can tell by how his eyes dart over to me between words.

"How about baseball cards?" Frank asks.

Orson laughs. "Don't spend all your retirement in one place, young man."

"Bah!"

"Well, this week, it's cards; last week, it was horse races."

Orson's eyes swivel back over to me. I bite my bottom lip. I think I see him heave an exasperated sigh.

"Hold your money for a few more seconds," he tells Frank. "Don't set it on fire while I'm gone."

"A fireworks company," Frank says with a laugh. "Now, there's an idea!"

With a finger point toward Frank that feels both oddly threatening and yet gives me *yes, sir* energy all at once, Orson finally walks over. He raises his eyebrows with a knowing grin. I can see the spark of curiosity in him.

"Come here often?" he jokes.

I put both elbows on the counter, lean forward, and tilt my head to the side. I come here, at minimum, two times a week, and he knows that.

"You're funny," I say.

"No, I'm not," he responds with a laughing scoff. His eyes trail down to my shirt, then back up again. For a second, I think he's checking out my chest, so I grin in response—score for me—but instead, he says, "I like the new logo."

"Oh." I glance down at my shirt.

The in-town yoga studio I work at part-time, Yogi Bare, just rebranded. The back of the shirt lists our new classes from the past year. I hoped they would feature the more inclusive programs I'd added for our older clients, but I can't blame them for being overlooked. They're not the most popular classes.

"I mean, I didn't make the logo," I say with a laugh.

"You didn't?" he asks, turning to wipe down the counter, his head cocked to the side. "It's purple. Isn't that your favorite color or something?"

I narrow my eyes with a smile. "You know what my favorite color is?"

"I notice things," he says with a shrug, his lips pulled up in a grin. "Wouldn't be a good bar owner if I didn't."

"I bet you notice a lot of things," I say, returning to my mission.

Eye on the prize. Sleep with the bar owner. The mysterious one who also somehow knows your favorite color.

His eyes dart between mine before chuckling.

"You want something," he says. "So, out with it, Poulos."

I like how my last name sounds on his tongue. He's the only man, aside from my friends, who can pronounce it correctly. I've got Frank, who says *pow-lohs*, or even Mrs. Stanley, who insists it must be *poo-loose.*

Poo-lohse, Orson says.

Who knew a properly said surname would get me revved up?

"I want something?" I ask, batting my eyelashes. "Whatever do you mean?"

"Nah-ah-ah. I know that look."

"What look?"

"You're lookin' for trouble."

My smile gets bigger, and I feel my whole body flush.

I like the low timbre of Orson's Southern drawl. It tugs at the edge of each word like a hook dragging a fish out of water. Even though Orson is older than me by only six years, he feels like an old soul. I'm convinced it peeks through sometimes in the small bits of gray starting to form in his stubble or in the small lines at the edge of his eyes when he laughs.

"So what if I am?" I ask.

Of course I'm looking for trouble. I might as well be uncapping my feather-tipped pen and preparing to write *Dear diary, I did a bad thing* tomorrow. But what is life without a bit of trouble?

"You're just bored," he says.

"Can't I be bored to your advantage?"

"Don't you have work tomorrow?"

"I don't like to linger."

Ooh, that was a good one, even for me.

Orson lets out something between another barking laugh and a grunt.

"I don't exactly make a habit of *going home* with friends," he says.

"I wouldn't say we're *friends*. More like friends of friends or friendly acquaintances who may or may not want to have more fun than they already are."

"Theo ..." His tone sounds like a warning.

His apprehension makes sense. In a small town like Cedar Cliff, friend groups overlap too much, and ours is like a Venn diagram two steps away from a complete circle. His cousin, Emory, is my friend's boyfriend. His other long-term friend, Bennett, is also one of my best friends. We might as well be in an intertwined soap opera. But I've never been one for the dramatics, so I cut to the chase.

"I heard you don't like commitment," I say.

His chin tilts up, and he smiles. "Ah, there it is."

"What?" I ask with a laugh. "As a fellow non-committer, am I not capable of being curious?"

His smile curves into a beautiful grin. "I'm sure you're capable of a lot of things, sweetheart."

Sweetheart, with the faint *t* and the swing of the *ar.*

"Wouldn't you like to find out," I say. It's not a question. It's a fact.

Orson looks away, biting the inside of his cheek, as if my observation pained him. Then, he lets out an exhale before squinting one eye at me.

When I had just turned thirteen, I once had some boy

at youth camp in a puffy camping vest tell me I wasn't like other girls. He said this while handing me a burned CD of bands I didn't know as I roller-skated away from him in the church parking lot.

I then told him that statement was ridiculous.

I am very much like other girls. Heck, I am the combination of every person you've ever met. I enjoy whatever music is popular because I like background sound. I choose my next book from the best-selling charts because it's almost always guaranteed to be good. I enjoy wearing any and all makeup styles, simply because I like trying new things. I like this, that, and everything in between, as long as it's fun.

So, when Orson stares at me from across that bar top with heat in his eyes, lingering on my orange yoga pants that hug my yoga-made figure and looking like he might be two seconds away from caving in to my thinly veiled one-night-stand offer, I'm not flattered. It's not because I'm *not like other women*, which is insulting to zillions of women everywhere. No, it's because Orson Mackenzie likes people, and I am very much the person he's looking for tonight.

With one final hope, prayer, and saving grace, I lean in and say, "I'm really good at keeping secrets. We're both adults, aren't we?"

That makes him laugh, and that's when I know I have him.

"Fine," he says. "You want to play, I'll play."

I squirm in my seat and grin back at him.

"Perfect," I say. "And since I'm here anyway, I'll even help you close down the bar. Because that's what friendly acquaintances do, right?" I walk behind the counter to grab a broom leaning in the corner.

Orson lets out another one of those low laughs, shaking his head and placing his large palms on my shoulders. He walks me backward until I'm on the opposite side of the counter again. It's forceful, and it sends my heart rate skyrocketing.

"Don't push your luck," he says.

"I don't need luck."

He grins. "I know. And that's what makes you dangerous."

3

Theo

I've been to Orson's house what feels like a million times for our town's Halloween parties, Christmas parties, Super Bowls, and neighborhood cookouts. But it's never been just the two of us. It feels like walking up to an empty chapel on a weekday. Dissonant yet oddly intimate.

Orson holds his front door open for me after he keys in. I look around. His house is utilitarian. Almost nothing is on the main floor, except a couch, a decorative mirror, a couple of side tables, and one lone box of mini peanut butter cookie snacks on the kitchen counter. It seems Cedar Cliff's main party host keeps his place a clean slate for parties.

The lock clicks shut behind me, and the sound echoes through the house like a final symphonic note.

Bring it on.

I make my typical one-night-stand move of running a hand over my partner's forearm, snaking my fingers up to his shoulder. It's a classic move—a flawless move—but Orson catches my hand mid-stroke. He pulls my fingers up to his lips, and he kisses the tips of them.

"No," he says, shaking his head. "I don't think so."

Well, that's a bucket of cold water to the face.

Don't think so? Have I misread this whole night?

"What?" I ask with a laugh.

Orson grins and grabs my face with both his hands.

"I just like to make the first move, is all," he says.

And then, with his hands caressing my jaw, he pulls me forward and presses his lips against mine.

His kiss is soft and gentle but purposeful, moving in tandem with my lips in a rhythm that seems well practiced. He smells like the bitter hops from beer, mixed with some natural scent of wood. It only adds to his warmth.

Orson trails his hands away from my jaw, reaching down to hook them into the crook of my forearms. He walks toward me as I blindly stumble backward into his living room.

I always thought Orson was shorter than me, but now that we're toe to toe, lips to lips, I realize he might just be my exact height. Honestly, I've never kissed a guy the same height as me. I think I might like it. I don't have to get on my toes or lean my head back. We remain at the same level. Evenly matched. Connected.

Orson's kisses start to get confident. Everything about him does—the way he presses into me unabashedly, how he fists my hair, how he lets out a low groan that has me moaning in return. I reach to palm below his belt, but he grabs both of my wandering hands and pins them above my head.

Oh. Hi there, cowboy.

He gathers my wrists into one palm, moving his other hand down the back of my arm, ghosting fingers over my skin that raise goose bumps in their wake. He rubs a thumb over my cheek, tracing lines across my jaw and down to my chin, when he slows his kisses.

But I want more.

He has set me on fire, ablaze from the inside out.

Eventually, we're gathering our breath with our mouths paused an inch away from each other. His lashes are thick and more beautiful than I remember. His full lips part to reveal a glimpse of straight, smiling white teeth.

"What do you want from me, Theo?" he asks. No, he whispers it. Murmurs. Low and husky and gritty on the tongue. Heady.

I don't know how to answer that now. *More of your lips? More of your surprising roughness? More of you?*

"A good time," I finally answer.

He tongues the inside of his cheek and slowly nods. "Uh-huh, and?"

And? Did he not hear me moaning inside his mouth?

"That's it," I say.

"That's it?"

My whole body arches into his, and he lets out a low *hmm* from his throat. It almost seems indecisive. I get it. One bad relationship could turn the tides of our small town and make our interactions difficult. But I'm too stubborn for that, and his kisses are too good for me to forget them now.

His thumb runs over my bottom lip, pulling it down and letting it pop back up.

Holy—

"Orson," I say with a sigh, "it's just one night. We'll have fun and then go our separate—"

But before I can say anything else, he swoops down and tosses me over his shoulder.

Good Lord, he just lifted me like I was a feather pillow.

His hand hooks behind my knees as the other soothes over the backs of my thighs before slapping me on the bottom.

"Ouch!"

"You liked it."

I did, which is why I tease, "I don't know. Maybe you can remind—"

He smacks my ass again, and I can feel the tremor down between my now-slick thighs.

The upside-down living room grows smaller and smaller in my vision as he walks forward until we finally round the corner into his bedroom.

Orson tosses me down, and I land on the bed, bouncing once with the throw. He leans over me, kissing along my sides, my waist, and then down between my legs. He shoves my leggings down and shifts my thong to the side, and then the world suddenly slows. Time winds down like a record player being adjusted to a different speed, and goose bumps roll over my body at the change of pace.

Orson drags the tip of his tongue along my slit. It's leisurely, as if he's taking his time to enjoy it. But while he's enjoying his appetizer, my heart rate is ramping up to a million. One second ago, we were ripping clothes off, and now ... now? I look down and see his hazel eyes staring up into mine, the movement of his tongue rolling against me, the heat of his breath causing my head to fall back.

"Oh my God—"

Then, time speeds back up.

His tongue finds what it's looking for—the spot where I've previously painstakingly had to direct most men—and I melt into the mattress. My nerves spark as each lash of his tongue is deliberate and calculated. I remove his baseball cap, running my fingers over his shaved head, letting the hair bristle my palm as I pull him closer. He lets out a low growl, gripping my hips and steadying me in place.

My head is swimming. No, *drowning*. Falling into the

black abyss of pleasure. It might last an hour; it might last ten minutes or maybe even thirty seconds.

All time is lost to his whipping tongue and grunts of, "You taste so good, sweetheart."

But in no time, my stomach drops, my head feels empty, and my orgasm barrels through me like a careless bull in a china shop. The plates and bowls inside me are broken. I am a shattered woman.

I'm out of breath as Orson places kisses along my inner thigh, moving up my stomach before he joins me on the bed. My spread thighs straddle either side of his knees.

"I'd like you to ride me," he says, "if that's all right with you."

My head falls back onto the pillow with a laugh.

I'd do a handstand and moonwalk my way off a bridge if he asked me to.

"Oh, I didn't wear you out already, did I?" he teases, reaching forward to run a thumb under my shirt and bra before tweaking my nipple, sending a shock through me right down between my already-aching thighs.

"You wish," is all I get out through my obviously tired voice. But I refuse to stop now. If I'm only having one night with him—and his wonderful tongue—I want to experience all that I can.

He grins, grabs a wrapper from the bedside table, and flips to lie down on his back. He tugs down his pants, and his full length pops out of his boxer briefs, bobbing in the air.

"Christ, Orson," I breathe out because, *Christ, Orson.* "I didn't know horses walked on two legs."

He laughs, but the cocky—*very* cocky—man says nothing as he rolls the condom over himself. I straddle his hips, hovering over him for a moment.

21

"Do you carry a permit for this thing?"

Orson chuckles while stroking a line down the side of my waist.

"You can take it," he says.

I almost cross my chest in prayer, but it almost—no, very much so—seems sacrilegious in the current moment, so I don't. Instead, I slowly lower myself down while his hands guide me every single inch. I pull up, then back down. Up, down. And when our hips finally meet, when I've taken all of him inside me, he lets out a low groan. I think I might need to save that sound for a rainy day.

His knees rise up, and he starts to thrust into me, soft, slow, sweet ... but, God, I don't want any of that. I'm practically itching for him. I heavily grind down, and as if taking my cue, he grips my hips and lets loose.

He goes for it. It's obscene. It hurts. It feels good. Great. Then wonderful.

With each subsequent slap of our skin hitting together, I let out an embarrassing moan akin to either a cat in heat or a coyote that's desperate for the moon. Heck, maybe he is my moon, and I am the waves bending to his pull.

"You take me so good, sweetheart," and, "That's my girl," are his repeated mantras as we move faster and faster and my body heats more and more and his breaths get heavier and heavier.

It dawns on me, right as our eyes meet, as I'm still riding this beautiful, surprising man, that this will not be the last time I sleep with Orson Mackenzie.

That thought remains blissfully in my mind right until he suddenly stops, blinks up at me, and mutters, "I don't feel so good, Theo."

4

Orson

I count the ceiling tiles above me to pass the time. It's quiet in the patient room. Too quiet.

After a few minutes in silence, Judy's sleep-deprived eyes finally find mine over her clipboard. She's lacking her usual white coat and instead bundled in a hoodie and pajama pants.

"So, you thought two in the morning was the best time to ring me up?"

I smile. "Not my idea, I promise."

I lean to the side, the paper beneath me crinkling as I do, and peer out into Judy's waiting room.

Theo Poulos sits with her legs pretzeled in her chair. My Atlanta Braves sweatshirt hangs loosely on her figure, and her yoga pants that were once on my floor are now back on her hips. She strokes her ring-filled fingers over the leafy plant in the corner of the white-walled room. She tucks a strand of her curly black hair behind her ear. When she looks over and our eyes meet, she gives a grinning wave.

Thirty minutes ago, I was close to having the best orgasm of my life, breathing in Theo's almond and oat scent, my mind swimming with the hottest image that I'd thought was only reserved for porn. And now, I'm here instead, in a cold doctor's office that smells vaguely like lemon-scented cleaner.

Judy clears her throat. "Can I ask you something?"

I look back at my friend as she places my chart on the counter beside her. I raise my eyebrows and lean back into our conversation, leaving the thought of Theo's smooth skin in the back of my mind.

"It's gonna be judgy, isn't it?" I ask with a grin.

"You're in excellent shape, theoretically," Judy says, ignoring me.

She folds her hands in her lap. I call it her doctor pose.

"You hittin' on me, Judy?"

"I know you work out," she continues. "But your blood pressure is too high. And thirty-five is when people start to feel their age catch up to them."

"Well, now, you're just being mean."

"I'm gonna prescribe you something, okay?" she says, scribbling on a pad underneath her stack of papers. "And I'll also give you some referrals for psychiatrists."

I hold my hands up and laugh. "Psychiatrists? Hey, come on ..."

"You overwork yourself at that bar," she says with raised eyebrows. "Then, this happens."

"What happens?"

"An anxiety attack."

I bark out a laugh. "That is not what happened."

She blinks at me like *I'm* the delusional one in this scenario.

"You get chest pains, right?"

I shrug. "Sometimes."

More like *all the time*.

But I'm accustomed to the chest pains. Judy is right; I'm thirty-five, I own a bar, and I have a constant low-level stress coursing through my veins. But it's never anything to worry about. And it's definitely not *anxiety*. It's small-business ownership. The worst diagnosis of all.

"And this time, you felt like you couldn't breathe?" she asks.

I laugh. Technically, yes. But I blame my lack of breath on the sight of a gorgeous woman bouncing on top of me, making cat noises. My head went foggy, and I knew if I felt her tighten around me one more time, I might pass out. And not in the fun way.

I felt better once she stopped riding me like a cowgirl high on too many drugs to count. But she was already on the phone with our only in-town cardiologist before I could pull my slowly deflating cock out of her.

"What's your point?" I ask.

"Cool it," Judy says. "Slow down. Stop working so much. Your daddy had issues with overextending himself, and I'm not gonna sit here and let you have them too."

True. It's why he and Mama moved down to Florida for their early retirement and a slower life. It worked for him. But I can't imagine a slower life. I love that bar more than anything in the world. I was raised in its kitchen, molded by its music, and forged into a halfway decent businessman under its hanging lights. People depend on The Honeycomb to stay around. It's a safe haven, and I can't take that away from Cedar Cliff.

"Plus," Judy continues, tilting her head toward the waiting room, "don't you wanna live for her?"

I look back to Theo, who is now standing and pacing in the waiting room, looking up at the ceiling, her mouth slowly moving, as if talking to herself. I smile, then quickly let it fall. Because I know I made a huge mistake tonight.

I let myself indulge.

Theo isn't a stranger to me. I've known her since she moved to Cedar Cliff at the age of twenty-two. I remember the way she hopped into my bar with a bounce in her step and a mouth that wouldn't stop talking. I watched in awe as she found best friends who absorbed her into their long-standing group within only one month. She's electricity personified, unable to sit still, unable to not get involved, unable to be anything but her God-given self.

I notice her more than others. And, sure, I could say it's because her group of friends are regulars or that Cedar Cliff is small enough to know everyone and their grandma too. But she also has a magnetism about her. I see her clear as day. She demands it.

I shouldn't have agreed to sleep with her. I don't want a committed relationship. I'm married to my bar, and I'm happy with that. But it's hard to deny Theo's magnetic pull. I'm not capable of saying *no*, especially not to someone I've admired from afar for this long.

I'm an adult. I can handle a one-night stand with my silly little small-town crush. Not a huge deal. It's fine.

"She's just a one-night thing," I murmur to Judy.

"I know," Judy snaps. Then, she levels me with a glare.

Oh. Should have seen this coming.

"What happened to dating Meghan?" she asks, reaching out with her clipboard to thwack me on the knee. "She's my *friend*, and she really liked you."

I toss my hands up in the air. "Hey! I had reasons!"

"Like?"

"She wanted to make it official," I say. "And I didn't. It didn't seem fair to keep stringing her along."

26

"Did you like her?"

"Yeah, she was nice."

Judy sighs. "Then, why would it matter if she wanted more?"

"I'm not looking for forever," I say with a shrug. And it's true. Much to my dad's dismay, Grandma Mackenzie's heirloom ring will rest in peace with her lovely soul. "I don't have time. I've got a bar to run."

"A bar cannot love you back."

"Speaking of more," I say, changing the subject when I realize the impossibility of explaining how The Honeycomb is all the *more* I'll ever need. "How'd your date with Landon go?"

She narrows her eyes. "Never set me up with someone again."

"Oh no, what happened?"

Judy swivels her chair to a pad of paper and whips her pen across it.

"He called me *champ* at the end of it," she murmurs.

I bark out a laugh. "Please tell me you're joking."

Judy lets out a low snarl that tells me she's definitely *not* joking and rips the top sheet from the pad.

"Stop playing town matchmaker," she says, waving it to me. "Stop working so much. Think about your own happiness for once and call one of the doctors on this list. Literally any of them."

I take the sheet of paper, glance over the names, and sigh. "I'll be fine."

"I know you'll be fine," she says. "You have a good heart. The best one. So, keep it safe, okay?"

"I'll think about it," I say with a grin. Then, I twist my baseball hat forward and tip it as I hop off the counter. "Ma'am."

I pull open the door and let it shut behind me. The sound echoes through the empty waiting room. Theo's head yanks over to me. Her eyebrows tilt in.

"Everything okay?" she asks.

I chuckle. Her concern is adorable.

"We're all good," I say. "And, hey, sorry if this doesn't count as part of your *good time*."

She laughs. "I don't know what you mean. I'm having a *blast*. Did you know Judy has over fifty ceiling tiles in her waiting room?"

I can't stop the slow grin spreading on my face. "Huh. I only counted up to twenty-five in my room."

"I win."

"Yeah, you win."

Suddenly, she's tossing something at me. I catch it midair, the bag crinkling in my palm.

"Got these for you."

I look down. It's my favorite mini peanut butter cookies. I look over at the vending machine, then back to her.

"How did you know I liked these?"

She smiles and winks. "I notice things too. I figured you needed a pick-me-up."

"I did," I say with a smile. "I do."

I place my hand on the small of her back, walking us out of the building. It's still pitch-black outside. The parking lot is lit by the glow of a lone streetlamp, and the only cars consist of my black Jeep and Judy's sedan.

"What's that?" Theo asks, tapping on the sheet of paper in my hand.

"Oh, just some names," I say. "Suggestions for psychiatrists."

"Psychiatrists?" she asks, taking it from me.

"Judy thinks I should see someone. I don't know."

"You should call."

She says it so suddenly that my head jerks back.

I laugh. "What?"

She rolls her eyes and lets out an exaggerated sigh, which only makes me laugh more.

"Well, I'm not sleeping with you if you're gonna *die* before orgasming."

"I won't die. But if I did, wouldn't it be a glorious death?"

She nudges my side. "This isn't something to mess around with."

"Yeah, I know. *You're* something to mess around with, and I much prefer that."

She bites her lip with a smile and halts in place. I like the way I can see her reddening cheeks in the moonlight. I open her passenger door, and she slides in. I lean through the open window.

"Thank you," I say. "For calling her."

"I don't need a dead man on my record."

I laugh. "All jokes aside. Seriously, Theo. Thanks."

A slow smile spreads over her face.

"Don't worry about it," she says, buckling her seat belt. "Just lookin' out for you."

For a second or two, we exist in each other's company. It's a weird sort of moment that somehow doesn't feel weird at all. I don't want her to leave. I don't want this to be the end. And I decide in that moment that it can't be.

"So," I say, leaning closer, "I know we said only one night ..."

"We did say that," she says. "And I *definitely* need to get home."

I smile. Because even though her words say one thing, I

can tell by the tone of her voice and the glint in her green eyes that she's playing along with my coy approach.

Theo isn't going anywhere else but back to my house.

"Oh, we should definitely get you home," I continue. "But ..."

"But?" She tilts her head to the side in mock innocence.

"Well, here's another option," I say.

"I'm listening."

"Your apartment isn't going anywhere."

"True."

"And my bed is very lonely and very big."

"*Very* big," she echoes with a grin.

I mirror her smile, leaning in and brushing my lips against her ear. I can feel the shiver roll over her body.

"So, what if ..." I whisper. "Well, what if I'm not exactly done with you yet?"

Theo's face flushes a deeper red.

"Mr. Mackenzie, my word," she says, her hand reaching up to her chest, as if gripping invisible pearls. She bats her eyes. It's all for show. Because I now know Theo is far from a blushing bride.

"Miss Poulos, do you mind if I steal you for just a few more hours?"

She smiles. "I thought you'd never ask."

5

Theo

I am, inevitably, late for work the next day.

And the day after that. And the week after that.

I spend eight solid days sneaking over to Orson's house, all without notice from our friends. Eight days of getting railed on every surface in The Honeycomb's back rooms. Eight days of calling Orson's name in every moaning noise I can muster, like some creature of the undead. But now, my sleepy zombie butt rushes down the midway toward the Honeywood Fun Park employee offices.

The faint sounds of preopening music filter through the sound system. My sneakers squeak on the blacktop. It's a sunny, beautiful autumn day in our theme park, and the jingle of my backpack's key chains almost overpower the roar of the roller coasters.

"Excuse me! Pardon me! Hey! Move it or lose it!" I bump past a few of the teenage employees, who give their supervisor—me—a small wave. And what a Rides supervisor I am. A beacon of professionalism.

I burst through the office saloon doors and place my

finger on the time clock system—removing, inserting, removing. It keeps blinking red.

"Come on, come on, come on."

Nobody would notice if I was late. Nobody, except …

"Theo."

Crap.

"Freddy," I respond through heaving breaths. I wouldn't normally advise nicknames for your park's general manager, but I've been working here long enough that he knows it holds no disrespect.

When the time clock finally beeps green, I twist on the spot and find Fred with his hands on his hips. His bright yellow Honeywood polo stretches over his stomach in an almost-blinding way. It looks like the already-risen sun that I should have been at the park to see firsthand. And beside him is one of my best friends, Lorelei, in her role as the new general manager in training.

"You're late," Fred says.

I hold up a finger. "I'm *fashionably* late."

His eyes dart down to my untucked staff shirt, which I start to shove into my shorts.

"Okay, so, sort of fashionable."

Lorelei stifles a laugh. What I love about Lorelei is that she takes things seriously, but only up to a point. A couple of months ago, that was proven when she had a secret relationship with the roller coaster engineer she was suing. Love is love. Plus, Emory is pretty cool—once you look past his grumpy exterior.

"You missed the supervisor meeting again," she says.

"I know; I know," I say. I look pathetic, but my big, worried eyes aimed at Fred grant me a small smile under that mustache of his.

Whew.

I love Fred as much as I would an uncle or that one family friend who always gives the best birthday gifts. And, thankfully, he feels the same way about all of us Honeywood longtimers.

"What am I supposed to do with you?" he says with a sigh.

"Uh, promotion?" I ask. "A raise? Ooh, free admission for life?"

"What we need is a role where all you do is talk," Lorelei says, pulling me into a *good morning* hug.

She's a hugger, and so am I. It works out.

"Oh, that sounds nice." I dig in my pocket to pull out my name tag and clip it to my shirt.

"I'll let this one slide," Fred says. "But only because I assume it's going well?"

Flashes of Orson's mouth roaming over my neck pass before my eyes. My face heats.

"What?" I ask.

"Yoga," Fred says.

"Oh." My heart drops. "Right. That."

That.

I've spent the last year cornering the market—or trying to—on geriatric yoga in our small town of Cedar Cliff. My part-time instructor job at Yogi Bare always has some older regulars, but when Mrs. Stanley expressed interest in specific sessions to help her hip pain, the owners didn't offer it. So, I took her on as a solo client. Since then, through word of mouth, I've taken on all the older people in town—even Frank, who keeps it secret because the retired mechanic might keel over if people knew he wasn't all man, all the time.

I love it. I love being able to help people whose specific needs might normally be overlooked. I love hearing their soliloquies about life, which normally keep me thirty minutes past our scheduled time. But to say it's not profitable is an understatement. My side classes weren't even included on the back of Yogi Bare's new T-shirt even though a partnership would be ideal. It's simply not their current brand.

So, I plaster on a fake smile and say, "It's going great, Fred."

He gives the biggest grin in return, which only makes my thumping heart chant, *Liar, liar, liar.*

"Good," he says. "I'm rooting for you, kid."

That makes one of us.

Last summer, I tried to go full-on business mode with this side hustle. I paid for online ads. I started social media accounts. I even posted courses online, which had a handful of sales. But when tax season came around, most of my earnings got dwindled down to nothing. What had looked like a good year turned out to be less than I made at Honeywood alone.

Fred grew accustomed to me taking early morning clients when I was on the grind. Being late last year was a necessity that he was fine with. But now? Well, I don't have the heart to tell him my business is not taking off like I imagined. I can't stand seeing that downturned mustache.

The employee office saloon doors swing inward, and my other friend Quinn appears. She's fully decked out in her Queen Bee gear. She's played the role for years, and the poofy pink ball gown looks just as natural as everyday clothing on her. The only thing differentiating her from the sunny character is her large scowl.

"Your brother," Quinn says, pointing a finger at Lorelei, "will be the death of me."

"Oh boy," Lorelei says.

As if on cue, Lorelei's twin brother, Landon, pushes through the doors next. He's tall, towering over the rest of us —even Lorelei, who is taller than most women I've met. Landon has a boyish smile hiding under his beard, as if taunting his sister's best friend is a prime-time activity rather than borderline horror, like it is for her.

"What'd I do this time?"

"You know what you did," Quinn says.

It specifies nothing for any of us, but I touch his arm anyway.

"You know what you did," I echo back to him.

He grins and sighs.

"Oh," he says, digging in his pocket, "I almost forgot. You got mail."

Fred exhales and rolls his eyes with a smile when I take the letter.

A few years ago, Fred might have given me a heavy speech about how "Honeywood's address is not your own," but I've moved apartments too often for that conversation to be worth it anymore. Plus, now, Landon, our head of security, sorts the mail, so it's out of sight, out of mind for my boss.

I recognize the handwriting on the pink letter as my little sister's. I rip it open, and I pull out pictures. They're all from her wedding this past winter. On the back of one picture is a small, scribbled note. While I imagine other guests' envelopes are filled with *thank you for your gift* and *we were happy to share our special day with you*, my note only has two words—*you're next*.

I gasp and mutter, "You little snot."

Callie is the second Poulos daughter to get married, leaving only me left. Those words are not a wish; they are a curse, and she knows it.

Fred, mid-typing on his phone's keyboard, looks back to me. He doesn't have to ask before I hand him the wedding thank-you card. After a few seconds of scanning it, he lets out a snorting laugh.

The photo Fred holds is a full shot of our family in the cathedral. Callie and her groom, Alex, are in the middle with smiles that light up the whole church. On one side is my oldest sister, Kassandra, and her sour-faced accountant husband, David, who looks upset he was dragged away from his abacus or whatever. And on the other side are my parents—Mr. Elias and Sophia Poulos, hand in hand, cupped instead of intertwined. Elegant and proper.

And then there's me.

I'm lying on my side up front with my hand on my hip, looking like I'm posing for a high school senior picture. I'm tan from a summer of working at Honeywood. My exposed thigh through the slit of my bridesmaid dress is toned from yoga. I have a big smile, second only to my newly married sister.

Fred hands the photo to Lorelei, who then hands it to Quinn.

"It's like you're taunting them," Quinn says with a barking laugh.

I notice Landon grinning down at her, as if admiring the sound.

Oh, he's so into her, and she doesn't even know it.

I snatch the photo back.

"If being happy is a taunt, then I don't want to know what's polite," I say.

"Well, are you?" Landon asks.

"Am I what? Happy?"

"No, are you next?" Lorelei finishes for him with a huge smile.

36

It's their twin thing. I swear they can read each other's thoughts.

I give the most exaggerated eye roll. "No, I'm not, *guys*."

I think about the prospect of settling down. Of my mom who spent every night doing dishes and playing the good wife. Of my sister Kassandra with David, who probably sit on opposite sides of a long, fancy dinner table. Even of Fred, who is now happily divorced.

Why would I settle down when I could instead have a week of passionate sex with the local bar owner? Or start a niche business from the ground up? Or work at a theme park, just for the insurance?

I glance at the words once more.

You're next.

My life is fine as is. It's all perfectly, absolutely fine.

And I'll be finer when I find Orson again tonight. Because what is life if you can't live on the wild side?

6

Orson

I adjust the box in my arms, sidestepping past the other leaning towers of cardboard boxes rising to Mrs. Stanley's ceiling.

"I really can't thank you enough," Frank says.

"Not a problem," I grunt out, heaving the box into the back of my Jeep.

"Do you have to take the flower pillows too?" Mrs. Stanley asks, holding her puppy close to her chest, like it's a safety blanket for the trauma we're putting her through.

"It all goes, woman," Frank responds.

"But I like those."

"The box was unopened," I say to her. "You didn't use them, right?"

She huffs, scratching below her dog's ears. "No."

I give her a weak smile, placing a hand on her shoulder.

"Then, Frank's right. It gets donated."

Frank and I have spent the last month helping my eighty-one-year-old neighbor clear out her garage. Mrs. Stanley's children finally re-blocked the home shopping channel on her television, but the reign of terror it held over this house remains. Boxes full of unused purses, cooking ware, dolls, and baseball cards—it could be a museum for all the advertisements in the last year. The last time they blocked the shopping channel, we only had to clear her bedroom of impulse purchases. Now, her whole house is a glorified storage facility. This will take months.

"I think we're full today," I say, closing my trunk and clapping my hands clean.

Frank's truck is also filled to the brim.

"We did good work today," he says.

I wrap an arm around Mrs. Stanley's shoulders.

She looks less than enthused, but still mutters an irritated, "Thank you."

"See you tomorrow?" Frank asks me.

"Sounds good," I say. It's an automatic response even if I haven't mentally scrolled through my social calendar to ensure I'm available. I'll make time.

But then I think of Theo and when she'll be coming over tonight. If there's time for her.

God, Theo.

A distraction above all other distractions.

I haven't gotten a lick of mental peace since she barreled into my bed one week ago. Licks of other things, sure, but peace? No, Theo is a mix of lightning and feral animal. She's He-Man's Battle Cat. A jolt straight to the heart.

I didn't expect us to keep going like this, but when she shows up at midnight with nothing but bare tanned skin under her Honeywood jacket, you don't exactly say no. Plus, one time, she showed up with a pack of blueberries, saying she hadn't eaten dinner yet. We proceeded to lounge naked while she tossed them in my mouth from across the room to see how many I could catch. I shouldn't like hanging out with her as much as I do.

I take my car full of Mrs. Stanley's boxes to donations before rushing five minutes down the road to The Honeycomb. I toss my bag into my office and push through the kitchen door to the area behind the bar.

My bar is big for what it is, filled with picnic tables, scattered high-tops, and the long bar top, adorned with stools, practically reserved for Cedar Cliff regulars. This small town's watering hole has been mostly unchanged since my dad retired, and it's in need of upgrades. A new side room with pool tables is next on the list, but even that is still months away.

I unlock the front door, placing a brick down as a doorstop to let the autumn breeze in. But out in the parking lot, walking away from Honeywood Fun Park, is an all-too-familiar pretty face.

My breath catches in my throat. Even after a day of work at a busy theme park, Theo is still effortlessly gorgeous with her messy black curls and flushed cheeks.

"Right on time," I joke.

"Accidentally," Theo calls over with a smile. "When do you get off?"

"When do you want to make me?"

Her smile grows, and the cheeky answer floats between us as she crosses the parking lot. I look behind me to see if anyone is walking down the sidewalk—this town is nosy as hell.

"What am I?" Theo asks. "Your dirty little secret?"

I tilt my head to the side. "Last I checked, I was yours." When she gets close enough, I reach my hand out and pull her into me. "But I get the feeling you like secrets."

My phone buzzes in my pocket. I pull it out. One of my new employees, Kailey, is going to be late. My chin falls to my chest, and I heave out a sigh.

I feel that familiar tug in my chest—the tension that feels like it's pulling up my neck and into my throat. I rub a circle over my heart, where the tightness rests. Normally, that dissipates part of it, but not all—never all of it.

I look up to see Theo staring at the rotating hand.

"You're stressed," she says.

I can't help the laugh that leaves me.

"I'm always stressed," I say.

"Did you ever call those people Judy wanted you to call?"

Her concern does something to my heart. Maybe makes it ache more or less—I can't tell—but I laugh it off either way.

"I can handle myself," I say, tucking a curl of hair behind her ear. "I've lived this long. I'm a big boy."

Her eyes dart down to my jeans and back up. She smirks.

"Oh, I know you're a big boy," she says. But before I can grin back, her eyebrows pull together. "But I still want you to call them."

Her care is endearing, if not misguided. I'm fine.

"How about"—I take a step closer—"instead"—I run a thumb over her neck and kiss the apple of her cheek—"you come by after work, and I bury my face between your legs?"

She bites her lip. "Gonna put me on the bar top?"

"Gonna put you wherever I like, sweetheart."

"I have a better option."

"Go on."

Theo arches into me. I pull in a sharp inhale when her hand finds its way beneath my belt, splaying out over the hardening length of me.

God.

"You can do whatever you want to me ... but"—she jabs my chest with her pointer finger—"only if you call a doctor."

My expression falls. I don't know how to respond. Nobody asks about my health unless it's Judy, but that's her job. And yet here is Theo, a woman I've been seeing for a little over a week, demanding that I look after myself.

I smile again. It's kinda nice to be worried over.

"Well, you do drive a hard bargain," I say.

She breathes out the words, "The hardest."

When she tries to pull her finger back, I grab her hand instead, pulling the fingers up to my mouth, kissing the tips one by one before tilting her palm out and placing my lips against the soft center. She sucks in a sharp inhale.

In the next movement, she's leaning in, kissing the column of my neck and running her tongue over the spot. It elicits a groan from me that I don't expect, forcing me to grab her hips to still her movements. As if I could control her anyway. I've never met a woman who matches me move for move. When I push, there's no pull. She just shoves right back.

"Fine," I relent. "I'll call someone. Tomorrow."

But I know if I'm not careful, it won't be my health problems that might end me. It'll be her.

7

Theo

"Did you get the card?"

I groan in response to my dad's question.

"Your mother insisted," he continues.

"I should have known Callie was just a good soldier, following orders."

I hear a creak on his end of the phone line—their screen door opening. A few more crunches of leaves, and he's likely walking farther into the backyard. I know where he's going.

"Mom is gonna kill you," I say.

The click of a lighter.

"Eh, I've survived this long."

I don't know if he's referring to my mom's anger or the cigarette, but he lets out a raspy laugh anyway.

I lie on the floor of Yogi Bare, humming out a disapproving noise during what should have been a quiet, wind-down to my session. Dad called while I was in the middle of my afternoon, relaxing savasana, and now, he's smoking. I'm no longer relaxed.

"You promised you'd stop," I say.

"Did I? I don't remember that," he says with mock aloofness. "Anyway, I've got three dates for you."

I groan. "Dad."

"Mother's orders."

"Who is the soldier now?"

"Hear me out."

"I'm not going on dates."

"Why?" he asks. "Do you have someone lined up already?"

"Yes, I've been putting myself through years of guilt-tripping simply to whip out a husband at the last minute."

He lets out a rasping chuckle. "Didn't ask for sarcasm."

"Didn't ask for you to be Mom's little helper."

"Theodora."

"Sorry. So, have you considered switching to vaping at least?"

"I had a set of twelve-year-old girls laugh at me the last time I tried."

"Oh, the horror."

"You try getting mocked by people a quarter your age. Let me enjoy my vices."

"You are a medical professional, sir."

"And you're being cheeky," he says with a chuckle. "Isn't that my job?"

I grin to myself. Out of all my siblings, I like to think I inherited my dad's rebellious streak. Except my rebellion came in the form of rejecting our family's tradition of entering the medical field and getting married.

I think it's a middle-child thing. I don't know if that's a scientific fact, like how nine out of ten dentists recommend certain toothpastes or something, but it's proven true for me. My two sisters became stable, licensed physicians and still

44

live close to my parents. I moved away and did anything but be stable.

"Stop avoiding the subject. Now, there are tons of eligible bachelors at the"—he pauses, and I can tell what follows will pain him to say aloud—"church."

I snicker. "Dad."

"Come on." I can practically picture him waving around the cigarette. He always talks with his hands. "Give me something to tell your mother or else it won't seem like I did my job."

I smile to myself. I know my dad would rather be watching old war documentaries or painting his miniatures in the drafty basement art studio. Instead, he's calling his daughter like a salesman slinging bachelors. He's very good at playing the dutiful-husband part: *Well, my wife said ...* The ol' ball and chain. The honey-do lists. The rigamarole of a marriage I do not crave.

It's quiet for a bit until my dad finally says, "You know your mother just wants you to be happy at the end of the day."

"Does she?"

"She does. She also asked me to invite you over."

"Will a man be waiting for me as well? A blind date?"

"No, we just want to know what's going on with you. Are you stitching clothing still? Gardening? Or is yoga sticking?"

"Yoga has stuck."

"That's fantastic. See? We just miss you, is all, Tomato."

I bend at the waist, pulling myself up and leaning my chin on my knee. He knows he's got me with the nickname. It's one of those nicknames that you're never sure how it came to be, but even in our oldest home videos, my dad calls me Tomato while I kick in a high chair.

"I know," I say. "I know. Dad, I—"

Then, I hear another voice in the background, my mom's thick and insistent one, yelling, "Is that Theodora?"

"Ah shit," my dad hisses. I hear stomping in the dirt. He's putting out his cigarette. "Yes, dear!"

I bury my head between my knees and groan.

"Don't give her the phone," I say. "Dad, don't give her the phone. Don't—"

Suddenly, the sound on his end gets noisy. I hear jumbling, mumbling, and fumbling before my mom's voice is no longer distant, but clear as day.

"Theo, when are you coming home?"

My muscles tense. I'm gonna need another session of yoga after this.

"Uh, soon," I lie.

"You know, Father Peter asked when you'd be coming to church again."

I have no intentions of coming home soon, and this is a good reminder as to why. I bury my head between my legs further. Maybe I can disappear if I go far enough.

"How nosy of him," I murmur.

"You should stop by," she says, ignoring my comment. "Lord knows you come to the city enough with those random online dates of yours."

The guilt. God, the *guilt*. The worst part is, it's not malicious—not really. It's so interwoven in my mom's system that it's become a cog in her machinery. It's just how she functions. And she wonders why I moved two hours away.

"It's hard to get away on Sundays for church," I say.

"From the theme park?"

"From my yoga business," I correct even though, yes, I meant Honeywood. "I'm starting to build some clients on the side. It's actually getting lucrative."

Nope.

I can feel myself grasping at straws, trying to play the prosperous daughter. But I can't compete with my sisters' successes, and I shouldn't try.

Her tone shifts, but only slightly. "That's great, honey. You know, you should talk to your sisters about this."

"Why?"

"They have business experience. Kassandra is about to hire on a new receptionist."

"Well, good for Kass."

"Have you considered helping her out?"

"Mom, I'm not going to be my sister's assistant."

"Why not? You work in a theme park and perform yoga or ... have you had any successful dates lately?"

My body ignites, like a gas tank heading to an already-raging bonfire.

"Are you kidding, Mom?"

"I'm just asking," she says. I practically picture her raising her eyebrows in faux innocence.

I hear my dad in the background, saying, "Okay, dear. Let's not ..."

"I just think she's being careless."

"You know I'm right here, Mom," I say.

"Well?" she asks.

"No, I haven't. And you know what? I should get back to my silly theme park and my plethora of careless dates and yoga, which, by the way, was meant to ease my stress. Except, right now, I am *very* stressed."

"Try walking a mile in your sisters' shoes. *That's* stressful."

I don't answer. I don't have the energy. The call is quiet. Too quiet. For a second, I wonder if she hung up. I pull the phone away from my ear to see the call time still ticking away.

There's fumbling again. Then, I hear my dad's voice replace my mom's. He clears his throat.

"I didn't know your yoga business was picking up," he says, as if the latter part of my and mom's conversation didn't even happen. "That's great, honey."

"Yeah, well ... it's going. Sorry for being the disappointing daughter, I guess."

"Theo ..."

I close my eyes and press my temple into my knee. "Sorry. I'm sorry. That was unfair."

"It was. Because you're not a disappointment. You never could be."

I know he means it, but I don't know if he means it like one normal person does to another or if he says it because he's my dad and he's supposed to think the sun shines out of my eyeballs.

"I should go," I say.

"Okay. And, hey, Tomato?"

"Hmm?"

"Life is short. Just do what you feel is right, okay?"

I hang up, tossing my phone to the floor and letting the slam echo throughout the empty studio. I lie back down and close my eyes.

Breathe in and out ... in and out ... following the breath ...

I try to imagine waves rushing in, taking hold of my thoughts, then pushing them back out to sea. If I'm lucky, my imaginary kraken will steal them completely.

It's all going to be fine.

It's all fine.

I'm like water. I adapt to fill the space I'm in.

When I moved to Cedar Cliff in my early twenties, I

found my four best friends within a week. When I needed insurance after I aged off my parents' plan, I made sure to hop onto Honeywood's. When I needed stress release, I started practicing yoga and quickly became one of the main instructors here at Yogi Bare.

Everything has been from my own hard work. My own drive.

I do love my life in Cedar Cliff. But sometimes, I feel like if I don't have either a husband or a budding medical career or both, I might as well be the one kid still living in my parents' basement.

But I'm happy here.

I am.

And I do what I want. When I want. How I want. And nobody will tell me otherwise.

8

Orson

I blink at the numbers on my screen—at the website I've
visited exactly one other time. I had to dig in my
office drawers and messy filing cabinet just to find the
login information for it, and I gotta say, I kinda wish I
hadn't.

"The insurance number, sir?" the voice says over the
phone.

I stare at the website—at the deductible that's so high
that I choked on a sip of my water when it popped up. But
then I forced myself to stop because I realized I couldn't
afford an ER visit either.

"Uh, can I just call you back? I need to look at my
calendar again." I let out a weak laugh. "You know, just not
sure what days work and ..."

"We open tomorrow at nine."

"Perfect," is all I say before pressing the key on my
speakerphone that ends the call. I stare at the numbers
again. The numbers from hell.

When my dad handed over The Honeycomb to me, he
glossed over a lot of the rough parts and romanticized the

50

rest. He made it seem like running a small business was the dream.

Make your own hours! Be your own boss! Carry on the family legacy!

And for the most part, that's all true. I love my bar. I love being a home for people like Frank, who is now intent on spending his retirement reviving dying toy stores, or Mrs. Stanley, who comes here with her puppy to escape her storage unit of a house, or simply to be a reliable source of competitive Wednesday Trivia Night for all the other beer drinkers in Cedar Cliff.

This town depends on this bar, and I'm happy to be the one running it.

But self-employment insurance is less than ideal.

It's not that I don't have the money to pay for it. The Honeycomb objectively does well with decent margins, which, for a bar, is rare. But I want to invest in expansions. My dream of a side room with pool tables and extra seating will never happen if I'm making regular doctor visits that carve out my savings.

God, Judy would kill me if she heard me debating between my personal health or the health of the bar.

"Why, hello, Mr. Bar Owner."

I lean around my computer to see Theo's loose raven curls pop into my office doorway, followed by her beautiful, grinning smile.

I instantly feel a wave of relaxation wash over me.

"A sight for sore eyes," I answer.

"I have more good things too."

"More?"

Her hand appears in the doorway, holding a packet of mini peanut butter cookies.

I laugh. "You didn't."

"I did."

"Close the door?"

She grins and tiptoes into the office, closing the door behind her and leaning back against it.

"You're gonna give people ideas," she says.

"Good. I have some ideas." I curl my finger in. "Come here, sweetheart."

She circles around the desk, dropping the snack packet, then plopping into my lap. As she does, she makes a point to lean forward, arching her spine and sliding her backside against me. I groan, biting the inside of my cheek.

"Naughty girl," I murmur, reaching around her with one hand, lowering it over the waistline of her shorts.

But before I can dip inside, she gasps. Her hand dives to the mouse on my computer.

"Orson, I've never seen a deductible this high."

I groan, leaning in to kiss her shoulder. I steal the mouse and close out of the window, leaving only my desktop with scattered files and the default landscape wallpaper.

She tosses her head over her shoulder.

"Orson."

"I know," I groan with a chuckle. "So, distract me from my misery."

"You know, I think I'm a bad influence," she says, tilting her hips backward.

I lean my head back on the chair, letting out a low moan.

"You're right," I grunt. "You're terrible for me."

"So, is this why you haven't made an appointment?"

"Let's talk about other things," I say. "Like how pretty your thighs would look, spread out on my desk."

I bury my nose into her neck, sinking into her familiar scent of almonds and oats. I run my hands over her bare legs. Every part of her is hard to my touch. You can tell she doesn't stop at teaching yoga; she's dedicated to the practice. Her body is lean.

I grab her hips and lift her up, turning her around so her bottom lands on my desk, crumpling a few papers under her thighs. I stand and step forward between her spread legs, trailing my palm down her neck and running my thumb over her chin.

When I meet her eyes, I expect them to be just as heated as mine. Instead, they are busy searching my face. Her full lips are slightly parted. For once, she looks serious. But even a serious Theo is somehow cute.

"What?" I ask with a laugh, planting a small kiss on the end of her long nose.

"Marry me."

She's off my desk in point-one second. I don't know if I pulled her off or if she jumped. But before I know it, she's on the other side of the desk with her palms splayed on the wooden top before I can gather my first breath.

"Marry me," she repeats with a sly smile.

She looks deviant, like she just discovered the solution to getting out of hell. I just didn't know we were in hell to begin with.

I could say a million things, like, *Why did that sentence even remotely enter your brain?* Or, *Please leave my office.*

But instead, all I can settle on is, "You're proposing to me in my bar?"

She bats her eyelashes. "Romantic, isn't it?"

I let out a strained laugh.

"Theo," I say, holding up my hands, "we're not ... why did you ask me to marry you? Good Lord."

"Why not?" she asks. "This solves so many issues!"

"What issues? My only issue is that we're having this

conversation instead of me being deep inside you. Do you see the disconnect here?"

Her cheeks flush, but it doesn't stop her from continuing.

"Insurance," she says. "Honeywood's insurance is incredible."

"Insurance," I repeat.

"I've literally never paid above thirty dollars for, like, anything. Ever. Hop on my insurance. Get whatever appointments you need for the rest of time. Easy-peasy."

"Insurance?" I say again, this time through a choked laugh. "We'd get married for insurance? Are you kidding?"

She leans over the desk. "Live life on the edge."

"Sweetheart, a legally binding lifetime commitment kind of seems like hopping right *off* the edge."

"It's perfect," she says. "I don't care if I eventually get married. Neither do you. It all makes sense. So, go to your appointments and get healthy as a horse to match that horse-sized cock of yours ..."

"Theo ..."

"And we can go on living our lives like the free-spirited people that we are!"

I'm at a loss for words. I keep looking between her eyes as if I'll understand the madness behind them any second now, but I don't.

Marriage.

Sure, Theo is funny. She's a wild child. She's my teenage wet dream come to life. But aside from her wheat beer preference or the fact that she loves blueberries or the color purple, I don't know nearly enough to *marry* her.

Life comes at you fast, I guess.

"This is nuts."

"Is it though?" she asks, biting her bottom lip.

I point a finger at her. "Don't be cute."

"There's literally no commitment to it," she says with a laugh. "We'll be fake married."

"But it's on very real, very legal paper."

She shrugs, as if to say, *Whoops!* She's too adorable.

I tilt my chin toward her. "And what's in it for you?"

She puffs out her chest. "To feel like I made a decision that helps someone else for once."

"You're kidding."

Her face scrunches up, and then something seems to shift, like a puzzle piece locking into place in her mind.

"Fine, I have another reason," she says.

"Go on."

"We can file taxes together," she says. "You get a massive cut if you're married and own a small business."

"How do you ..."

"My sisters run businesses. And I'm trying to get my yoga business off the ground, and taxes are murdering me. I get you a big cut, and we're still coming out positive in the end."

"I'd need to see my tax guy ..."

"How about this as a sweetener?" she says. "We can divorce whenever. I won't even ask for alimony."

I pause, opening my mouth, then closing it before letting out a small chuckle.

"How generous of you."

"Think about it."

I sigh, ripping my baseball cap off, slapping it against my thigh, and running a hand over my shaved head. But no amount of rubbing the magic eight ball is going to provide the answer I need.

Even after only a week of hanging out, I kind of like

Theo. And I can't afford to like Theo. Especially with this proposal on the table.

"Think about it," I echo with a weak laugh. "Think about it, she says. We're sleeping together."

"So?"

"Well, don't you think marriage would make that complicated?"

She scoffs. "No."

She's so young. So naive. So hopeful.

"Nobody else has to know," she continues. "We can keep living our lives as is."

"And what do we do when you find someone else you'd rather marry?"

"Won't happen."

"Or maybe when we stop messing around?"

She shrugs. "It's just a piece of paper. Who cares?"

"Okay," I say slowly. Then, my eyes catch on the snacks sitting on my desk. And my chest tightens.

I walk around the desk, taking her hand in mine, entwining our fingers together. "And what if it gets more complicated than that?"

"How?"

"Well, what if we fall in love?"

She doesn't skip a single beat before responding, "Impossible."

I bark out a laugh. At first, it's something small. I can't help it. This woman is so *sure* of herself—that falling in love with me would so far-fetched—that I actually believe her.

And then it hits me as well.

Impossible.

Because she's right. Of course she is. I'm married to my bar. I always have been. Always will be. I might sign papers, but at the end of the day, I'll be here. And I want it that way, don't I?

I find myself laughing more. Almost hysterical. Theo joins in on my laughter. Then, we're cackling together, soaring through the possibilities of it all.

"Can ... can you imagine?" she says through breathless laughs.

"Oh, and what ... what if I got you a ring?" I ask through my own laughter. I can barely get the words out. They sound so ridiculous.

"Or—or what if I wanted a *big* wedding?" she throws in.

I'm leaning back against the desk, clutching my stomach. She's up against the door, laughing with snorts, like some adorable piglet.

"I didn't know you snorted!" I say.

"Only for my husband!"

We bust out into laughter again.

She's wiping tears from her eyes.

I'm doing the same.

We finally settle down, letting out small breaths, little oohs, and giggles. Tiny murmurs of, "Good one," and, "Hilarious." The tension in the room feels cut. The ache in my heart has dissipated on its own. Theo makes this seem easy. Possible.

"But, seriously," she says, slumping against the door with a grin, "I don't really see that happening."

"What?" I ask, returning her smile.

"Us falling in love."

"No?"

"Absolutely not."

"Yeah," I say with a final engine backfire of a laugh. "Yeah, me neither."

9

Theo

Now—Seven Months Later

I stare at the back door of Judy's office. My car is still running. I grip the steering wheel, winding my fingers over the top of it.

A sense of déjà vu rushes over me. Everything about this—the trip here, the starry night sky, the sense of foreboding ... I've been in this moment before, seven months ago. And when he called tonight, as I celebrated the best month of my yoga business yet, it felt only natural that his voice would be the one I heard. After all, my success wouldn't have been possible without his help—without our arrangement.

After our call, I left with only a quick word to Ruby who said she understood if I was late coming home. It's not like her couch is going anywhere anyway. At least, not in the next week.

The back door to Judy's office swings open, and then he walks out.

My husband.

Orson Mackenzie.

My heart rises up to my throat, and for a second, I think I might be sick. Or maybe I'm gonna pass out. But I know I'm sober enough that neither is from alcohol. My nerves are because of him.

My husband looks good, walking across the parking lot. Orson walks with a type of swagger—with his thighs spread, as if they're too muscular to be closer; with his large work boots crunching over gravel, like he owns it; and with his broad chest filling out his T-shirt with The Honeycomb's logo. For once, he's not wearing his baseball cap. I notice his hair has grown out into a nice cut. And when he spots me— when he gives me that same earth-shattering grin—I'm frozen in place.

I have no conversation starters on hand. What do I discuss with a man I haven't spoken to in five months?

I get out of my car, running to him. I awkwardly place a hand in the crook of his elbow. He stiffens under my touch.

"I don't need help," he says with a chuckle.

"Says the man who called his wife in an emergency."

Orson laughs. Low, vibrating. The same good-natured laugh I hear each week at The Honeycomb. But from a distance.

"Judy made me," he says with a weak smile. "You're my only emergency contact."

"Oh. Right."

It's funny how a simple sentence can have my blood both rising and sinking all at once, like fever chills. I can't decide if I'm sad or hurt.

"I'll follow you home," I say.

"I'm fine," he says with a laugh. "I fell at the bar. No harm, no foul. It happens."

And he does look fine. In fact, he looks like he didn't fall at all. But Orson has always been resilient like that.

"Really, I don't mind," I say.

"What?" he asks. "You think I can't drive?"

"Your brain might be rattled."

"*Your* brain might be rattled," he says, reaching out to lightly knock against my head. "Your breath smells like alcohol."

"I'm sober enough."

"I know. You're not dumb enough to drive drunk."

I grin, closing my eyes to breathe in his usual scent of hops and wood—a smell so unique to him that it almost feels like the first day of school. The hallways that you forgot about over the summer. The comforting scent that comes rushing back with good memories and *home*.

Except Orson isn't my home.

The truth is, I haven't been this close to him in months. I arrive to the bar slightly late so I'm not sitting alone at our group's Trivia Night table. I never offer to place our beer order. I even once brought a sandwich from home so I wouldn't have to order food. I've gotten very good at avoiding my secret husband.

But if he's at Judy's, then he needs me. And I'm going to do my part.

"Just let me follow you home," I say.

"But I'm headed back to the bar."

"The bar?"

"I still have work to do," he says with a grin.

"It's after midnight."

He shrugs, taking backward steps to his Jeep and swinging his keys around his finger.

I end up following him the two miles down the road from Judy's office to The Honeycomb.

We pull in the back lot, and he parks, raising his arms, as if to say, *See? Made it alive!*

I smile back. Good. I did my emergency-contact duty. I picked up my husband at the doctor's office. I made sure he was fine. I deserve a gold star, honestly.

I give a good-bye wave, but then he comes over in a lazy half-run toward my car.

No. No, no, no.

My heart rushes into my chest, and I swallow when he places a hand on my window. He spins his finger in a small circle to signal me rolling down my window.

My gut instinct is to zoom out of here with my wheels spinning out behind me. But I don't—I can't when he's looking at me with that smile that shows part of his white teeth. So, I roll down the window. After the first inch, I almost stop it there. But then I realize how petty that would be, so I let it continue down.

I'm fighting all kinds of impulses today.

Orson leans a hand on the roof of my car.

"Thanks," he says.

"Thanks?" I didn't mean for the word to come out in a sarcastic way, but it does. I shouldn't be surprised Orson felt the need to run over here after a fall that landed him in the doctor's office, just to say *thanks*.

"Yeah," he says. "And I, uh, actually have your tax documents inside, if you want a copy."

"Oh," I say. *So, he only came over here for business.* "Yeah. Sure."

I stumble out, accidentally pushing him with the door and getting an, "Oof."

I give an awkward, "Oh, sorry," and he mutters, "Nope, it's fine."

We're a mishmash of awkward moves, like playing

Twister in high school with your crush. Except this is far less fun.

I follow him through The Honeycomb's back door, watching as he walks to his office. I hear the distant clang of the keys hitting his desk.

I haven't been back here since we were ... doing whatever it was we did last fall. The bulletin board no longer has the giant poster for Honeywood's autumn play promos. Instead, it's replaced by a flyer for the upcoming reopening of The Grizzly. There's a prep list for a new menu over the stove. But more notably, part of the wall that was once enclosed now has two double doors leading to an additional area.

I push them in and emerge into a large, empty room. The crisp smell of new wood is everywhere. It's colder than the kitchen. In one corner lie rolls of carpet. In another is uninstalled drywall.

Orson's boots clunk on the concrete behind me, and he exhales.

"It's coming along," he says, as if we were mid-conversation. "Hoping it'll be done by the time The Grizzly opens."

"Or Journey."

"Huh?"

"Great Forest Journey."

"Oh yeah. Forgot about that one."

Honeywood's headlining roller coaster, The Grizzly, is getting rebuilt this year along with a new indoor ride, The Great Forest Journey. After Honeywood Fun Park was bought out last winter, the new owners have hit the ground running with new additions.

Our small town is practically waiting on pins and needles for when it's all complete. We don't know how busy we'll be after the plethora of renovations, but if the influx of new guests due to the increased hype is any indication, I'm willing to bet local businesses will explode. And it will be a very profitable mushroom cloud.

"Anyway, here ya go."

I feel a nudge at my back, and my body freezes on impact. Orson chuckles. I grab the small stack of papers, peering at both our names smack dab in the center.

Orson Mackenzie and Theodora Poulos.

I never changed my last name. Why would I when it's supposed to be a secret?

"Thanks," I say. "Was it a lot?"

"No. I saved a ton actually. Even with your stuff added. Plan worked."

Plan. It is a business arrangement after all. But my stomach still flips at the statement.

"Thanks for filing," I say at the same time he says, "How's your family?"

We both pause, and he laughs. He's changing the subject. I let him.

"Fine," I say. "Good. My dad asks about you sometimes."

He nods, sucking his teeth with a tsk sound.

"And your mom?"

"She's fine," I lie and instantly feel bad about it, so I amend with, "Well, I mean, she's a queen at holding grudges so ..."

"Still mad?"

Mad is an understatement. Our surprise elopement caused a rift in the Poulos family that I hadn't expected. Or maybe I was just naive. I think a part of me knew eloping was a bad decision. Somewhere deep down, after years of watching big wedding after big wedding in our cathedral, I knew. But Orson didn't.

"Very mad," I answer.

"I'm sorry."

I shake my head. "Don't be."

He lets out a low laugh to break the tension, running a hand over the back of his neck and down his chest. I watch as he still rubs over the same spot he used to. Right over his heart.

He must still have pain, even with all the visits to a psychiatrist that come through my insurance bill. I wonder if he's taking something to manage stress. I wonder if he's lightened his workload at all. Judging at how often I see him at the bar, I bet not.

He sees me looking at his hand and drops it instantly.

"Hey," he says, catching my gaze. "We should get dinner sometime."

"What?" I ask.

"Let's catch up. I wanna hear all about your yoga business." He nods to the papers in my hand. "Your profits were impressive."

He's just being nice. Orson Mackenzie is always nice.

"We shouldn't."

"Theo." With the tilt of a smile at the edge of his mouth and the downward nudge of his chin, he levels me with a stare. "No offense. But I'm over you. I promise."

I blink at him. I can't think of anything to say to that. Not as my heart melts down to my stomach.

Last fall, we spent two months in faux married bliss. Two months of getting our lives together with the new, exciting benefits of a legal marriage. Two months of giving and receiving mind-blowing, non-committed orgasms. And it was great—up until I showed up one night to see him at the end of the bed, rolling a box between his palms.

A box that looked an awful lot like it housed a ring.

"I'm over you. I promise."

I suddenly feel like a steaming pile of garbage set out in Georgia's summer sun. Possums might as well ravage every piece of me.

But didn't I make him feel the same way? Didn't I leave his house and never return? Don't I finally deserve this comeuppance?

"Sure," I say. "Let's do dinner. I'm free after work tomorrow."

"Wanna meet at The Bee-fast Stop?"

I swallow and nod.

I can do this. I can totally have one silly little dinner with him. The man I rejected months ago. The husband whose heart I shattered to pieces.

10

Orson

I run through Honeywood Fun Park's parking lot. I'm late for my dinner with Theo. I told my cousin, Emory, that I'd help him at his workshop, and I lost track of time. Again.

I jiggle the iron gate. It catches on the magnet. A skinny teen behind the ticket booth window has her pink sparkly lips pursed.

"Where's your ticket?"

"Holly," I say, leaning on my forearms on the window's ledge, "The Honeycomb alone sponsored sixty percent of your prom. You're kidding me, right?"

"Mr. Mackenzie, the student council appreciated that. But I take my job very seriously."

"You're a menace," I say with a laugh. I open my wallet and pull out my vendor card, slapping it against the glass. "How's this?"

My vendor pass is littered with holographic stickers, one piled on top of the other, with the glittering numbers of years past torn and peeled. The laminated yellow Honeywood logo is nearly orange, and the edges are sticky with pocket lint.

Holly squints at my card, then back up at me a few times, as if she's the bouncer at a bar.

"This doesn't look like you," she says.

I bark out a laugh and nod. "Yeah, yeah, just let me through."

She's not wrong though. The picture taken ten years ago has me with a shaved head and a hungover, dazed expression. I'd been partying that night, before my dad told me he was giving me our family's bar. Now, my free vendor entry card is frozen in time—a time when I didn't go to a doctor's office at midnight.

Last night, I told Theo I fell, then rushed her away from Judy's office before she could learn the truth—the fact that I called my doctor friend at midnight on a Friday night just to say my heart didn't feel right. By the time I was sitting in her chair, I was embarrassed. Like a boy who had cried wolf. My heart felt fine.

"Why didn't you call your psychiatrist?" Judy had asked.

"Because it's midnight."

She leveled me with a look. I gave her back a weak smile.

"Orson ... I told you to cut back on work."

"I'm fine," I said. "False alarm."

"You aren't fine," she said. "It's been seven months, and clearly, something isn't working. What meds do they have you on?"

"I'm fine," I repeated.

Because I am. I know I am. I'm busy, sure, but I have been for most of my adult life. I take the meds I'm prescribed to take, and that's that.

Holly hands me back my ID, and the gate to Honeywood unlatches. I grab it with one hand, pushing outward.

"Get a new picture, Mr. Mackenzie!" Holly calls.

I look at my watch. I'm only two minutes late.

I weave through crowds of families and children and strollers. I bypass the fountain of Buzzy the Bear with glittering coins at the bottom. I watch the drop of The Beesting, the screams of guests ripping through the sky. Honeywood Fun Park is a cacophony of music and conversations and rattling roller coaster tracks, but when I open the creaking door to The Bee-fast Stop, it's replaced by classic rock and the smell of their signature all-day pancakes.

I scan the park's themed restaurant—the wooden high tables and booths, the wall full of pictures of famous people who have dropped by, the cardboard cutout of Buzzy the Bear in the corner, giving a huge thumbs-up—and pause when I find Theo in the corner, waving me over.

Suddenly, I don't feel so hungry. But Theo has a way of disarming me like that, even all these months later.

"How was work, dear?" I jokingly ask as I slide into the booth across from her.

She laughs. "Busy. I actually got a peek at the new animatronics for Journey today."

"Oh yeah?"

"Queen Bee in a wedding dress is weird."

"Why's she in a wedding dress?"

"The ride ends with her and Ranger Randy getting married."

"Blegh," I say, letting my arm fall over the back of the booth. "Who needs marriage as a happy ending?"

She gives me a wide smile, which I return. A little inside joke to lighten the mood.

"So, how's life?" I ask.

"Life is ... life," she says with a laugh.

"Yoga business good?"

"Thriving," she says, tipping her drink to me.

I clink my water cup back.

Good. She's gotten everything she ever wanted. A successful side business. Freedom. It was all worth it.

"Heard Frank bought your apartments," I say. "How's living under his fist?"

She leans back in the chair.

"Frank," she mutters, the lick of bitterness on her tongue.

I laugh. "Not good?"

"I mean, it's fine. He can spend his retirement how he likes. Real estate was his best option, I guess. But he decided to renovate to make it nicer and accidentally blew a hole in my unit."

"Seriously?" I say, stifling a laugh.

She tosses her straw wrapper at me.

"It's not funny," she says, pulling her bottom lip in to capture her own laugh. "I had to move."

"Ah. Where ya living now?"

"Ruby's couch," she says with a snort. "For only the next week. Then ... eh, who knows?"

My back stiffens. "What?"

"I'll figure it out."

My fist clenches next to me. Theo might not be my real wife, but she is legally my *wife*. And I don't want her couch-surfing.

"Why not get a new place?" I ask.

"Well, I have stuff I wanna save for," she says, tracing a line over the napkin in front of her. "Like my own yoga studio or something."

"What about Lorelei?" I ask. "Or Quinn? Don't they

have spare rooms?"

"Quinn moved in with Landon. Lorelei with Emory. You know how it goes."

"Okay," I say, biting back my words. But then they explode out in a mess of, "Well, I have a spare bedroom."

Shit.

I don't know why I said it. It just came out. But my chest feels lighter at the idea.

I can't stand the idea of my wife existing like a vagrant on the wind. I'm sure she loves the freedom, but it doesn't sit right with me. Plus, I can't imagine a reality where Theo isn't doing her best. And if she's not, what was the whole point of this arrangement anyway?

What was the point of getting my heart broken?

It only took me two months to fall for her. Two months of messing around, calling each other husband and wife with stupid grins on our faces. Playing house, like two children who didn't want to grow up. But then it hit me one night as I ran a single finger through her dark curls, watching as she snored next to me like a worn-out puppy. I knew I didn't want another woman in my bed anymore.

I wanted Theo.

But you try telling the noncommittal woman you married that you want commitment. You try seeking out your grandmother's heirloom engagement ring and rolling the velvet box around from hand to hand as you tell this free-spirited woman that you might just be falling for her. I used those exact stupid words too.

"I'm falling for you," I said, sitting on the end of my bed, looking over to her as she sat next to me in silence.

For a split second, for even a fraction of a second, I remember how she leaned into me. I remember the hesitation. And it was that millisecond of hope that got crushed in the fist of reality.

"I ... can't," she said. "I can't. This is just ... for fun, right? It's for fun. I've got my business, and you've got—"

"No, you're right." I nodded, pocketing the ring box. "You're absolutely right."

I should have known. Theo had said from the very beginning that she wasn't looking for anything serious. Heck, so had I. Even in our vows at the courthouse, we'd both let out little secretive giggles, like we'd fooled the world.

The thought of marriage hadn't been on either of our radars. Until it was for me.

And so she walked out of my house, leaving us only talking one or two times over the past five months to share items for taxes or discuss billing or something equally as transactional. Because that was why we did it to begin with. That was the point.

"Move in with you?" Theo says with a disbelieving laugh.

"Sure," I say with a shrug. "Why not?"

"Oh, no, no, no," Theo says. "I'm not playing this game again."

"We're playing a game?"

"Marry me. Move in with me. Where does it end?"

"You've already done so much for me," I say. "I've got my doctor's appointments handled. Plus, there's so much going on in the bar right now that I'll barely even be at home. We wouldn't even cross paths."

"I can't afford—"

"I'll charge you the cheapest rent in town. Free."

She laughs again, a small snort coming out with it. I

would say I forgot that sound, but there's no way I could have forgotten it even if I tried.

"You're kidding," she says.

"Should I be?"

When I say that, her face falls. I think it finally hits her that I'm far from joking.

Maybe I should be. That would probably be the smarter move. But I've learned my lesson. I know my place with Theo now, and I should have from the beginning. She doesn't need me; she needs freedom. She's a bird that can't be caged, and who am I to try? I can only do my best to help her soar.

"Think about it," I say, echoing her words from seven months ago. "Just think about it."

"Look how well that worked last time," she says.

"Pretty well, I'd say. Your business is thriving, and so am I. This marriage—"

"Shh."

She bites her bottom lip and looks around the restaurant, as if waiting for someone to overhear us. Nobody we'd run into here knows our secret, except three people—one of who is Honeywood's general manager, Fred. And he's been good at keeping Theo's secret insurance change to himself.

"This marriage," I continue with a whisper, "is supposed to be beneficial. Let me help you."

She blinks. "You're serious."

I lean in and twist my baseball cap forward.

"You *are* serious," she says with a laugh.

"Come on. Move in with your husband. How bad can it be?"

11

Theo

"No, you can't just ... ugh, *pick a card*, Landon."

"But I want to know why I can't move there."

"Landon, I swear ..."

Even with the irritation in her tone, Quinn still leans over and places her head on Landon's shoulder. He smiles, kisses the top of her head, and picks a card. They've come a long way since they got together six months ago. But aside from their happiness, I've pretty sure Lorelei is more stoked that Quinn is now on the path to true sisterhood. Well, sister-in-law-hood.

"Is it our turn?" Lorelei asks, smiling at the two of them.

Emory doesn't wait for the answer before he's drawing a card for him and Lorelei. His jaw looks so much like Orson's. Emory doesn't share much with his cousin, but their manly jawlines must be a family trait.

I shift in my seat and try to think of something that *isn't* my husband's beautiful face.

"Oh, easy," Emory finally says, his low, confident voice booming through Ruby's living room. "We got this."

Emory Dawson is all confidence. I guess that comes

with the territory of operating your own roller coaster construction business. I'm convinced it's part of why Lorelei loves him so much. I swear they'd have glorious sex on a roller coaster if they got the chance.

"Oh, we definitely got this. *So* easy," Lorelei echoes with a smirk.

Emory leans back, wrapping a huge arm around the back of his girlfriend's chair.

"It makes me uncomfortable when they're confident," Ruby says with a smile.

"They're bluffing," Quinn mutters with a shake of her head.

"You wish," Emory says.

Bennett playfully knocks over his stack of coins. Emory levels a non-menacing glare at him, but Ruby gives Bennett a secret high five.

This is how it always is with our friend group on board game nights. Emory and Lorelei getting competitive. Quinn and Landon play fighting. Bennett and Ruby messing with everyone else and hiding behind their inside jokes.

Then, there's me.

I'm the scorekeeper. I'm always the scorekeeper. But I don't mind. I'm the odd woman out, so it makes sense. As long as I'm with friends, that's all that matters. And right now, it's neck and neck. I would care more—especially with how Lorelei and her brother, Landon, exchange glares—but I'm distracted tonight. Because all I can think about is Orson's offer.

"Move in with me."

My gut reaction was to immediately say no, but then my mind drifts to the other thing he said.

"I'm over you. I promise."

God, that hurt.

Orson said he was over me with the confidence of a man unaffected by feelings. I guess I can't blame him.

"Fifty points," Bennett says.

"You're kidding," Emory breathes.

"Nope."

I smile as Bennett and Ruby break down their final points for the round, far surpassing the two other scheming couples. Emory and Lorelei are visibly upset they didn't win. Quinn and Landon are too busy taunting them to care that they didn't either. But I wonder if Ruby and Bennett discovered the secret. Maybe being *just friends* works. Maybe Orson and I could do that. He seems to think so.

When everyone finally leaves and Ruby and I are alone, I finally blurt out my thoughts.

"What if I moved in with Orson?"

Ruby sputters into her water glass.

We both sit on her couch. Bedsheets are stretched under me and partially scrunched in the corner. They somehow both barely fit the couch and are too big for it. The unfortunate fate of a fitted sheet on anything but a bed.

"What do you think?" I ask.

"Are you kidding?"

"Maybe," I say. "I don't know. Is it crazy?"

She traces a line through the condensation on her cup, but doesn't respond.

"Okay, so that's a yes," I answer for her.

Ruby is the type of person who doesn't rock the boat. Lucky for her, I'm the one who leaps in and breaks a hole in the bottom.

When Orson told me he was falling for me, there was a part of me that wondered if we could make it work. Maybe I could come home to his smiling face and dry humor. But then my future flashed before my eyes, and I knew how it would inevitably end.

Life would get difficult. Maybe we'd get in a fight about dishes or laundry or something else. We'd stop sleeping together. We'd start saying *yes, dear* in a sarcastic tone, and we'd start rolling our eyes at the other person's jokes. We'd sit on the couch, resenting the fact that the other person dragged us away from the life we could have had. A life of freedom.

I know what a typical marriage becomes. I've seen it with my parents, my older sister, and countless people in our church. And I like Orson too much to subject either of us to that.

But so much time has passed since last fall. His admission of, "*I'm falling for you,*" has come and gone. That box he held in his hand when he said it—the velvet box I never asked about—is just a distant memory. And if he can forget it, then so can I.

"You think it's a bad idea," I say.

"Kinda," Ruby responds with a small shrug.

"Tell me why, Rubes."

"Do I really need to?"

"It's not like we're getting together or anything," I say. "And that's fine. Seriously. It's *fine.*"

The clarification sounded more damning than it should have.

"It's just another arrangement," I tell Ruby. "And I can't stay here."

"I'm so sorry, Theo. I—"

"No, you've got Bennett's mom staying with you starting next week. I get it."

She winces. "Do you really have nowhere else to stay?"

I slump. "No. But, hey, maybe this can help me save

money. Maybe, after all this, I can get my own studio." I point a finger at her. "Come on. You know I've talked about that."

"Yeah, I know," she says softly. "But don't you remember your wedding?"

Ruby sure does. She and Bennett were the only ones who attended.

"I do," I say. "I remember."

"Right. And you couldn't stop laughing."

"It was awkward! Why wouldn't I?"

"That's my point though. Do you think you'll just laugh your way through the awkwardness of living with him?"

"I don't see why not."

She sighs, pulling a pillow into her lap and hugging it to her chest.

"What? You think I can't do it?"

"No, just ..." She sighs, then laughs, waving her hands beside her head. "Gah, everyone is stressing me out! Stop planning marriages!"

I laugh with her as she falls against the cushions with her typical sweet smile.

Ruby doesn't mention Bennett's name in that sentence, but she doesn't have to. He's the only other person in our group with a marriage problem.

Sort of.

After he proposed to his girlfriend, Jolene, last fall, it's been an unspoken source of stress for all of us—not just Bennett. Mostly because that lug of a man stomps around like a troll under a bridge all the time, consumed by wedding planning. Even his mom decided to come back into town and help. Ruby offered to play host, like the good best friend that she is. An offer she made *before* she knew I needed a place to crash. I can't blame her.

"Orson and I are both adults," I continue. "We can do this. I mean, what other options do I have? Plus, you only live once, right?"

Ruby giggles. "You sound so confident."

"I am."

"So, you'll just ... move through life without a care in the world?"

I shrug and pick up my phone, scrolling down my list of texts, past our friend group's ongoing chat and past my family's group chat, which is dominated by my dad and Callie. Kassandra, Mom, and I don't talk at all.

"I already move through life like that," I mumble. "I can handle a bit more drama."

I then open the empty text thread for DO NOT CALL —the name I entered for Orson five months ago. After I stared at my phone day after day, wanting to do exactly that. But things are different now.

I shoot a text to Orson. All it says is, *I'm game.*

I show it to Ruby, who sighs.

"Okay then," she says in that wistful tone. "Cheers to life-ruining decisions."

I pick up my water bottle and clink it with hers.

"That's the spirit."

12
Theo

"Box," Orson says, holding out his arms.

I release the box I'm carrying into my husband's open arms. When his hands slip over mine, I instantly jerk them back. He notices and laughs. I laugh too. Like we're telling the punch line to a very bad joke.

Okay, so it's been a little awkward. But that's to be expected. To our credit, we've tried not to be. I bought his favorite mini peanut butter snacks and put them in a makeshift thank-you basket, and Orson surprised me with new purple bedsheets and a tiny flashlight in the guest room's side table. He's tried to be welcoming, but a fact remains—this is weird.

Orson walks off with my box of stuff in his arms, wearing blue jeans that fit too well around his tight butt and the type of black T-shirt that I swear all hot men just buy in bulk online.

Bennett walks up to me, carrying three stacked boxes, also wearing the hot-man T-shirt uniform.

"This is a bad idea," he mutters with a shake of his head.

I grab the leather band holding his hair in a bun and rip it out.

"Hey!"

I toss it to Ruby, who catches it midair, shifting the trash bag full of my unfolded clothes to her other hand.

Bennett snorts, puffing and blowing part of his long black hair out of his eyes. "Just because you don't want to say it's bad doesn't make the bad decision go away."

"They're making an adult decision," Ruby says. "And it's their life to do as they wish."

Bennett's face looks exactly as it did when I first told him I needed help moving into Orson's house. His mouth twisted to the side, his eyebrows rose, and he clucked his tongue in disapproval like my yia-yia used to do when I snuck extra Christmas cookies from the jar.

"You'll regret it," he grumbles.

"She won't when she sees him in a towel," Ruby singsongs.

"Gross," Bennett says.

Ruby laughs. "If I were married, I'd probably *want* to see my husband in a towel. And Orson isn't exactly bad-looking."

I gasp and smile. "What happened to your modesty?"

"You think Orson is good-looking?" Bennett asks.

Ruby's eyes swivel to his.

"Yes," she says with a laugh, "I do."

"He's already married, if case you forgot," Bennett says, leaning down to her.

She sticks out her tongue in defiance.

"I did mention he's over me, right?" I say to him.

"No," Bennett says. "But Ruby told me."

"Of course she did."

You can't say something to one of them without the other finding out. Ruby and Bennett are just that—Ruby and Bennett. Bennett and Ruby. Two names always lumped in the same breath, which is why when Orson and I needed a witness to our wedding and I asked Ruby on account of the fact that she's the quietest person in our friend group, I shouldn't have been surprised to also get a call from Bennett, saying he would be the stand-in best man. I think he just wanted to watch our courthouse train wreck.

This is also why, even though all of our friends would be elated to help me move, we only have the help of the dynamic duo.

"You know what *does* sound really attractive to me?" Ruby says.

"What's that, Rubes?" he answers.

"Pizza and wings."

"I like how your mind works."

They high-five—something they do often. Like their own form of a secret handshake. I wonder if that comes with the territory of having a best friend.

"I'll tell Orson to order some," I say.

"Already demanding your husband do things?" Bennett teases.

I narrow my eyes. "You're on thin ice, mister."

"Ooh," Ruby says under her breath.

They walk into the house, still muttering little jokes between them.

I head back to my car, grabbing the last box from my backseat. This is it. After this, I'll be moved in. I'll be living with my husband.

That's not so bad, right? Just a place to rest my head for a while, and then we'll part ways again. Easy-peasy.

I lift my leg to kick my door shut. But I barely reach so I nearly stretch into a full split to kick it closed.

"I could never be that flexible," Orson says.

I almost jump in the air. I didn't realize he was standing behind me. My hand goes to my chest, and I lose traction on the box. Orson catches it as it slips out of my hands. I can hear every item rattle and clank—my roller skates, my jewelry—and then ... *buzz*.

His eyes widen.

My eyes widen.

Bzzzz.

"What is that?" he asks, but I see the slow grin on his face.

We both know exactly what it is.

My little pal. My helpful hand. My *vibrator*.

I see Ruby and Bennett coming back over, laughing with each other. Totally not entrenched in the awful situation I'm suddenly in. I didn't consider the fact that I'd be using my sex toys in the same house as my not-husband husband. I just packed up my stuff and went on my way.

But here we are, with the buzzing between us and Orson's steadily growing smile.

I quickly remove part of the box's lid, dip my arm in, find the buzzing vibrator, and twist it off right as Bennett and Ruby walk up.

"Last box?" Bennett asks.

Orson tongues the inside of his cheek, adjusting the box in his grip, and nods.

"Yeah," he says. "I've got it though. Seems like there's some sensual—I mean, *sensitive* stuff inside."

Yep. Definitely awkward.

13

Orson

Theo has *toys*. I shouldn't be surprised. Not with the way she used to ride me like a cowgirl in the rodeo. But as I lie in bed the next morning, blinking awake in the blurry darkness of my room, still as a mummy in a tomb, I realize my ear is itching for any sound of *buzzing* in the guest room next door.

I wince. I'm getting secondhand embarrassment for myself.

I grab my glasses from my bedside table—a necessary crutch before I put in my contacts for the day—and then head toward the kitchen. I slow as I walk past the guest bedroom, now Theo's room.

The door is still closed. That makes sense with the barely risen sun. Theo strikes me as a woman who stays in bed as late as she can. When I was twenty-nine, I did the same. That hasn't been my life in years though.

I walk to the coffeemaker, upending the bag of pre-ground coffee and filling the pot with whatever portion of sink water seems to make sense. I've never been one for measuring. Whatever amount I've been blindly dumping in for years has worked out so far.

But then it hits me.

How does Theo take her coffee? Does she measure it out precisely, or is my bachelor lifestyle of dumping it all in willy-nilly not ideal? Heck, does she even like coffee?

I rummage through my cabinets, as if expecting something else, like tea, to magically pop up. But I know I don't have anything else.

That's okay. It'll all be okay. She knew what was getting into by moving in with a perpetual bachelor, right?

I grab an Atlanta Braves coffee mug and start to pour from the pot. But then my eyes trail over to the glass door leading to my backyard.

Holy shit.

Positioned on all fours with her ass pushed to the sky is my very attractive, *very* untouchable wife.

Theo is practicing yoga in tight pants—so tight and ruched that I worry about the comfort of her ass in them—and a strappy sports bra that shows off her lengthy spine and muscular back.

Good Lord.

She slowly walks her legs forward until she's literally folded in half. In that new pose, her ass looks like a damn peach.

When she rises, exhaling a deep breath, I let out a deep breath with her. I didn't realize I'd been rendered speechless and breathless at the sight of her flexibility. Not that it's new to me. I've had sex with her enough to know she can bend every which way she and I prefer. But my infinite dry spell doesn't exactly make this sight easier.

We stand there together, me watching with wide eyes

from the kitchen and her with her face turned toward the rising sun. She's—

SHIT.

I let out a yelp as my coffee pours over the rim of my cup. I shake my hand out, coated in steaming coffee, and throw the pot back on the counter. I rush to the sink and place my hand underneath the running spout. The back of my hand feels like it's been stung by fifty wasps.

I forgot I was pouring coffee. This is exactly what I get for ogling my wife.

I hear the back door open behind me. I swallow, keeping my waist pressed to the sink because, considering I made the dumb decision to walk around only in boxer briefs and watch my wife bend into precarious positions, the tent in my underwear is far from appropriate.

"Are you all right?" she asks. "Thought I heard a yell."

"Yep," I say, strained as the water rushes over my thumb. "Just peachy."

Don't say peachy. It'll remind you of her ass.

Great. Now, you're thinking of her ass again.

"Coffee," I clarify. "It spilled on my thumb."

Her hand touches my bare shoulder because, yeah, I didn't put on a shirt either, like an inconsiderate jerk. But Theo's palm is just as soft as I remember it. Except the last time I felt it, it was wrapped around my—

"Let me see your hand," she says.

I swallow, trying to think of literally anything but her ass hiked in the air. I focus on the aching burn on my hand. No, I think about The Honeycomb's payroll. I think about how the Braves missed the playoffs years back. I think about Mrs. Stanley's stacked boxes in her garage.

Yes, Mrs. Stanley's boxes are what cause me to go from raging boner to something more manageable.

I face Theo, grabbing the tea towel from the counter as I wrap it around my coffee-roasted hand.

"It's fine," I say, wincing. "I, uh, didn't think you'd be awake yet."

I wait for her to answer, but her eyes are too busy halting at my chest, roaming over every inch of it, like she's reading a book. After a few awkward seconds, her eyes finally snap back up, and she swallows.

"I like to do yoga with the sunrise."

A slow smile creeps onto my face. I can't help it. Theo was checking me out.

"I can see that."

"You're a morning person too?" she asks, clearing her throat and opening cabinets until she finds the coffee mugs.

"Yeah, I have to go to the bar."

She squints at me. "But The Honeycomb doesn't open until the afternoon."

I shrug. "Well, I go and get ready for the day, then run errands and stuff. I have some weekly visits with people in town."

"Do you spend all day out?"

"Most days. Told you I wouldn't be around much."

"Hmm."

I wish I knew what was going on in her mind, but all I see instead is how her bottom lip slips between her teeth in concentration, which has me thinking, BOXES, BOXES, BOXES, over and over.

"Well, anyway, I'm gonna go take a shower," I say.

"Yeah, I should too," she says. "I've got a punctual streak going at work now."

"Do they give you gold stars?" I joke.

"Actually, yes," she says with a grin. "Well, I give them to myself."

"Wait, really?"

"Yeah. It's the only thing that motivates me." Then, she narrows her eyes. "Don't judge me."

"No judging," I say. "I've always liked gold stars."

"Oh, it's not just gold stars. I cycle through lots of different stickers."

"Why? Gold stars are the best ones."

"I like variety."

"Why switch it up when tried-and-true works?"

"I've always liked your consistency," she says with a laugh.

Our eyes dart between each other's. Then, we both laugh, each of us looking away at the same time.

"Well, shower time, right, roomie?" she says, nudging me with her elbow.

"At the same time?" I ask with a laugh.

"Should we not? Is there not enough water pressure?"

"Well, considering I only have one shower ..."

Her eyes widen in realization. "Ohh."

"Yeah," I say with a grinning nod. "*Ohh.*"

"Well, you can shower first," she says. "Your house and all."

"It's your house now too," I say. "Seriously. Take all the coffee you need. Kick your feet up. Do yoga naked next time. I don't mind."

She smiles. "I forgot how funny you are."

"I'm really not."

This somehow makes her laugh, letting out a small snort.

"Oh my God." She covers her mouth with her palm but still snorts into it. She shoves my shoulder. "Go shower."

"Yes, ma'am."

I'd be lying if I said the place where our skin connected

didn't strike a match in my soul. But regardless of what they say, you can definitely teach an old dog new tricks. And this old dog knows better than to think anything of it.

I grab my cup of coffee and turn to walk to the bathroom, but before I can shut the door, Theo calls, "Cute glasses, by the way!"

I give a final wave, then close the bathroom door behind me. I tug it an additional time to get it to latch.

But the conversation between us still lingers, even once I turn on the water and stand under the hot stream.

This was a bad idea.

14

Theo

"The squishy bits are what you need to watch out for."

"Disgusting."

"You're tellin' me."

I hop down from the ledge and onto the drained floor, into the heart of our new ride. Our very under-construction ride.

The large building on the far-left side of Honeywood Fun Park previously housed a dark boat ride that has been shut down for years. But after Honeywood's sale last fall, our new owners are trying to utilize every building we have. I think they're going for the *we're under new management, so expect only great things* approach. But that's resulted in lots of changes in a very short period.

The water channel for the ride is drained, so the four of us—me; our general manager, Fred; general manager in training, Lorelei; and head of maintenance, Bennett—walk along the empty track. As Rides supervisor, I only sort of need to be here. But Lorelei insisted on it, saying I had a special job for this ride opening.

I thankfully made it right on time for the final inspection before they refill the channel with water. I even placed a Buzzy sticker on my agenda to celebrate another day of being on time. Even if Orson does think the sticker system is silly, it works.

A piece of so-called squishy bits squelches beneath my sneaker.

"Ew!" I practically yelp.

Bennett laughs. "Told you. It'll get a deep clean this weekend."

"And this is really gonna be open by the end of summer?" I ask.

Lorelei nods. "Animatronics done. Boats done. We just need to refill the tunnel and get you"—she pokes me in the side—"training all the skippers."

I laugh. "Skippers?"

"That's what we're calling the tour guides," Fred answers for me.

"You mean, chaperones."

Lorelei—her face suddenly so serious that it has me curling my lips in, begging not to laugh—says, "We've had too many uh-oh babies on The Canoodler. We've learned our lesson."

"Well, that takes the fun out of a dark ride," I say.

"Probably for the best," Fred mumbles.

"Y'know, I had my first kiss on The Canoodler," Bennett says with a smile.

"With the back of your hand, right?" I ask.

His face falls, and he grunts, "No."

"Let's hope not. Poor Jolene."

"Oh, did you ever pick the flowers for your wedding?" Lorelei asks.

Then, I add, "Or is Jolene making you practice with your hand now too?"

"Theo, I swear ..."

"Was it roses?" Lorelei asks, continuing to attempt a change in subject, like the elegant mediator that she is.

Fred doesn't say anything. I don't think he likes hearing his surrogate kids talking about their teenage shenanigans.

"Yeah," Bennett finally grumbles. "We chose roses."

"Boo," I say with my hands cupped over my mouth.

"Well at least I'm not being called a skipper."

Lorelei pats Bennett's bicep. "I think roses are lovely, Bennett. And, Theo, you're gonna do great with these skippers. I just know it."

I laugh again. "Okay, but seriously, please stop using the word *skipper*."

"Why?"

"It sounds ridiculous."

Bennett snorts. "Don't tell the skippers that."

"Can I at least be named head skipper?" I ask. "Or something slightly cooler since I'm the trainer?"

"How's captain?" Fred asks.

"Isn't that the same thing?"

"Yes, but it sounds better," Lorelei says with a smile.

"Good point. I'll take it."

We spend thirty more minutes walking along the track, the three of them taking notes on who knows what. Maintenance or construction or maybe even the squishy mold bits that need to be removed, like, yesterday. I'm just here to get out of work with the excuse of "training," so I balance on the edges of the track, tiptoeing along the path until I look up and see an empty area already lit with pink and white lighting. A few men in khakis and polos play with wires.

"What's going on up there?" I ask.

"That," Lorelei says, clutching her clipboard to her chest as it puffs out with pride, "right there will be the

Queen Bee and Ranger Randy animatronics. Their wedding scene." She laughs. "Quinn is gonna hate it."

Honeywood characters Queen Bee and Ranger Randy were forced together last fall by the demand of guests. Quinn, playing the role of Queen Bee, was less than enthused. Well, until she and Landon—Ranger Randy—fell in love, that is. Plus, it's what ultimately got our park on the radar of buyers and allowed us to expand like we have. Never say the customer isn't right because, sometimes, they are.

But as I look at the empty space, I realize it is yet another wedding haunting my life, like the ghost of Marriage Past, Present, and Future.

"I should get going," I say, finding a ladder nearby. "See what newbie is freaking out today."

"Are you gonna be at trivia this week, or do you have another client?" Lorelei asks.

"Oh, no, I'm good to go for trivia."

I don't correct her and say that I didn't have a yoga client last week. I was instead packing up my stuff from Ruby's living room. But Lorelei doesn't need to know that. It'd open the door for too many questions.

Questions like, *Why did you move in with Orson?* Or, *Are you two dating?* Or, *How did his erection look in his boxers?*

Okay, so she wouldn't ask that, but that doesn't mean the thought hasn't left my mind since this morning.

I can't erase it. Even not fully erect, Orson is ... a lot. Formidable. Like a soldier ready for battle. A soldier with a bayonet, whose spear I've never been able to forget.

I take a final glance at the empty space where the married animatronics will go, and that unsettling feeling—

the urge to see him in his boxers again—deflates like a balloon.

After work, I meet up with Mrs. Stanley at Yogi Bare for a quick hip session. We wrap up around eight, and then I record a few videos for my social media marketing and head home. Well, to Orson's house. My house? I don't even know. Does being his wife count as partial ownership?

Legalities.

Literally.

I key in, tossing my fob onto the bare counter. I make a mental note to place a bowl there later.

Orson's house is still utilitarian, just as it was months ago. There's next to nothing on the main floor. Very bachelor-esque. Very *not expecting a wife*-esque.

But seriously, who doesn't have a key bowl?

I cross over to go to my room, but I notice an arrangement of items on the kitchen table that weren't there this morning.

Two boxes of assorted teas. A small stack of fluffy white towels and a purple loofah with the tag still attached. Four different kinds of face masks. And ... tampons?

Did Orson buy all this for me?

What a silly question. Of course he did. Unless the dude uses tampons for his nose bleeds—hey, if it's ridiculous but it works, it's not ridiculous—I'm pretty sure it's all for me.

I feel a tiny little butterfly flutter inside my chest. It's nothing though. He has always been caring—for everyone in his life, even his fake wife.

I grab a face mask packet and follow the sound of a television coming up from the spiral staircase. I trail a hand along the railing, adorned with orange string lights, likely still left over from his Halloween party last fall. I descend to the bottom floor.

When I reach the last stair and dip my head below the drop ceiling, I instantly get a new vibe. This area looks completely different from upstairs.

Whereas the top floor is empty and bland, the downstairs is—dare I say—cozy. The furniture is a mismatch of styles and patterns. Sports paraphernalia hangs on every wall, ranging from framed, signed jerseys to other collectibles stored in shadow boxes. There's even a small piano in the corner with the seat hidden under a stack of folded blankets. But the main centerpiece is a large television mounted on the far wall and, in front of it, a long couch with Orson reclined on one end.

He's in a gray Atlanta Braves T-shirt with black-and-red checkered pajama pants. He's wearing the same circular glasses he wore this morning. His short hair is damp, and he smells of wood and lemongrass. He must have just gotten out of a shower.

A slow smile spreads over his face when he sees me.

"Hey, you." His voice is low and croaky, like a man who talked all day and is enjoying the quiet around him.

I can't help the smile I return to him.

He pats the area of the couch next to him. "Sit. Don't be shy."

I laugh. "Like I ever could be."

He chuckles, like the thought is ludicrous to him as well.

I sink into the couch cushions next to him. While the leather couch upstairs looks stiff, this cloth feels well loved. Broken in. Comfortable.

I look down at the mask in my hand, then hold it up to him.

"Did you buy these for me?"

"Are they okay?" he asks. "Do you not like that brand?"

I smile, feeling a warmth in my body that fills me from my toes up to my neck. "No, it's a good brand."

"Good. Figured you should feel at home. I'm a provider, you know."

"Ah, my husband," I say wistfully.

"Your husband," he echoes with a chuckle. So gentle, like his voice could tame a panther.

We both turn back to the TV, and instead of enduring the awkward quiet, I continue talking.

"My dad is a big TV guy, so this," I say, gesturing to the giant TV in front of us, "he'd love this."

I swallow at the thought of it—the fact that I haven't seen any of my family in months.

"Do you talk to them much?" Orson asks.

"Just my youngest sister and my dad," I say. It comes out as more of a mutter than I intended.

Out of the corner of my eye, I think Orson might be looking at me.

"Do you miss them?"

I shrug. "Sometimes."

All the time. Constantly. My dad with his raspy laugh. My mom with her dead plants on the windowsill, pretending she has a green thumb. My youngest sister, Callie, with her punny jokes, which are worse than my dad's. Even my older sister, Kass, with her resting bitch face and eye-rolling husband, David. Those two might look like they're straight out of a Tim Burton movie, but they're *my* Tim Burton movie.

I look over and see Orson still staring at me. For a

moment, I wonder if he can read my thoughts. Though I hope he didn't hear how I compared my oldest sister to *Corpse Bride*.

Not far from the truth though. Her wedding day was a mess of sour faces and hesitation and ... dullness.

I stood at the end of the bridesmaid row, clutching white flowers, crossing my chest and shoulders every time, "Father, Son, and Holy Spirit" was repeated, watching them at the altar, unsmiling. And I felt numb.

They were getting married because it was what they were supposed to do. David's parents were friends of my parents. He didn't go to our same church, but it still made sense.

But not for me. And part of me feels solace that I went a different route. At least until I realize that's why my family and I are estranged to begin with.

"So, what are we watching?" I ask, settling into the cushions, pulling my legs up to my chin.

I rip open the face mask packet. Orson watches me slide the gooey mask out. I lean my head back and lay it on my face.

"The game," he answers.

"What game?"

"You look like a serial killer."

I swivel my head toward him, and I swear he flinches.

"That mask is horrifying," he says with a laugh.

"What game?" I repeat with a grin.

A small smile spreads on his face, and he faces the television again.

"Baseball, Michael."

"Michael?" I ask.

"Michael Myers."

I laugh. "Rude!"

"I'm not the one wearing a mask."

I stick out my tongue, and he laughs.

"Okay, so baseball?"

"Yes," he says. "The Braves are playing."

"I've never understood the rules to baseball."

Orson's head whips back to me.

"Never understood ... what? What do you mean?"

I shrug. "Sports aren't really my thing."

"Oh, not under this roof. I'm gonna make it your thing."

Except the way he says *make it* sends the area between my thighs burning. Orson Mackenzie should know better than to do things like that.

"Let's start with the innings," he says.

"Pause there. What are innings?"

"Oh, Poulos ..."

I grin as I remember just how much I liked the way he said my last name.

15

Orson

"Has Theo been acting weird to you?"

I practically stumble over the chair in front of me, which is odd, considering the chair wasn't in my way at all.

It's Wednesday Trivia Night at my bar, and Lorelei always comes early to help set up with my cousin, Emory. It's always funny, watching him take chairs from her as she pulls them off the table, his thick eyebrows turning inward as he slowly gets more frustrated that she's actually doing labor with her bad hip.

"Isn't Theo always weird?" I say with a laugh.

Lorelei smiles back at me, but it lasts only a second before she twists her lips to the side. "Hmm. I don't know. I went over to Ruby's, and all her boxes were gone."

"Maybe she put them in storage," Emory says.

"She would tell us."

"Maybe she's seeing someone."

Lorelei sits up straight, blinking at Emory like he just invented something new.

"Maybe she's seeing someone," Lorelei echoes.

I let out a nervous laugh. "Wouldn't she tell you that?"

Lorelei looks to me and nods. "She would ..."

The front door opens, and Bill, our trivia guy, comes in, lugging his equipment. All three of us rush over to help him, and the conversation is forgotten. At least by everyone but me.

I'm doing my best to throw our friends off the scent, but it's not an easy task.

I watch as, one by one, Theo's friend group arrives, coming to the bar and ordering their beer. Theo's group of friends used to consist of five people, but it's grown with the addition of partners.

The core group used to be only Theo, Lorelei, Quinn, my buddy Bennett, and his best friend, Ruby. But since then, they've added my cousin, Emory, and Lorelei's twin brother, Landon, who is a beam of light beside his girlfriend, Quinn's, crossed arms and sarcasm. Their long table is full of laughter and small-town gossip.

Watching from a distance, I can't help but wonder what the hell Theo and I were thinking. How long can we seriously keep our living situation, our marriage, a secret?

"Is it weird, knowing your wife is right over there, not talking to you?" Bennett asks later in the night, leaning on the bar top with Ruby next to him.

"Is it weird your fiancée doesn't come to trivia?" I shoot back.

Ruby pulls her lips in and looks away, eyeing something —probably anything—on the wall to avoid my awkward, and, okay, insensitive comment.

Bennett's fiancée, Jolene, rarely comes to Trivia Night. I swear she only lives in Cedar Cliff for Bennett's sake, which makes me worry he'll get snagged away the moment they say *I do*. I worry more what that will do to Ruby, who has been joined at the hip with him since elementary school. But that's not the only thing that concerns me about his wedding.

Bennett grunts, "Uncalled for."

"Sorry. But don't make fun of my wife, and I won't make fun of your future one."

"How about we make fun of nobody?" Ruby suggests, her eyebrows turned in, as if begging for the subject to be changed.

"And where's the fun in that?" I ask with a smile.

I hear the screech of a chair and see Theo leaving their table and walking over.

"Incoming," Bennett mutters.

Ruby elbows him.

"Figured it was safe if y'all were here," Theo murmurs to Bennett and Ruby as she climbs onto a barstool. She doesn't need to explain. We all know what she means. She and I have ignored each other for months. It might be obvious if we started acting buddy-buddy now. She looks between the three of us and squints. "Wait, were y'all talking about me?"

"No," Ruby says slowly, but she's not a good liar. "We were ... discussing tuxes for Bennett's wedding."

Theo grins. "I don't believe you. But, oh my God, Bennett!" She hits his arm. "You don't have a tux yet?"

"Should I?" he asks.

"Yes," all three of us chorus back.

"How do *you* know that I should?" Bennett asks pointedly at me.

I shrug. "You work in a bar long enough, you hear some bride complaints. You're three months out, man."

"Well then," he says, drawing in a long sigh, "yeah, I probably need one."

"I keep telling you that," Ruby whispers with a small smile.

He grins. "Yeah, aren't you supposed to keep me on track or something?"

Ruby is Bennett's best woman or maid man or whatever it is the two of them are calling it nowadays. Their joke changes week to week.

"We should go to Atlanta soon," she says.

"Wait, why leave town?" I ask.

"Believe it or not, a tux shop is the one thing Cedar Cliff doesn't have. Lorelei's parents are handling the flowers. Landon says he'll cater. But tuxes?" Bennett slashes his hand in front of his throat, as if saying, *Not a chance.*

I look over at Theo, but she's too busy staring down at her phone, looking at a text. The group thread is labeled *Poulos Party* with a beach ball and a balloon emoji around the name. It's the second time I've seen it pop up on her phone. I wonder if it's her family text.

We haven't talked about her family much since she moved in. She changes the subject before we can, but I know she misses them. I can just feel it in the change of the air whenever they're brought up.

This is why I blurt out, "We could go with you."

Theo's head pops up. "Who is we?"

"You and me, wife," I say with a grin.

I think I see her posture falter, and a shuddering breath leaves her lips, but only for a second. I wonder if the word *wife* does something to her, but I try not to think about it more. Not a good route to go down.

"Why?" she asks.

"We could visit your parents."

Her eyes widen. "Are you *insane*?"

"I'm not doing anything Saturday," Ruby says. "We could go then?"

"Oh," I say, my body instantly deflating. *Well, there goes that idea.* "Maybe not. I can't leave the bar in the middle of a weekend."

"Come on," Bennett says.

"And who will run this place, huh?" I ask. "I don't even take holidays off."

Theo looks at me weird. When I follow her eyes down, I realize she's looking at my hand that is absentmindedly rubbing over my heart. I didn't even notice I was doing it. I lower it back down and look away, playing it off with another laugh.

"You should go," Theo says.

"No, I don't think—"

"Okay, I'll be the bad guy," Bennett says. "It's my wedding, and you're a groomsman. I demand you come and get fitted too."

"Guys, come on."

"Nope, you need to come with us," Ruby says with a grin. Her face looks red, as if demanding something is uncomfortable for her.

Bennett barks out a laugh. "Get 'em, best maiden."

I look to Theo, who bites her lower lip before placing a splayed palm on the bar. She's a woman with a plan.

"How about this? I'll see my parents if you take one day off," Theo says. We look at each other, and I can see the challenge in her eyes. The fire. "Don't you want me to see my family, husband?"

Well played, Poulos.

"You're a monster."

She grins. "I know."

16

Theo

O rson is already waiting for me in Honeywood's parking lot by the time I get off work on Saturday. He's in his black Jeep, leaning with his elbow out the window, his eyes shrouded by aviators. The glasses make him look like the hot cop on the squad that breaks all the rules. I swear he knows it too.

"Ready to go, sweetheart? Ruby and Bennett are already halfway there."

Sweetheart.

That word still does horrific things to me.

I clear my throat. I don't know why I'm nervous. I've been living with Orson for over one week now, and it's been fine. It's been doable. But we also barely cross paths. Being alone together in a car for two hours? With nothing but maybe the radio? I don't think I'm mentally prepared.

But I said what I needed to say to get Orson away from his bar. Orson needs a break that he won't give himself, so I did it for him, like the good wife that I am.

I go around to the passenger side, grabbing the handle at the top to climb in. The whole car smells like him.

"Can I pick the music?" I ask.

"Only if it's good music," he says with a playful smile.

"Cool. So, classical only."

"Hey, don't knock piano."

I almost call his bluff and play Mozart the whole way there, but all my joking confidence falls apart when I see his *hand* grip the wheel. The way it rests so casually on the top while the other handles the gearshift. Veins sprout over the back, twisting over his forearms. I swallow, trying to ignore the threat of pressure between my thighs.

I pick something remarkably normal and unoffensive, then look out the window as we drive away from Cedar Cliff.

"Proud of you for doing this," he says.

"Hmm? What?"

"For seeing your family."

"Oh. Right. Well, it's a bad decision."

"Good thing we're full of those."

Too many at this point.

Last night, I paced the den with my phone in my hand, tossing it up in the air and back down, tapping it against my palm, then slumping in the chair.

"You have to call," Orson had said.

"I know, you jerk."

He grinned at me from the opposite side of the couch.

"I told Kailey to cover my shift. It's only fair."

"Yes, yes, I know," I said, burying my head in my hands.

"Call."

I leveled a glare at him, then finally called my parents' house. Thankfully, my dad answered, and he seemed over the moon about me dropping by. I didn't ask whether my mom was too.

"And you're bringing Orson?" he asked. Because of course he did.

"Yes."

And I feel just as weird about that answer now as I did last night.

When we make it to the wedding shop, Ruby and Bennett are already there, sifting through styles, laughing together, as if they were at a stand-up show rather than a place with too much formalwear. They eventually pick out a few styles, and Orson and Bennett go to get dressed.

Ruby and I sit on couches, waiting, browsing cat videos on our phones together, but when the boys finally come back out, I thank God that my phone is pulled up to my face because my cheeks instantly heat at the sight.

Orson adjusts his cuffs and looks around the store. Even stuck with pins for alterations, Orson looks like the tux was made for him. It's cut right at the shoulders, tapered in toward his waist, pinned up at the ankles. If there were a picture next to the definition of *smolder*, his wistful expression would be it. The way he clutches his lapels and shakes out the tux jacket feels like a moment lost in time. A snapshot that should be in a cologne magazine ad. And when his hazel eyes finally find me sitting on the couch, I'm frozen to the spot.

I once heard Meghan call Orson her *short king* and he does, in fact, carry himself like royalty. With the way his chin tilts up. With how sharp his jawline is.

Orson is kingly in his own right.

"Well?" Bennett asks.

I look over to him instead—anything to break away from Orson's gaze. Bennett's long black hair drapes over the all-black tux. He looks good, too. Though, he also looks uncomfortable. But when I look over at Ruby, her bottom lip is pulled in, and she's nodding repeatedly, like a bobblehead.

"Yep," she says. "Looks great. That's the one for sure."

I meet Orson's eyes, wondering if he also noticed just how flustered Ruby seemed, but he's already gone back behind the curtain. And I already miss seeing him in his formalwear.

While Bennett and Orson pay at the counter, I look around with Ruby. But I'm not focused on whichever bow ties or belts or wallet clips are available. I'm distracted by my husband.

I look at the window, seeing his reflection from across the store. Even without the tux, he still holds himself tall. I consider that maybe my family event won't be so bad with him next to me. I wonder if maybe, just maybe, we could survive it together.

But when I look back to the rack in front of me, I see another set of eyes peering from the other side. Green eyes too much like my own, which I didn't anticipate seeing for another thirty minutes, minimum.

My mother.

17

Orson

"Mom," Theo says.

I hear it all the way across the store.

Theo's eyes dart over to me, and when her mom's follow, I tense.

Sophia Poulos stares, assessing me where I stand. I raise my hand in a wave. Then, I keep it there. Like a man getting arrested. With that gaze, she might as well be bringing me in for questioning anyway.

"Orson," she says.

"Nice to see you, Mrs. Poulos."

Theo's mom is not my biggest fan. After last fall, when our elopement came to light, you would have thought we had told her we robbed a bank. I've never met Sophia in person, but the one video call we had was less than successful. We haven't spoken since.

"Theo," she says, "what are you doing here?"

"Me? What are *you* doing here?"

"Picking up a dress cleaning kit for Callie."

Theo pauses, and I've never seen her look so small. Like

the mention of her sister makes her feel lesser than. I don't like it.

"We were just about to head over actually," Theo says.

Her mom's face brightens. "Perfect."

"Yep. Perfect."

Awkward good-byes are exchanged along with cringing glances between Bennett and Ruby.

"Don't say a word," I murmur to them.

I follow Theo back out to my car, opening the door for her and leaning through the window after she climbs in. She's stiff in her seat.

"Everything okay?" I ask.

We watch her mom drive off in a sports vehicle far nicer than my ruddy black Jeep.

"Well, considering I haven't talked to my mom in months, no, I'd say I'm not feeling my best right now."

Theo's hands wring her lap. I reach out and take one. I run a thumb over hers. I hope it's okay, but I'm not sure what else to do. She lets out a breath of air through her nose. I can't tell if it's a laugh or not.

"It's gonna be fine."

"We could just bail," she says quickly. "You know, there's a skating rink between here and Cedar Cliff."

I chuckle. "I don't know how to skate, Theo."

"You can learn," she says. I can hear the desperation. "Come on. Be adventurous."

"We're just dropping by for a bit."

"You don't just *drop by* at my parents' house," she hisses.

"Be adventurous," I whisper, echoing her words back at her.

"No," she whispers back.

"It's just one dinner." I finally get in the driver's seat,

starting the engine. "You gonna give me directions, or do I need to pull out my GPS?"

She groans, grumbling something that might be a curse word, and then says, "Take a right out of here."

From there, I drive where she tells me to. It only takes ten minutes for us to pull into a neighborhood with black iron fences and sidewalks along every yard. It's nothing like Cedar Cliff. Not one single crack in the pavement or dandelion in sight.

When we finally pull up to the driveway, another car is already parked there. A simple black Audi.

Theo groans. "You've gotta be kidding me."

"What?" I ask.

She unbuckles her seat belt like it offended her. "My sister is here too."

"Is that good?"

"Not good. The opposite of good. She doesn't think much of me now."

"Why?"

But Theo leaves the question unanswered.

We walk up the front walkway, lined with rose bushes. Vases of tulips are on the porch, which is surrounded by finely trimmed hedges. We arrive at the open door, where an older man with a long nose canopying a thick mustache waves. I already know him as Elias Poulos.

"Tomato!" he calls.

"Hi, Dad."

"And, Orson! About time we met you in person, son!"

Son?

I barely make it on the porch before his palm is clapping me on the back, his other shaking my hand like we're old golf buddies.

"Well, it's nice to officially meet you, Mr. Poulos," I say.

"Please," Mr. Poulos says, "call me Eli. Or Dad. Up to you."

Dad?

Eli stands there for a moment, looking between us, his grin so wide that his mustache can barely keep up. Then, he waves his hands in the air like a man exasperated by the silence.

"Come on in, you two. Come in."

I pass the threshold into unknown territory. There's a chandelier above our head. A side table with another decorated vase, full of tulips. A wall with framed religious icons and a cross. And the woman next to me—my wife—slowly gets redder and redder by the second, her small hands clenched into fists.

The moment her dad rounds the corner down the hallway, I grip her hips and tug her into a small hallway to the right. Her back lands against the wall.

"Okay, tell me what I'm missing," I say. "He wants me to call him *Dad*?"

Theo's eyes dart between mine, and she pulls that plump lip between her teeth, like a child caught stealing candy.

"He still thinks we're happily married."

"We are."

"But ... not fake."

My heart sinks. My breath catches in my throat.

"Theo. No. You didn't tell them?"

"Hey! It's your fault they think we're madly in love."

Oh, right. There's that.

Do you ever get secondhand embarrassment for yourself? For a decision that still shakes you by the shoulders in the middle of the night, only to have the soul-crushing memory capture your sleep?

Well, I've been having secondhand embarrassment for myself for months now.

"Okay, that's not fair," I say. "I only called your dad."

"Yeah, to ask for his *blessing*," she whispers. "What year is it? I don't have a dowry in the form of three apples and a donkey."

I take a step forward, placing my hands against the wall on either side of her head, caging her in.

"You married a Southern man, sweetheart. I might be many things, but disrespectful isn't one of them."

Her face falls, but her eyes dart between mine.

"I made a mistake, okay?" I continue. "I didn't mean to rat us out. Just felt like the right thing to do."

Eli's voice calls from the kitchen, "We've got spanakopita in the oven!"

I sigh, rubbing the bridge of my nose with my thumb and forefinger. This is ten times worse than I thought it would be.

"I really thought you'd told them it was fake," I mutter, "when everything went down."

She shakes her head and sighs. "I couldn't. It would have made things worse."

"They would have been over it by now."

"Really? Would they have? Because my mom found out through Mr. Spanakopita in there that I was *getting married*." She says the last part through gritted teeth, grabbing a fistful of my shirt and shaking it. "If I'd said it was only for *insurance*? You're kidding me. They'd never be over it. I already probably can't take communion. We should thank our lucky stars Father Peter isn't here to give us judgy eyes."

In the heated motion, we both bump into a side table with another vase full of tulips.

"Okay, what's with all the tulips?" I ask.

She sighs. "They're my favorite. Mom always puts out our favorite flowers when she knows we're coming to dinner."

"That's sweet."

"She can be when she wants to."

Theo laughs a little even though I can tell she's frustrated. I laugh with her to ease the tension.

"Okay, let's just—"

"We have to pretend," she interrupts.

"No," I say slowly. "We'll come clean."

"Orson, stop trying to be a gentleman."

"It's called having integrity."

"Are you saying I don't have integrity?"

"Absolutely not," I say with a laugh. "I'm saying you're being ridiculous."

"*You're* being ridiculous."

Then, a voice from behind us says, "What are you two whispering about?"

Theo looks over my shoulder, and her face instantly falls. I follow her gaze to see a woman who looks remarkably like Theo and yet not at the same time. Thinner. More angular. And holding a glass of wine clutched in a talon-like fist.

She's taller than me. Although that's not that difficult. But I can tell with the way she tilts her chin up that she relishes in that fact. I get this from time to time, and when I was younger, it might have bothered me. But now, I appreciate the heads-up. It's like a free red flag, given willfully and unknowingly.

Theo snorts. "Kass, did you take your wine to the bathroom with you?"

Kass scrunches her nose and spits out, "No."

"Except you're holding wine and leaving the bathroom, so ..."

"Is this your sister?" I ask with a smile.

"Unfortunately," they both chime at the same time, which only makes me smile wider.

Ah, sisterly affection.

"And you are ..."

"The husband? Yes, he is," Theo says, entwining her fingers in mine and clutching my palm hard. It almost hurts. "His name is Orson."

"You've caused a lot of problems around here," Kass says, taking a sip of her wine.

"I'm a bit of a troublemaker," I joke.

She laughs with me, but it has an edge to it.

"By the way, it's your turn to set the table," Kass says to Theo.

Theo sticks out her tongue in a younger sister kind of way, and then Kass walks off with another swig of her wine.

"Aren't you lucky you married the nicer sister?" she says with a grimace.

"No, I married the succubus sister," I say.

She pushes my shoulder with a laugh.

"So, what happened?" I ask.

"She's just bitter that I'm having fun with my fake husband and she's not."

"Seriously."

Theo sighs. "Seriously? She kinda got dragged into our mess. Mom thought she knew I was planning to elope and didn't tell her. And Kass being Kass, she got mad and said some not nice things. They must have eventually connected the dots, so now, I'm the mutual enemy. Plus, I think Kass is mad I got to elope and miss the big wedding tradition when she didn't."

"That's a lot."

"Family drama. Don't recommend it."

We leave the hallway, and she reaches back to take my hand. I disentangle from her.

"No," I say with a laugh. "I won't lie for you."

"I'm not talking to you unless you pretend to love me," she says, grabbing my hand again.

Instead of continuing to argue, I roll my eyes, hook my free thumb in her belt loop, and tug her toward me.

"Brat."

She grins, pulling me around the corner and into the lion's den.

18

Theo

I wish I could say my childhood home is the same as I remember it—maybe a comfy couch, where we watched home movies on or the same fridge, where we hung our turkey-shaped finger paintings—but that wouldn't be the Poulos house.

I lead Orson to our living room with floor-to-ceiling windows, a recent addition from the past ten years; an open kitchen, from the past five years; and a grand piano that might as well still have the price tag on it. There are even two uncomfortable, purely decorative chairs that I'm sure are only intended for the guests my mom dislikes the most.

My mom is funny in her own way.

"Orson, how do you take your steaks?" my dad asks from the kitchen.

"Rare," I say quickly.

"Attaboy." My dad laughs and clinks his tongs.

Orson gives me a side-eye because I know he likely doesn't take his steaks that way—nobody in their right mind would. But my father has always liked his meat still mooing.

Best to start Orson off on the right foot with him. Or at least a slightly better foot.

My dad actually likes Orson. As much as it pains me to admit it, I think he appreciated the gesture of asking for his blessing. It was my mom who called with enough rage to scare the Father, the Son, and the Holy Spirit, then stopped communicating afterward.

My dad makes conversation with Orson in the kitchen, like they're old buddies, ranging from talk about Orson's bar ("an entrepreneur!"), his love of sports ("I'm more of a golf guy, but I respect a man who can appreciate a good game!"), all the way to safety—somehow?—("I see your hand is burned. Can't be too careful in a kitchen!").

I walk away with a grin. I take a step into the den, where Kass sips her red wine on the couch and thumbs through her phone. We pretend like the other isn't there. I guess that's just how we are now. Not that we were ever close before. She's always been the cooler older sister who has higher priorities that don't include her younger sibling. But this cold shoulder behavior is just excessive, if you ask me.

"He's cute," my mom whispers.

I jump, not realizing she was behind me. "Jesus, Mom."

"Would have looked cuter in a tux in the cathedral."

There we are.

"We did what worked for us," I say.

Kass snorts. "You always thought you were exempt from everything."

"I did not."

My mom gives a high-pitched, "Hmm. My little rebel."

It doesn't carry the adoring weight she wants it to. I understand the implication. I didn't take over Dad's business, like Kassandra. I didn't go into the therapy field, like

Callie. I didn't get any form of a college degree. I didn't even graduate high school with honors.

I look toward the kitchen to find Orson staring at me again. He gives a lopsided smile, the kind that accentuates the small lines beside his eyes. He draws me in like a moth to a flame, so I flit over to him on light wings.

Orson doesn't care that I didn't become a freaking doctor.

When I reach him, he wraps his arm around my waist, placing a small kiss on the side of my head. And the gesture, though I'm sure is just for show for our little game of pretend, still makes me feel warm. When I lean my head on his shoulder, he only pulls me in tighter.

"You okay?" Orson whispers.

"Just my mom."

"I'll watch out for your knife at dinner."

I lightly punch him in the stomach, and he chuckles.

Orson offers to help set the table, which has my mom waving him off. She hands me the plates instead, but he grabs them from me anyway.

"Is this the *Southern gentleman* bit?" I ask him.

He grins and takes the utensils too.

We sit down to dinner, the centerpiece holding a vase of tulips—both my and Kass's favorite flowers, which is convenient—but right before we say the blessing, I hear the front door open and three quick beeps from the security alarm. Turning the corner in thick-rimmed glasses, adjusting his tie, and looking bored to even be here is my sister's husband, David.

"Who's this?" he asks without preamble, nodding his chin toward Orson.

David is, for lack of a better word, a *snot*.

"Orson," Kass answers from down the table, "Theo's husband."

Orson grins and says, "Nice to meet ya."

He reaches out his hand, and David responds with the simple up, down, up of a businessman's handshake. Then, he takes a seat next to my dad. He doesn't explain why he's late, but nobody asks either.

It's quiet after we say the prayer. Only the distant humming from the stove's fan and the sound of forks and knives clinking against the china. When I reach for my own knife, I notice it's missing.

Orson gives me a small smile.

Hilarious.

"You have a lovely neighborhood, Eli," Orson says.

Dad smiles. "Thank you. We've lived here for thirty years. We like the neighbors well enough."

Mom snorts. "If Mrs. Johnson would cut the plant near her mailbox."

"Y'know," I chime in, "when we were kids, we would try to guess what everyone did to afford living here."

"Theo," my mom hisses.

"Callie and I always thought they were FBI agents, spies, or gangsters," I continue.

My dad lowers his fork. "Ah, that explains the tree house with *no guns allowed* sign."

"They watched *The Godfather* way too young," my mom says.

"I won't apologize for introducing our children to good cinema."

"Scared them half to death."

"Remember the safety fort?" my dad says to me with a wide smile.

"Safety fort?" Orson asks.

118

I can see the look of concern in his eyes, and I laugh.

"We didn't want the gangsters to get us," I say.

"I'd find the girls sleeping in the same bed all the time," Dad continues. "Curled under blankets. Flashlights out. They said they were hiding from the Godfather."

"Like he was the bogeyman," my mom says. "Eli, you gave them a bogeyman."

"The jowls," I say with a faux shiver. "They scared me."

Orson laughs and holds up his fingers, making his voice stuffy. "*You come to me ... on the day ...*"

"Yes!" my dad says at my husband's admittedly very good impression of Don Corleone.

A smile breaks out on my face at the whole exchange. At Orson's joyful laugh. At my dad's continued impression, continuing the movie quote with, "My daughter would be married ..."

The mood breaks when my mom says loudly, "So!" She sits up straight, huffing out air. "Orson, you own a bar."

The laughter dies down at the change of subject. My dad wipes his eyes with a napkin. The echoed clinking of forks continues.

"Yes, ma'am," Orson answers.

"And does Theo help out at your bar?"

Orson tilts his head side to side, grinning at me conspiratorially. "Sure. From time to time."

Mom squints, as if she doesn't believe him. I can feel my face reddening.

"My yoga business is actually doing really well, Mom," I say. "I keep pretty busy."

"Oh. Yoga," she echoes.

Orson clears his throat. "You know, I learned a while ago it's best to just let Theo do what Theo wants," he says. "Why cage a bird that needs to fly?"

My fork freezes halfway to my mouth. My breath is caught in my throat, but I'm not sure how because my heart is pounding like a hammer, begging to be let out.

Orson isn't smiling but is instead looking at me with a pointed glance. It's like he can see right through me. And maybe, just maybe, he can. Because that is the first time anyone has accurately voiced how I feel.

I'm a bird, born into a cage. And I just need to soar.

Why is that so hard for my family to understand?

My dad smiles, which is why my mom doesn't look at him but instead darts her eyes to Kass, like she's searching for someone to commiserate with. To my sister's credit, she doesn't look back, but she does blink at Orson like he's some alien she's never seen before.

All my mom says in return is, "Well."

And that's that.

The rest of dinner is fairly quiet aside from David discussing business with my dad as if none of us were in the room. The laughter of gangsters and security forts is forgotten.

After dinner, I help clear the table, then make my way to the backyard. I don't tell anyone where I'm going, only wanting to escape into the cool night air for a bit. Seconds after, the door opens and shuts again. My dad walks up beside me. The sound of his Zippo clinks open, and then the glow of an orange bud is at his mouth.

"You promised you'd stop smoking," I say.

He exhales a puff of smoke, leaning away so it doesn't get near my face.

"When did I say that?" he asks with a wet, coughing laugh.

I sigh. "What am I gonna do when you die?"

"Are we also going to discuss what my tombstone will say?"

I laugh. "Maybe."

He takes another drag. The smoke billows from his nose like a dragon.

"You seem like you're doing well," he says. "I'm proud of you, Tomato."

"That makes one person."

"Orson seems proud too."

"Okay, so two. But Mom ... God, it's like, even with a successful business, I'm still not good enough."

My dad looks at me with his thick, graying eyebrows tilted in before taking a step closer and placing an arm around me. He tugs me in toward him—a rough motion because the guy doesn't really do hugs.

"Ah, middle child syndrome," he says. "Life's a bitch, isn't it?"

I snort. "I'm the forgotten child."

"Never," he says without hesitation. "If anything, I worry about you more."

I lean my head against his shoulder as he pats my back.

"Eventually, it'll just be Mom and Kass at that table, and I won't stand a chance."

"God, give me more time, won't you?" he says through choked laughter. "I'm only sixty-five."

"Papou died at seventy," I say.

He places the cigarette to his lips once more.

"Then, I have five more years," he says. "I'm enjoying my sins while I can."

From the house, I hear the low tones of a piano. We both turn and see Orson sitting at the grand piano. My mom stands beside him, her hands winding together. She almost looks nervous. I wonder if she thinks he'll break it. But then, after what looks like a short conversation, he slides over on the seat, and she sits down next to him.

Orson's hands move over the piano keys, sending out beautiful notes. His deft fingers, which I remember feeling so rough and callous against my skin, now look like they belong in a museum of art.

"Orson plays?" my dad asks.

"I guess so," I say with a small smile.

"Don't you know your own husband?"

Before I can answer, there are additional chords on the piano, and I see my mom's hand flying over the keys now. Orson continues to play, but his tones sound softer. He's letting her be the star.

I smile. "He's a great guy."

"You didn't answer my question."

I side-eye my dad, but his eyes float down to my ringless finger.

Something I've always admired about my father—something I wish I'd inherited—is how observant he is. He can read between the lines. I wish I were like that, but I tackle things like a child blindly swinging a bat toward a piñata.

"No ring?"

"He needed my help," is all I answer. And the second the words leave my mouth, I realize how true they are and yet how ridiculous they sound out loud. What I'm really saying is, *Someone* actually *needed me*.

"Well, it seems like he needs it again," he says. "Let's go rescue him from your mother." My dad discreetly puts out his cigarette under a potted plant.

We both go back inside, and when there's a break in the music, my dad purposefully says loud enough for everyone to hear, "Theo, you should get your trumpet out and play with them."

I cut a glance at him, and his thick eyebrows bounce up, then back down.

"She was last chair in band," Kass chimes in from the couch.

"And it's so loud, Eli," my mom says with a wince.

"It's not for everyone," my dad says, nudging me with his elbow. "But it's still wonderful."

My dad leaves the room with a wink and his hands in his khaki pockets.

Orson twists around in his seat, placing his gorgeous piano-playing hands on his knees. "I'd love to hear you play."

His ability to look so genuine and mischievous at the same time is a mystery to me, but I can't help but smile at him in return.

"No, you wouldn't," I say.

"No, I really think I would."

"Oh, wow, look what I found!" My dad waltzes back into the room, holding up my trumpet case from high school.

"Piano and trumpet don't even go together!" I say with my hands in the air.

Kass holds up her palm with wide eyes, as if to say, *Exactly.*

"I think it'll be nice," my dad says. "Sometimes, the unexpected combinations are the best ones."

He places the case at my feet.

I look from it back up to Orson, who tilts his head to the side and gives me the slowest, most beautiful grin.

"Come on, sweetheart. Play music for me."

That alone has me bending over and flicking open the trumpet case's latches.

19

Orson

I take an exit that isn't ours. Five minutes after that, I pull into a parking lot and turn off the engine. We both stare at the building in front of us lit in neon purples and pinks with the words *Supernova Skate* at the top.

"Figured you needed it after tonight," I say.

Theo's lips curl into a smile as she says, "Thank you."

I pat her knee. "You were adventurous. Now, it's my turn."

We walk inside and stop at the counter to pay. I pull out my wallet. Theo tugs out her mess of receipts, cards, and ID, lumped together by a purple hair tie.

She shoves it through the window at the same time I put my card through. The employee looks between our outstretched hands, but I knock my knuckles against hers and shove my credit card closer to him. The attendant hesitantly takes my card.

"I hope you fall," Theo mutters, sliding her card back into her hair tie and pocketing it.

"Only if you catch me when I do."

We walk through the doors. Theo lets out a sigh.

"Don't you just love this?" she says.

"I ... guess?"

Based on her reaction, you'd think we'd entered a spa. It is far from it.

The navy-blue carpet with neon accents is stomped flat to the ground. The air smells like burnt popcorn. The skating rink is lit with blinding bright lights, including a spinning disco ball sending beaming squares over all the people whizzing by on the rink. The walls are covered in airbrushed murals of roller skates, planets, stars, and what might be Buzzy the Bear in an astronaut suit.

"Is that ..."

"Oh, yeah, that's definitely Buzzy," she says. "Not their intellectual property and totally illegal. We'll fit right in with our illegal marriage."

I bark out a laugh as we walk over to the counter to collect our roller skates, then find a free spot on the long bench to lace them on. Theo finishes before me, instantly stepping onto the rink and zooming down the length of it. I don't know what I expected, but I should have known Theo would be a natural at skating.

She winds past dancing adults, toppling children, and teenagers who look like they're too cool for school. She holds her arms out as she soars, but I can't imagine it's for balance. I wonder if she just wants to feel the air flowing through her palms. I wonder it's the freedom she craves— no, the freedom she *needs*.

She slides one foot out and rotates in a semicircle. She's now skating backward, waving to a small kid, who stumbles in place, attempting to wave back. When she takes the final curve back to where I sit, she comes to a sudden brake right in front of me.

"Aren't you full of surprises?" I say with a laugh.

"Could say the same for you, piano man," she says. "Since when do you play?"

I stand up, wobbling on my feet.

"I took too many lessons as a kid," I say, trying to walk forward. "I think they wanted a world-class musician rather than a bar owner."

"Your parents didn't want you to take over the business?"

"No. They actually wanted other things for me. But I always kind of liked the bar."

She nods more to herself than me.

"Want a walker?" she asks, tipping her chin over to the rows of white-and-red contraptions that look like they belong in a retirement home storage closet.

I glance out at the rink again, seeing only children gripping them. One falls right on the spot, the clattering of the walker falling with him.

"Yeah, I think I can do this without one," I say.

But my feet slip, and I have to hold out my arms to steady myself. Theo loops her arm through mine.

"Embarrassed to use the walker?" Theo asks with a giggle. "Think you won't look cool anymore?"

I laugh. "I don't care what I look like. I just don't want a walker to injure me more than I already will be."

As if on cue, another kid falls across the rink. The walker causes a racket on its way down and pummels his head. He gets up like it didn't even happen. Kids are resilient. My mid-thirties ass isn't.

A slow smile spreads over her face.

"You've never been one to care what people think, have you?" she asks.

"Not one bit. And you?"

She grins. "Never."

"The trumpet proved that."

She pushes me lightly, and I feel the skate slip again. I windmill my arms and catch my balance before the skates can rip out from under me. I'm impressed by own ability to stay upright, so I glance at her with a grin. She's already poking out her bottom lip, as if impressed as well.

"Okay, try walking like a penguin," she says.

"A penguin?"

"Side to side. Like this."

She imitates the motion of a penguin waddling on ice with her arms held out and her weight shifting from one foot to the other. I mirror the movement and get a laugh from her. But it does push me forward.

Penguin it is.

Eventually, I make it to a low wall, looking like an aquatic animal and hearing Theo's stifled laughter behind me the whole way. I place one foot on the concrete rink. A teenager soars way too close to me. My skate immediately slips. Her hands grab my forearm, and instead of going down, I stay upright with Theo holding me up.

"My feet are strapped to two tiny cars," I say. "This should be illegal."

"Side to side," she repeats, sliding her palm into mine and keeping her other hand in the crook of my arm.

We skate slowly around the rink, trying to stay on the outside to avoid the crowds of people passing us. At one point, another child almost barrels into us—pretty sure it's on purpose too, the punk—making Theo laugh. I love her laugh. I love how genuine it is. How un-cute it is with its loudness and guttural snort. It's undeniably her.

We make it around the rink, and I finally clutch the lip on the wall, pulling myself back onto the carpet and falling onto the bench seat.

"Wanna go again?" she asks.

"Give me a second, sweetheart," I say with a laugh.

She plops down beside me, leaning back and closing her eyes. We sit there for a moment, taking in the beats of early 2000s pop hits and the electronic symphonies from the nearby arcade and laser tag. I wonder how often younger Theo came here. I wonder if this—the fast speeds and pumping music—was her safe place from her parents' judgment.

"You should have told me," I finally say. "About how your parents treat you."

"My mom's reaction to our wedding didn't tip you off?"

"Fair," I say with a laugh. "Your dad's reaction was so … tame though."

Theo snorts. "He's just happy someone is putting up with me. After I moved, I'm pretty sure he wanted someone to watch over me and make sure I wasn't being the token wild child."

"Why did you move?"

"Do you really need to ask?"

"Humor me."

She sighs. "Expectations. Dinner after dinner of my sisters doing amazing things and me just being … me. I wanted a change of pace. Something new. I honestly didn't think I'd stay in Cedar Cliff past a year, but then I found the crew, and I knew I couldn't leave."

The crew. Lorelei, Quinn, Bennett, and Ruby.

"I've never found a group of people I love as much as them. Who understand me like that. Well, except …"

"Except?"

"You. With the whole bird comment thing. That was a nice touch."

I don't tell her it wasn't a *touch* or anything to be nice. It was just fact.

Her feet roll front and back on the carpet.

"Y'know ... I never asked what he said when you told him."

"Who?" I ask.

"When you told my dad we were getting married."

"He was confused." We both smile at that. "But I told him that you were the kindest person I knew. And that I couldn't wait to marry you."

She blinks at me. "Did you mean it?"

"That I actually wanted to marry you seven months ago? No," I say with a laugh.

She laughs with me, and I can practically hear the wheels turning in her head. The *I knew it* echoing through her mind.

I settle into my seat, tightening my crossed arms over my aching chest and continue, "But did I mean it when I said you are one of the kindest people I've ever had the pleasure of meeting? Absolutely."

She sighs, her hands winding in her lap. It's always odd to see Theo curl in on herself. She has so much day-to-day confidence, but any compliment sets her off-balance.

"He likes you," she says.

"Parents tend to."

"You have the same sense of humor."

"I'm a funny guy, according to you."

"Well, you know what they say. You always marry your dad."

"Yikes," I say.

"Big yikes," she echoes.

We both laugh.

Then, she says, "Sorry about Kass though."

I nod in understanding. But Kass is not my sister, and it's not my place to say how she resembled a viper more than a human, so I don't say anything.

"Your mom was nice today," I offer.

"By the end of it," Theo grunts. "She didn't say anything to you, did she?"

"Only if we would have a real ceremony one day."

Theo lets out a massive laugh, head back. Little squares of light from the disco ball beam over the apples of her cheeks, reflecting on the whites of her teeth. The column of her throat is raised to the air in delight. It's glorious, and I want to trace the length of it with my palm.

"No," she says. "Courthouse was good enough for our arrangement."

I swallow down the word *arrangement*. The clinical nature of it. But that's all this is. I know that.

"Nothing could be good enough for you," I say.

"What does *that* mean?" she asks with another laugh.

"I mean that you deserve so much more than a court-house or even a cathedral. You deserve the world. Nothing less than mountaintop vows for you, Theodora Poulos."

She stares at me, her full lips parting before she tucks the bottom one in between her teeth.

"Well, lucky you, I prefer courthouses instead."

"Lucky me."

We both look out at the rink, and I feel her head land on my shoulder. Her perfume is all around me, even above the stale popcorn. I can't help but close my eyes and lose myself in it.

There was a time five months ago when I might have wondered where this would go, if this small source of affection meant anything. But I can't let myself get distracted.

I've got my own issues to worry about. The bar. The renovations ...

"You keep doing that," Theo says.

"What?" I ask.

She points to my hand, which now runs over my chest. I didn't realize I had been rubbing out the tightness.

"I'm fine," I say, dropping my hand back down.

"No, you're not. Are you nervous because you're not at the bar?"

I give her a side-eye and smirk. "Maybe."

"You don't trust anyone but yourself to run that place, do you?"

"Yes, I do," I say with a laugh. "But I just ... I like being there. It's my home. I like seeing the regulars. Making sure it's all running smoothly. When I'm away for even one day, I feel lost, like the place has moved on without me."

"Moved on? It's your bar though."

"It's hard to explain."

"I think I understand," she says, and then after a moment, she sighs. "No, I definitely understand."

Of course she does. I think about how her sister looked down on her. How her mom didn't respect her decisions. I think about all the times I've seen her with those four best friends of hers. How much of a fifth wheel she's been to Bennett and Ruby's best friendship and Quinn and Lorelei's unspoken sisterhood.

Maybe for once, Theo needs someone exclusively in her corner.

"Okay," I say. "From here on out, we're a team, all right?"

"A team?"

"We tell each other everything. No being left out or forgotten."

A slow smile spreads over her face. But it's big. Bigger than one I've seen on her before.

"Sounds an awful lot like a real marriage and not a fake one," she finally says.

"No, it's friendship." I wiggle my shoulder so that it bumps her head. She laughs. "Think you can do friendship with ol' me?"

"Oh, I'm really good at friendship."

"I know you are," I say, rubbing her arm. "So, let's do that."

"Deal."

"Should we shake on it?" I ask.

"Ooh, absolutely."

She holds her hand but then instantly pulls it back. Something passes over her face.

"Wait," she says. "Best friends get secret handshakes."

I laugh. "They do?"

She gives a *duh* look before saying, "Oh, heck yeah."

We come up with something that is too complicated. A slap on the back of our hands. A flick of a middle finger. Our thumbs wobbling in front of each other. Ending with two finger snaps from me and three from her. It's complicated, but I wouldn't forget it for the world.

Because Theo deserves to be seen by someone.

"Ready to go again?" she asks, throwing her thumb to the rink.

"Yes," I say. "But I'm gonna need that walker."

20
Theo

The Great Forest Journey is more work than I bargained for. But then again, that seems to be a trend in my life.

"Stop laughing," Quinn says with her arms crossed. She leans against the counter in Yogi Bare as I look over the script for the ride.

"Isn't this supposed to be funny though?" I ask.

The Great Forest Journey—or Journey, as we're calling it—focuses on a swamp in the Honeywood Forest. The guests take a gondola-type tour on the way to Queen Bee and Ranger Randy's wedding. They get lost on the way, and the skipper of the boat tries to haphazardly navigate them back. There are bears, creepy crawlies, and a very scared boat operator.

"The script is great," I tell Quinn, who twists her lips to the side in disbelief. "I promise."

"I sure hope so."

The curtain for the main studio in Yogi Bare pulls to the side, and Mrs. Stanley peers her head through. "Move it or lose it."

"You staying?" I ask Quinn.

She shakes her head. "Nah, I should get back to the park. Just here to drop off this weirdo."

Honey, Quinn's mentor at Honeywood and the creator of the park, pops her head out. Her white hair has a tint of bubblegum pink to it. When I first met her, it was cotton-candy blue. I can only hope to still be as feisty at her age.

"Party pooper," Honey says. Her head is stacked on top of Mrs. Stanley's, like they're a pair of Muppet totem heads. Or that heckling duo in the box seats.

Quinn sighs. "This is the last time I drive you anywhere."

I give Quinn a hug before she leaves, and then I walk into the yoga studio, the script left behind.

Yoga that day consists of my regulars—Mrs. Stanley, Honey, Bill, and Frank. When we finish, they chat and gossip, like usual. Eventually, they ask how business is going for me, and I shrug.

"Good. I have y'all."

"That's it?"

"Well, and social media helps," I say. "I put out videos, get paid for the ads, you know ..."

"What you need is a place of your own," Honey says.

I laugh. "I can't afford that yet."

"Don't you have sponsorships?"

"Well, sure," I say. "Companies reach out with yoga gear." I snap the waistband of my leggings. "These came from some company."

"Are you going to piggyback off this place forever?"

I shrug. "Meghan doesn't seem to mind for now."

Meghan, my friend, who used to be a coworker, is now the manager and owner of Yogi Bare. She lets me host my own classes here.

"Can this town even support another yoga studio?" Mrs. Stanley asks.

Frank's eyes widen. "Why? Is there a building up for sale?"

"Chill out, buddy," I say with a laugh. I can tell his retirement money is still burning a hole in his pocket. "While it would be nice to have my own studio, I'm not even remotely financially ready for that."

I'm slowly building my savings, and it's mostly due to Orson's help and free rent. But I don't tell Frank—Mr. I Renovate Without Asking—that he's the reason I needed my husband's help in the first place.

"Ooh, have you tried modeling the clothes?" Mrs. Stanley asks. "With hips like yours, I would."

I wince. "I think you're talking about a different industry altogether."

"Oh. Hmm," she says, looking down at her own crop top that holds her boobs in like a seat belt. "Could be a good moneymaker."

"Uh, maybe not."

I should probably keep a better eye on feisty Mrs. Stanley.

Bennett's face scrunches up. "Please no."

"It's your thirtieth!" Lorelei says. "We have to!"

Bennett tosses a look at Quinn. They normally agree on things like this, but even she shrugs.

"Don't look at me. I agree with Lore," Quinn says. "If I had to endure a night at Dripping Honey for my thirtieth, you guys have to suffer too."

"Oh, Dripping Honey," I say, staring off wistfully. "A birthday not forgotten."

"I'm still finding glitter," Ruby mutters.

My friends and I are in Honeywood's parking lot, sitting in the back of Bennett's truck, the cool summer night breeze winding through our hair. We all waited for Lorelei to get off work so we could go to Ruby's house for dinner, but somehow, the thread of conversation got lost between the five of us. Now, it's two hours later, and we're still in the parking lot, discussing Bennett's and Ruby's upcoming birthday party.

"We really don't have to celebrate this year," Ruby says, winding her hands in her lap.

We always celebrate Bennett's and Ruby's birthdays together, but ever since we started discussing their thirtieth, neither of them has been excited. Something about turning thirty settles different with each person. I, for one, think I might just jump off a cliff when it's my turn. But that's just me.

"Why wouldn't we?" I ask. "And who doesn't love tradition?"

"You're one to talk," Bennett says.

I pull my lips in and snort out a laugh.

True. I shirked my own family's traditions for a court-house wedding. But this is different. It's Bennett and Ruby. Their birthdays are one week apart, and they've had joint birthday parties ever since I met them. I think it extends back to when they were kids, but honestly, who knows with those two?

"Ooh, what if we hosted it in the park?" Lorelei suggests.

Ruby's eyes widen. "How many people are y'all planning to invite?"

"Who cares?!" I say, throwing my hands in the air. "You're gonna be thirty!"

Lorelei claps her hands. "I'll talk with Fred!"

"Does, uh, Jolene have anything planned already?" Ruby asks. "We shouldn't step on her toes."

We all fall silent. We always kind of forget about Bennett's fiancée.

Bennett clears his throat. "I'll ask her. But Honeywood should be fine. She's good at planning stuff, so she can probably help."

"Perfect," I say quickly. "The more, the merrier!"

Bennett gives Ruby a quick look before averting his eyes again.

Quinn pulls out her phone. "Ooh, I bet Orson can provide some booze connections again. We can buy it from him at cost."

"I'll ask," I say at the same time Bennett does.

Lorelei's and Quinn's eyes shift to us.

I curl my lips in.

Oh. Right.

I'm not exactly supposed to be close to Orson, am I? That's Bennett's job. And yet, in the last couple of weeks since the skating rink, things have been going well with us. We have our morning coffee, we discuss the day, and then we go our separate ways. He's constantly at other people's houses or at the bar, renovating or setting up for who knows what? But sometimes, he gets home at a reasonable time, so we'll sit in the den and watch a baseball game.

It's easy. It's simple.

But I'm also not supposed to be this comfortable with Orson. He's Bennett's friend.

Quinn narrows her eyes. "You're still curious about him, aren't you?"

"What?" I laugh.

"Oh, come on. You've always talked about Orson. Just sleep with the guy and get it over with."

"Not all of us harbor secret feelings for years," I say.

She twists her lips to the side and crosses her arms. "Touché."

After Quinn started dating Lorelei's twin brother—a man she had fantasized about since high school—she's been a little less prone to judgment.

Though that doesn't stop her from muttering under her breath, "I still think you're curious."

I laugh it off. "He's not my type."

But even the sentence makes me uncomfortable, as if I talked about him behind his back.

"I'll talk to Orson," Bennett says, changing the subject. "I think he's got a lot on his plate with renovations and stuff, but he'd be down."

"Perfect!" Lorelei takes a quick swig of her beer, then goes back to typing on her phone. "Now, the balloons ..."

But as we continue, I think about what Bennett said.

Orson *does* have a lot on his plate. I think of all the times he's come home late. All the times he's seemed tired with his only relief being baseball on the TV. Orson is constantly exhausted, but he's also always chipped in for events anyway.

I guess I've never considered the other side. That maybe he helps *too* much. Maybe Orson gives *too* much. And I wonder if maybe, just like how I keep things to myself, he ever feels like he's bottling up things too.

21

Orson

"If you look on your left ..."

"There's a giant shark?" I interject.

"Stop making me laugh," Theo says, tossing a blueberry at me.

We're sitting on the floor in the den, bowls of snacks between our outstretched legs—her blueberries, my mini peanut butter cookie snacks—while she tries to memorize her new script for The Great Forest Journey. So far, we've barely made it past the second page, and I already have a graveyard of blueberries surrounding me.

"Line?" she asks.

"Nope, I'm not feeding it to you," I say. "You know what it is."

"Come on. Feed it to me."

My chest tightens at her words, and when I look up, she's holding back a grin. Theo knows what she's doing. She wouldn't be Theo if she didn't, the flirt. She bursts into laughter at the same time I do.

"Can we take a break?" she whines, running fingers under her eyes and tugging at the skin.

"Fine. You deserve it, I guess."

"I definitely don't," she says.

"I was trying to be nice."

"You're just lucky this isn't a musical," she says. "Then, you'd have to hear me sing all night long. You couldn't possibly be nice."

"If it's anything like your trumpet skills, I'd have to give Quinn a piece of my mind."

She tosses a blueberry into her grinning mouth before glancing over to the keyboard sitting in the corner of my den, then back to me. She's been looking at that piano a lot lately.

"What evil thoughts are you thinking?" I ask.

"Nothing."

"We promised no secrets, friend."

She eats more fruit, chewing for a moment before tilting her head side to side and saying, "Okay, fine. I was thinking that you play piano beautifully."

"Ah, my only talent."

She tosses another blueberry at me.

"You're gonna clean these up, right?"

"You've got other talents," she says, bypassing the comment.

"What?"

"Sometimes, talents aren't in skills, but with people."

I smile. "Go on."

She shakes her head with a playful laugh. "No. Now, you just want a compliment."

"No secrets," I whisper, leaning in with a pump of my eyebrows.

She inhales, her eyes pausing on mine before she sits up taller.

"Fine. You're kind," she says. "And honest. And nothing really bothers you. That's a talent."

My chest tightens, and I want to rub the ache, but I resist. I don't want her to question me, as she very much likes to do.

"Happy?" she asks.

"Very." I flick my chin to the piano. "Your mom told me you were supposed to learn how to play. What happened?"

"I was a brat."

I laugh. "Ah, right, so that hasn't changed."

"Ass," she says. "My little sister, Callie, is a natural though. Beautiful piano player. You'd like her. Much more poised than yours truly."

I can't imagine liking any Poulos sister more than I like Theo, but I don't say that. Instead, I say, "Well, do you want me to teach you?"

Her eyes light up, and without hesitation, she drops her bowl. "Ooh, yes!"

She scrambles from the floor and flips an invisible coat-tail out behind her before sitting into front of the keyboard. Her fingers hover over the keys, doing her best maestro impression. Then, her hands slam down, only to make a discordant organ noise.

"Your sister has nothing on you," I say.

She sticks out her tongue.

I stand and walk up behind her.

"Okay, put your first hand here," I say, pointing to the keys.

She moves her hand to the general direction, but doesn't commit to a key.

"Here?" she asks tentatively.

It's funny to watch Theo attempt something new. It always starts with full confidence, but then she curls in on herself, like she's scared someone's going to tell her she's silly for trying. I wonder how often that's happened.

"Hmm, not exactly," I say. "May I?"

"May you ... what?"

I reach my arm over her shoulder, running my fingers over the back of her hand, trailing them over her knuckles and to the tips, mirroring her hands with my own.

"Oh," she says, blinking. "Oh. Yes."

I chuckle, and I think I hear her pull in a hiss of air.

I like how soft her hands are. It's such a contrast to my fingers, which have had the prints seared off by bleach and hot grills. It almost feels greedy, getting to touch her.

For one split second, a second I barely consider, I wonder how my grandmother's engagement ring would have looked on her hand.

I shake the thought from my head.

Lightly, I press her finger on the key, and a single clear, keening note rings through the den.

After a beat, she whispers, "I'm a genius."

"You deserve a gold star."

"Hey, don't make fun of the sticker system. It works."

"Now, this ..." I move her hand where I want, and she lets me. I reach my other arm around, placing my second hand over hers. Her head leans back into my chest. My heart beats faster, and I wonder if she can feel it pounding against her head. "This is the first chord I learned."

I press on her fingers at the same time she lowers them herself, letting out the harmonious chord. We stay silent until it fades away.

"Pretty," she says.

Theo tilts her head back on my chest, blinking at me upside down.

"Think I could be a pianist one day?" she asks.

I laugh, trailing my thumb over the back of her neck, using my forefinger to smooth back a stray curl behind her ear. I don't know why I do it, but it feels right. And it only causes her to grin wider at me.

"Yes, I do," I say. "I think you can be anything you want to be, Theo."

Theo's face slowly falls, and she removes her head from my chest. I wonder if I said something wrong.

We ultimately go back to the ride script, the piano forgotten for now.

22

Theo

"Nope, that way."

"Which way?"

"Good Lord, sweetheart."

"Which way?!"

"Just follow. Follow. Follow. And drop. Wait! Slowly!"

But down the folding table goes, and I immediately cover my mouth with my hands. Orson runs around to the other side to inspect the damage. We breathe a sigh of relief when both the floor and the table appear undamaged.

"Close one?" I say with a wince.

"Yes, because I would have had your hide if the new floor had been scratched."

I give a sheepish smile as he points a finger at me.

"Don't think I still won't either."

He would. And I know he doesn't mean it in *that* way, but I remember how he used to mean it. And the thought raises my blood pressure just a bit.

I'd be lying if I said I didn't imagine him doing a lot of things he used to do. I've had too much quality time with Buzzy lately. And not Buzzy the Bear, Honeywood's mascot. I mean, my vibrator, which will need new batteries before the month is up—I guarantee it. But it's the best I can do right now. I know not to sleep with my husband.

However, that doesn't mean I can't admire his cute, tight butt when he climbs up a ladder to install the projector.

The spare room in The Honeycomb is still mostly a blank slate, but it's progressed a lot. The newly installed hardwood I almost scratched up is beautiful—beautiful enough that when someone mentioned that he should have a town movie night, Orson agreed.

"Drill," he demands, holding out his hand.

"Ooh, love it when you say it like that."

He peers down at me with a lifted eyebrow. "Theo."

"Right. Drill."

Sometimes, I push my limits, but who wouldn't when faced with Orson's crooked smile and very delectable ass-filled jeans?

Familiar faces pile into the room while we finish setting up. Mrs. Stanley is in the corner, building a pillow fort—no, castle—fit with a large blanket tied around her dog's neck. Honey shuffles over to sit with her, and they put a sign saying *no boys allowed* on the outside.

Orson stands at the front, picking up a case from the table and waving it in the air. "The Wi-Fi doesn't work in here yet, so we're living off a DVD. And Quinn provided it, so blame her if it stinks."

There's collective laughter, and Quinn tosses him the middle finger. She sits in between Landon's legs in a matching pink pajama set. Landon wears the same set in red. He pulls her into his chest and places a kiss on her forehead.

Everyone is in some form of nightwear. Even Emory is

145

wearing a gray henley that looks fit for sleep. Lorelei is next to him in a Bumble the Bee set in yellow, as is her usual color of choice.

Orson starts the movie, and after clicking off the light, he joins me and Ruby in the back of the room. I open the quilted blanket we're sharing to allow him to scoot in. He looks over to the opposite side of Ruby, at the vacant pillow.

"Where's Bennett?" he whispers.

I can see Ruby's face redden a bit, but then again, Ruby's face is always a different tint of pink or red. Or maybe it's just her spattering of freckles that makes her look that way.

"He's with Jolene," she whispers back. "I think they're visiting her parents."

"Good," I say. "I like having you all to myself."

I curl closer to her, and she giggles, leaning her head on mine.

But the good feelings do not last long.

The movie Quinn chose is scary. Like, really scary. There's blood, machetes, and jump scares, all set to an off-key symphony. After thirty minutes, I have my set of blankets pulled up to my chin, and I've kicked Quinn in the butt at least twice.

"What is wrong with you?" I hiss.

"Shh."

I squint my eyes just in case something happens again so I can close them that much quicker. I miss the next scare because of this, but when I glance over at Orson, his jaw is clenched tight, and he's absentmindedly rubbing a hand over his chest. I tap him on the shoulder. He hops off the floor a bit.

I snort. "Scared?"

His hand drops from his chest, and he scoffs. "Of course not."

"Aww, you are."

But he's not the only one. When the serial killer appears in the window, there's a low rumble of dissent throughout the room.

And when the heroine knocks him down, only to turn around and check on her unconscious friend, everyone erupts into, "Don't turn your back on him!" and, "Unmask the guy first!" or simply, "You're dead now. You're dead!"

Even Mrs. Stanley's dog barks, causing Orson to jump again.

"You are so scared," I say.

A slow smile spreads on his face.

I snake my hand over to his, and our fingers entwine. But when he turns back to the movie, his free hand rubs over his chest once more, and my smile fades away.

"Orson, are you awake?"

It's the middle of the night. The only light in his house is the moon shining through the glass door in the kitchen. The rest of the house is pitch-black. And that movie did bad things to me.

I stand in Orson's doorway with my arms wrapped around my middle and my back pressed against the door-jamb. It's a defensive position. You know, just in case something sneaks up on me from behind.

I hear the sound of his mattress squeaking and the rustle of a comforter being thrown to the side.

"Orson?"

His low, sleepy drawl answers with, "Get in here, Poulos."

I tiptoe through the room, and right before my feet reach the underside of the bed—because no monster will be grabbing me tonight, no, sir—I hop in.

"Ouch."

"Sorry."

I adjust so that my knee doesn't knock against one of Orson's limbs again.

"Couldn't sleep?" he asks.

"No. I kept seeing the ..."

"Grinning face?"

"Yeah, that one."

He chuckles, and the sound of it is better than the blankets keeping me warm.

There's a creak in the kitchen. I scoot closer to him, and he wraps his arm around my waist.

"What was that?" I whisper.

"Shh, it'll hear you," he says.

"Stop it."

He grabs his glasses from the side table and steps out of bed.

"What are you doing?" I ask.

"Going to look so you're not scared."

Then, I remember the monster under the bed and pull him back.

"Wait, it's too risky."

"Then, come with me."

I don't want to, but if it means saving his life, then I can be brave. I need to be brave.

Orson walks to the doorway, and I follow behind him, staying close enough so that the warmth of him never leaves me. I reach out to grab a handful of his shirt but instead run my palm over smooth, bare muscles.

Oh.

He's not wearing a shirt.

I whip my hand back to my side.

We both peer out into the living room.

"Okay, you go check your bedroom," he says. "I'll hit up the kitchen."

"We're going to split up?" I ask. "Did you learn nothing from the movie?"

He chuckles. "Fine, okay. Bedroom first."

I follow him into my bedroom, our backs never leaving the walls. He tiptoes to the closet. And when he peeks in, disappearing for a moment, I turn back to the doorway, and that's when I see it. A shadow.

I do what any sane person would do and rip open my bedside drawer and grab the flashlight Orson gave me on day one in this house.

I'm fearless. I am independent. I am woman.

I aim the flashlight at the shadow, but when I can't find the switch, I panic.

I panic hard.

A bloodcurdling scream leaves my mouth before I can stop it, all the tension spewing out of me like a shaken-up bottle of soda.

Orson screams from the closet.

I'm pretty sure we're going to die.

Orson emerges, sprinting to the bedroom light switch and turning it on.

The shadow is just my towel from the day before.

Orson looks to me, eyeing the flashlight in my hand, and starts laughing. Full-on belly laughing. Cackling.

"What?"

"Really? That was going to protect you?"

I look down and realize I'm holding not my flashlight, but something purple and silicone. My vibrator.

"Are you gonna buzz the bogeyman to death?"

Then, we hear another creak, and within seconds, the light is turned off, my vibrator is thrown on the bed, and we're both rushing back into his room, jumping under the covers.

"What if ..." he starts, then turns to me with a gasp. "What if it's ... the Godfather?"

"Oh, you ass!" I say, slapping his bicep.

He bursts into laughter and wiggles his fingers. "Don Corleone has come to finally get you!"

"Shut up! Shut up! Wait." I narrow my eyes. "You disappeared into the closet."

"Okay?" he says through a small laugh.

"How do I know it's you and not some ... other person who *looks* like you?"

His laughter dies down.

"Fair point. Secret handshake?"

"Secret handshake," I agree.

We do our odd combination that we've perfected over the past couple of weeks, ending with his usual two finger snaps and my three.

I let out an easier sigh. "Who knew that would come in handy?"

But then wind whips outside the house, and I curl closer to him. My hands clutch the curve of his bicep, and my other may or may not palm his built pecs. I feel no shame in fear.

"It's just branches," he says.

"Are you just saying that to make me feel better?"

"No. We actually have trees."

"I don't believe you."

He laughs, pulling me down so we're both lying on our sides. Then, he tugs me in toward him, his knees pressed into mine, my back against his chest. We lie there like that for a second, me counting the stars outside as his chest rises and falls behind me.

"I can feel every breath you take," I say. "And every movement you make."

"Are you singing me lyrics?"

"Maybe."

He doesn't answer after that.

"Are you actually going to sleep?" I whisper.

"Yes," he says, his breath rustling the hair at the nape of my neck.

"What about the serial killer in the house?"

"They've moved on."

"How do you know?"

He nuzzles into my hair and sighs.

"Shh," he whispers. "Let's go to sleep, sweetheart."

But I wasn't lying. I can feel every breath he takes. And every single one, I follow with my own until I can feel both our hearts settle down.

And then, light as air, I drift off. And I feel safe.

23

Theo

I'm settled in our house's den after a long day of spiel memorization, followed by yoga class. I've been zoning out to the baseball game on the TV. I still only sort of know what's going on, but it's a weird type of solace. A reliable routine. Orson isn't here with me, but he should be coming home soon.

The moment that thought crosses my mind, I stiffen in my seat.

Is this what I've turned into? Someone who waits for their roommate—no, their husband—to come home? Someone with a—gasp—*routine*?

I change the channel to a new show on a network I never watch. It's some travel documentary about small towns.

Better.

I hear the front door open upstairs and instantly mute the show. The rattle of keys land into the bowl I bought for the counter. Then, heavy footsteps come down the spiral staircase.

Orson gives me a smile, but it's weary. He looks ragged again.

"How was your day, dear?" I ask in my most over-the-top 1950s voice.

"I deserve a gold star," he says, rounding the couch and slumping into the cushions with a soft *plompf.*

Normally, I can smell the bar on him—only the good parts, like the bite of hoppy beer or the musk of firewood—but it looks like he went to the gym after work. His hair is damp from a fresh shower, and he smells like his lemongrass soap.

"I have something better than gold stars," I say.

"You do?"

I lean to my side and hold up two face masks with a grin.

"Tangerine or rose petal?"

Orson chuckles, running a heavy hand over his face.

"Um ... rose petal," he says.

I blink at him. I expected more resistance. More of, *It's been a long day, Theo. I'm tired.* Or, *It's got pink packaging. That's for women.*

But not Orson. He doesn't ask questions. He just *does.*

Giddy now, I rip open the packet and pull out the floppy mask.

"Slimy," he says with a laugh.

"It feels good, trust me."

"Trusting you."

I crawl toward him, the tips of my newly painted toes touching his thigh. The black sparkles complement his dark denim, like stars in the dusty night.

I tilt my chin. "Lean back."

He stares tentatively at the mask now drooping with goop as I unfold it. But he does as he was told, putting pressure on the back of his seat so the footstool pops out. He reclines back.

I lean over him. Suddenly, I realize the last time we were in this position was months ago, when we were doing far less innocuous activities. He always liked to rest his hands on my hips when I rode him like a cowgirl gone wild. And when I glance down, I see his fingertips twitch, as if he's remembering that fact too.

Nerves zip through me, down my arms and directly to my fingers that hold the—admittedly super-slimy—mask. It drips onto his face. Orson winces and turns the moment the mask gets near him.

"Stop," I say with a laugh.

"I didn't know it'd be cold."

"Trust."

He growls a bit but turns back. I place it down over his face, and he hisses in a breath. Running a finger over his high cheekbones, the curve of his jaw, the dip near his chin, the arch of his nose, I press the mask into every crease until it's flat. And when I'm done, I lean back and stare at him.

Even under a mask that arguably makes every person look like a serial killer—with only their eyes and faint traces of their lips visible—Orson still looks attractive. How is that even possible?

"It's cold," he says.

I roll my eyes. "You're such a baby."

"You next, if you're so brave."

He leans up, his head continuing to tilt back, lest the mask slide off, then fumbles around for the other packet.

I lean against the back of couch. The middle seat doesn't seem to recline, so I sink into the cushions as much as I can. I close my eyes.

I hear him rip open the top, and then I feel the cool mask on my own face. I hiss in a sharp inhale.

"Oh-ho-ho, who's the baby now?"

But it's not just the chill of the mask. It's his hands on me. I forgot how rough yet also surprisingly gentle his hands were. I feel like a deer in headlights as he pats the mask down, running a thumb over my chin, my cheeks, and my forehead. After a few seconds, I open my eyes.

Orson looks at me with his head tilted to the side.

"Well?" I ask. "Still pretty?"

"You're always pretty."

He shifts over to sit back on his side of the couch, and I'm left pressed against the cushions, sucking in air and swallowing back the stuttering in my chest.

You're always pretty.

I expect him to change the channel, but he doesn't. He only unmutes whatever I was watching. I can't remember what it was.

I stare over at him as he watches the TV. I don't care that I look like a creep. I care even less about my stalker-like tendencies when his hand starts running over his chest again.

"How're your doctor's appointments going?" I ask.

"Going," he says, but the answer doesn't feel complete.

"We promised we'd be honest with each other."

He side-eyes me with a sly smile.

"I'm going," he repeats and then turns back to the TV. "I went today actually. She says I need to work less."

"You do work a lot."

"I do."

"And you shouldn't."

"Maybe."

I laugh. "No maybes."

"I love it though."

I smile, taking in the way he relaxes when he mentions it. How his hand steadies down to his thigh. I don't think it's specifically the bar he's stressed about or even the work itself. It's everything surrounding it. The people who depend on the bar day in and day out. Regulars who unload their problems on him. The events he helps with around town. The renovations.

"Let's do something fun," I say.

"Oh?"

"Yeah. Let's ... I don't know. Go on a road trip."

"You're kidding."

"I'm not."

"Theo, I can't leave town for a long period of time."

"Orson," I say, mimicking him, "you do too much for this town. Get out of it. Live life a bit."

"I like doing things for people," he says. "Plus, you help people out too. What's the difference?"

"I'm me," I say. "I'm the vacation friend. You—"

He cuts me off. "The vacation friend?"

"Yeah. I'm the friend who's fun for a few days, but by the end, you're tired and just ready to go home. I'm a good time, but that's about it. But you, Orson Mackenzie, you linger, and people know that. I think they take advantage of you sometimes."

At first, I think he's quiet because I blabbed too much, but then I'm not so sure.

His brow is furrowed. His lips are drawn into a thin, straight line. He's serious, and I've never seen him like this.

I wonder if I offended him. If maybe telling him he gets taken advantage of was taking it too far. But then he holds my chin in his fingers and runs a line over my jaw with his thumb.

"Theo, you're my everyday friend."

I shake my head. "This is what I'm talking about. You—"

"Theo," he repeats. "Stop it."

His jaw is set. His eyes dart between mine. And the longer we sit there in silence, the more my stomach drops. My body feels like it's collapsing into the couch. And while I expect my heart to be racing, it instead slows. A wave of calm flows over me. I realize we're exhaling in the same rhythm, taking in each other bit by bit. Breath by breath.

"You look ridiculous in your mask," I say.

He doesn't laugh. "I'm serious."

"So am I. It really is like Michael Myers is giving me a pep talk."

Orson gives a slow nod, then releases my chin.

"I see you, Theo. Even in the dark, behind your mask, I promise I see you."

I pull in a sharp breath. I lean back, letting my heart catch up to my increased breathing. He sits in his reclined seat, and we stare at the TV like nothing just happened.

We watch a couple minutes of the documentary.

And when the commercial hits, advertising the next baseball game in the city, I blurt out, "Let's go do that."

From beside me, Orson laughs. "Do what?"

I nod to the TV and swallow. "The game. Let's go watch baseball in person."

"That might be the hottest thing you've ever said to me."

"Oh, I doubt that," I say.

He chuckles, but doesn't tell me I'm wrong.

24

Orson

"I don't like the Kiss Cam," Theo says. "Seems like too much pressure."

"Okay," I say. "Then ... we'll just flick them off if it comes to us."

She smiles. "I like your style, Mackenzie."

It's the middle of June, and we're sitting in the sunniest part of the baseball stadium. Theo leans back in her seat. She's stretched out like a woman tanning on the beach with her bare legs propped on the railing in front of us. I can see a slight shimmer of sweat glistening right beneath the skirt of her red dress. I avert my eyes.

Of course Theo is sweating. We all are. But her tan skin is far more attractive than the guy two seats down from us in a sopping shirt and sagging hat, who looks like he just crawled out of a swamp.

Theo takes a long sip from an obnoxiously large and skinny souvenir cup.

"Frozen wine," she says with a smack of her lips. "Genius."

"Just wait until you get a hot dog."

"Is that supposed to be a euphemism?"

I chuckle. "Not everything is, sweetheart."

"Bummer."

For her first time at a baseball game, I'm surprised by her tolerance. I've taken friends and dates to games before, but it's always too hot, too boring, or too crowded. It's a baseball game. Of course it's all three of those things. But I haven't heard a single complaint from Theo—only demands for more food.

She places her drink down to join the other stack of discarded cardboard containers, napkins, and buckets of devoured snacks.

"I think I'm ready for one of those hot dogs."

I chuckle. "I don't know how you still have room."

"Hush. I haven't eaten all morning. I'm treating myself."

We get up, walking back toward the concessions window, but before we can reach the long, winding line, she halts in front of the fan store. She peers through the window, oohing and aahing at the jerseys. I follow her while she walks in. She grabs a tag and lets out a low whistle.

"Dang, no wonder you frame these," she says.

I reach into my pocket, open my wallet, and hand my card to her. "Buy whatever you want."

She blinks down to my card, like I just handed her a cursed totem. "You're kidding."

I laugh and nudge it to her again. "I'm not."

"Okay, sugar daddy," she says with sarcasm, but she doesn't take the card.

"You came to the game with me. The least I can do is buy you a few things."

"You just want to watch me walk around the house, wearing a jersey."

I grin, raising my eyebrows. "In *only* a jersey, if I'm lucky."

She looks from me to the card, then back before finally snatching it from my hand.

There's a weird undercurrent between us now that I can't pinpoint. We flirt. We touch. But despite that, an unspoken line is still drawn in the sand. I wonder if this is what it's like to be best friends with a woman. She calls me *sugar daddy* with a shining smile, and I tell her I'd like to see her naked. That's totally a thing friends do, right?

Theo grabs a hat and puts it on, tipping her hips to the side in some ridiculous pose. I laugh, taking off the hat and replacing it with another one. I roughly tug the bill down in an exaggerated move that makes her laugh.

"You look good, Poulos."

Her eyes dance between mine, a moment suspended in time.

"I do like this one better," she says, and then she takes it off and looks at the price tag. "But I'll just get the jersey. I can't ask you to spend more than that."

I shrug. "Up to you."

We get to the register, but I see her eyeing that hat a bit more.

Once we check out and get in line for hot dogs, I tell her I'm going to the bathroom. Before I walk over the ropes, Theo grabs my hand.

"Hey. I'm having a great time."

I smile, bring her hand to my lips, and kiss the back of it. "Good."

Being away from Cedar Cliff is oddly freeing. I like that we can be ourselves and goof off like we do behind closed doors. If our friends ever caught us, it would look suspicious, and I know for a fact that Lorelei would try to coax some truth out of us. But there is no truth. Theo is my friend and roommate and legal wife. I'm not going to bleed my heart out on the floor in hopes that this will become something more. I'm happy with how it is.

Happy.

Back at the fan store, I buy two of the hats in the style she liked—one for her and one for me—and return to the concessions line. But after I weave through the crowds and find Theo again, there's another man talking to her.

I freeze.

This guy, with his chewing tobacco tucked in the bottom of his lip and an arrogant laziness in his face, seems like he's hovering over her. Theo is leaning away from him.

I feel my chest start to ache. But then it turns into something else. Irritation. Anger. A twist in my gut. A heat that spreads through my chest, up my neck, and to my face.

I walk over, climb over the ropes, and give this man a once-over. Theo looks relieved to see me. The man does not.

He narrows his eyes, tilting his chin to the air, as if to accentuate his height over me. I can tell he's sizing me up.

He's likely close to six feet tall, looks like he exclusively eats unseasoned chicken and broccoli, and probably says things like, *Take a joke, man!*

But I don't have time for him today. Not when he's that close to Theo.

To my wife.

"Is there a problem here?" I ask.

He lets out a scoffing laugh.

"We're just talking," he says, giving Theo a sly smirk, as if she were in on whatever joke is coursing through his hamster wheel brain. "There's no problem here."

He places a hand on the small of her back, and Theo's eyes widen.

My whole body feels hot.

I take one step forward.

"Funny," I say. "I seem to have a problem with you putting your hands on my *wife*."

Theo's head whips to me, her eyes wide and every disgusted expression she had for him erased. I can see her chest rising and falling.

I don't know what makes me do it, but I reach my palm out, run a hand over her cheek and down the length of her neck. A show of possession. But that's just it. A show. Enough for his hand to drop from her waist.

But then Theo melts into my touch. Her cheek buries into my palm. She lets out a long sigh and closes her eyes. She's also putting on a performance, and it's a damn good one. I'll give her that.

I lean my head in to kiss her on the cheek, but when I do, her head moves, too, and suddenly, our lips meet.

It happens so fast. It's an accident, a weird fumble of our faces. A mistake we'll laugh over later. But she doesn't pull away. And neither do I. Then, Theo's lips start to move. And mine do too.

We're kissing. I'm feeling her soft lips on mine for the first time in months, and we're back in our old rhythm, as easy as relearning a bike.

But it's wrong. I know we shouldn't be doing this.

I try to be kind, closing each kiss with a small peck, as if signaling that it can be the last one. That, yes, this is where we end this silly, goofy moment.

But Theo doesn't take the cue.

She keeps moving her mouth, and I keep following. When she exhales, I inhale. Her fist curls into my shirt, tugging me closer, and her tongue runs over my lips ...

I lose it.

I clutch her jaw, trailing over the back of her neck, thumbing over her cheek. She fists my shirt harder—not lightly pulling, but roughly *jerking* me closer to her. Our tongues meet. She lets out a small moan against my mouth. Her hand scrubs over my stubble. She bites my bottom lip. I bite her back.

It isn't until I hear some woman say not so kindly, nor so quietly, "Christ, get a room," that I finally slow down. That I finally pull back even though Theo's still clutching my shirt and breathing heavily, eyes closed, as if willing me back.

I trace my thumb over her jaw, and she finally opens her eyes and looks at me. Her lips are full and swollen. Her cheeks are red. Her eyes look dazed.

I feel exactly how she looks.

We both look to the guy who got us in this situation in the first place. His grin from seconds ago looks slapped off his face.

"Told you I was taken," Theo says through a heavy breath. "But better luck next time."

"I'm not exactly feeling hot dogs anymore," I say, trying to swallow my way through the words.

"No, me neither," she says, tossing a side-glance to the cocky dip-chewing guy who looks like he could choke on it any second. "Plus, I can get my own delicious, *massive* hot dog at home."

She glances down below my belt. I let out a strangled laugh at her horrible joke.

"Pretzel instead, dear husband?"

"As you wish."

I give one final look to the man whose face is now the color of beets—though whether that's from embarrassment for himself or for us for making out in public,

I'm not sure—and we exit the line without another word.

When we move to a separate concessions line, we don't talk. What is there to say? How do we possibly broach the subject when she's still breathing heavy and my jeans zipper is still painfully strained? We stand in silence until Theo finally notices the bag in my hand.

"What's that?"

"Hmm?"

"Are those the hats?"

"Oh," I say. "Yeah." It's all I can get out.

She digs in the bag and pops one on her head. "You went back for them?"

"Yeah. You couldn't stop looking at them."

Her bottom lip pulls in, and she smiles. I think I see her glance over her shoulder at the guy still waiting in the other line, now feverishly texting on his phone—probably about the crazy couple he met at the baseball game.

"Thanks," is all she says.

I don't know whether she's talking about the hats or the weird man. But it doesn't matter. What's done is done.

We end up getting more snacks than we could possibly need, including my favorite mini peanut butter snack and Theo's hot dog. And for the rest of the game, Theo holds my hand—even though it's far too hot to do so. If I try to give her space and pull away, she only grips my palm harder, keeping our hands entwined.

The Kiss Cam does shine on us eventually, and we both flash our middle fingers until it quickly pans away. Just like we agreed. We laugh the whole time, Theo's snorts echoing down our row.

Happy.

That's it. I'm happy.

25

Theo

I wake up to an alarm that isn't mine and an arm draped over my stomach.

Orson lets out a low groan as he rolls away. I instantly miss his warmth, and it's not even cold in his bedroom. The alarm is turned off, and he tosses back over toward me, pulling me against his chest again and nuzzling into the crook of my neck.

"We really gotta stop doing this," he mutters in the low, husky whisper of a waking man. I'd die to hear that again.

"Say that again," I say.

He chuckles. "What?"

"Nothing," I say. "I have nightmares, so think of this like charity. Plus, I like being spooned."

I scoot closer to him so that we're completely flush from neck to ankle. But that's when I feel something ... else.

I clear my throat.

It's not that I don't like what I feel. It's that I can remember *exactly* how *that* feels. My quickly hardening nipples remember it too.

165

"I seem to have a problem with you putting your hands on my wife."

The sentence, the low growl of it, and the gruff nature of his possession haven't left my mind since the baseball game. And then I kissed him. And the secret I will take to the grave? I did it on purpose.

The ache was too much. The slickness between my thighs would have killed me if I hadn't gone for it. Was it irresponsible? Absolutely. But was it amazing? I wish I could say that it wasn't, but, God, Orson's mouth knows what it's doing. *He* knows what he's doing.

And that's exactly the problem.

I slink out of bed and away from the temptation. I go to the kitchen to start our coffee.

"Hey, no," he groans from the bedroom. "That's my job."

"I don't have to go to the park until later," I say. "You're the one with the bar to run."

"You haven't done yoga yet though," he mutters back, his voice muffled into the pillows. He's still not fully awake.

"I am perfectly fine with having coffee before yoga."

He lets out a low moan that has my heart rocketing upward.

Get. A. Grip. Theo.

Orson appears behind me with a yawn. I turn to see him stretch, his shirt riding up, revealing the small line of dark hair trailing underneath his boxers.

Nope. Stop, stop, stop. Just look away.

Ever since we started sleeping in the same bed, he started wearing a shirt at night. It's a gift and a curse. Now, all I get are sneak peeks. It's a constant tease.

"It's gonna be a long day," he says.

"What's on the agenda?"

He shrugs. "Bar stuff. Helping Frank at his place. And Mrs. Stanley. Then gym. Then more bar stuff. The usual."

"Need help?"

"Why?" The word comes out a half-laugh, half-yawn combination, the latter interrupted by the former.

"To help," I say. "That way, you'll make it in time for dinner."

"Oh God, I forgot about that."

Tonight, we're going over to Lorelei and Emory's house to finalize plans for Ruby and Bennett's birthday party. With the hectic summer of new ride openings, it was difficult enough getting everyone together, which is why we can't afford to miss it.

"So, I'll meet you at the bar after work?" I continue.

"No, no," he says, waving me off. "Enjoy your night." He scratches behind his ear. "Though I coulda sworn you had something else on the calendar."

"Let me help," I say. "Seriously."

He looks at me with squinted eyes.

"I want to," I say, answering a question he didn't ask.

He chuckles, reaching up to knock his fist against my chin playfully. "We'll see."

He's not accepting my help in any way, but I don't care. I'll show up at the bar right after my shift. I'll answer emails, sling drinks, or whatever else he asks. I'll even flirt with patrons to get him more tips. He'll just have to deal with it.

"Okay, shower time," he says with a final stretch. "Leave me some coffee? I've got Mrs. Stanley's hallway to tackle today."

"Godspeed."

He lets out a grunt in response and heads to the bathroom. I don't take another breath until the door closes behind him, but then I exhale it out in one fell swoop, like pent-up electric energy leaving my body.

"I seem to have a problem with you putting your hands on my wife."

It's irresponsible to be having fantasies about him. We're *married*. And it hurts my brain to consider how backward that thought process is, but that's how it has to be. If we start messing around, we'll fall into the same trap as last time. We'll get feelings.

From Orson's bedroom—the bedroom that isn't mine, but one I also haven't left in a week—I hear my phone going off.

Perfect. That's what I need. A phone call. A distraction. Maybe my dad wants to chat. Maybe I can get breakfast with someone this morning.

Instead, I'm greeted with four texts from Quinn and a couple of missed calls from Lorelei.

What the—

Then, it hits me.

Oh no.

Today is skipper training day.

I check the time.

And I needed to be there five minutes ago.

Crap.

I quickly shoot a text to Quinn and Lorelei, apologizing and saying I'll be there as soon as possible. Then, I turn to the left and glance in the mirror. I haven't washed my hair in a couple of days. I still smell like a grungy baseball stadium and hot dogs and sweat.

Crap, crap, crap.

I run to the bathroom, stopping at the closed door. I already hear the shower water running.

Why in the world doesn't he have two showers in this house?!

My heart is racing. My body is tense.

Think. Think. Think.

I can't just kick Orson out of his own shower. I can't ask him to step aside either. I can't ... well ... I also can't be late for this training.

Okay, just ask if he can jump out for two seconds. It can't hurt to ask.

I reach out my hand to knock on the bathroom door, but after my knuckles hit the wood once, the door with the weak latch suddenly swings in.

And there he is.

Orson Mackenzie.

My friend.

My roommate.

My husband.

Naked in the shower.

It's not anything I haven't seen before, but I forgot about it. *All* of it. Of him. How tight his ass is. How his strong calves represent a man who lives on his feet. I forgot that, as his hands reach up to lather his hair, he has back muscles that shift with every single movement.

I swallow so hard that I let out a breathy exhale.

With his hands still in his hair, Orson twists on the spot, and, *yep*, there's that *other* piece of him I grew accustomed to.

I let out a weak whine.

"Theo?" he asks, unfazed by the fact that I'm in the doorway, just watching the shampoo suds slough down his chest and over his abs.

Christ.

I stammer out a weak, "I ... there's a ... shower. Need. Running late."

"What?"

"I should be at Honeywood," I finally get out. "I forgot today is training day."

"Oh shit," he says.

We stand there for a moment, blinking at each other. The only thing between us is the clear, slightly fogged shower wall and the tiled floor that seems a mile long.

Finally, his hand reaches out and pushes the shower door open.

"Get in," he says.

My eyes dart from his abs up to his face, where his eyebrows are raised expectantly.

"What?!"

"If you need to shower, then do it," he says. "It's nothing I haven't seen before, but I promise I won't look."

"I ..."

"And close the door," he says with a grin. "You're letting out the heat."

I blink for a few seconds before closing the bathroom door behind me and leaning against the wood.

My heart beats wildly in my chest. My thighs, which might have been partially under control earlier, are now clenching together, tighter than ever. I'm in the middle of wondering if I'll actually do this, but then one additional *ding* from my phone says Lorelei and Quinn might murder me if I don't.

It's nothing. This is nothing. We both need to shower. We've seen each other naked before. Many times.

This is fine. Absolutely fine.

I slide my sleep shorts off, hooking a finger into my

panties and dragging them down with them. For a second, I'm standing there like a dumbfounded Winnie the Pooh until I finally rip my shirt off too. Completely naked, I tentatively walk toward the shower, creak open the door, then step in.

To his credit, Orson steps to the side and doesn't look away from the showerhead. But even with his no-peeking promise, it's still a tight fit.

He hands me my loofah, preloaded with shower gel.

"Oh, uh, thanks," I say, sliding it over my shoulder and down my arm. And then finally over my chest and around my breasts.

I cast a quick glance over. His eyes are like lasers on the showerhead as the water beats down over him.

I grin. "You really are a Southern gentleman, aren't you?"

He lets out a strained laugh. "I keep my promises, sweetheart."

My eyes drift down of their own accord, taking in his slick chest, speckled with brown hair, the slight V that points down to—

I rip my eyes away before I can wander more.

If I don't want him seeing me, I should at least be respectful and do the same. The peek before I got in doesn't count.

We're quiet as we pass shampoos or move around to share the flow of water. When he's not underneath the showerhead, he holds himself in his hands, making sure to glance out of the clear shower wall.

After what feels like both the quickest and slowest shower I've ever had in my life, I step around him and open the shower door. But I find myself pausing in place.

The words return to me.

Julie Olivia

"I seem to have a problem with you putting your hands on my wife."

Adrenaline courses through me, and I don't know why the next sentence comes out of my mouth, but the words leave before I can stop them.

"You can look if you want," I say. "Like you said, nothing you haven't seen before."

I peer over at him. His jaw is tightly clenched. Droplets of water trickle over his cheeks, dripping off the end of his nose. His eyes level with the shower tile.

I give him a couple of seconds, and with each passing moment, my body heats.

Oh God, how embarrassing for me.

What in the world was I thinking? Here I am, naked and desperate for his eyes on me that I'm literally asking him to look.

I've hit rock bottom.

But then Orson finally looks over, and his eyes feast on every part of me—from my chest down to my stomach to my long legs and then rising back up, pausing at the area between my thighs and then again at my breasts.

Then, selfishly, I steal my own glances in the process. And that's exactly what it feels like. Stealing. I roam over his body like a thief, capturing images of his hard abs, the corded veins over his forearms, and then down to the length of him. Long. Rock hard. Heavy by the weight of it, pumped with blood.

My eyes shoot up to meet his, and when I do, the edge of his lips pull into a slow, tantalizing smile.

I step backward out of the shower, shut the door, and grab a towel. I don't even dry myself completely before opening the door back to the living room and letting the rush of cool air be the relief I need from the heat.

26

Orson

It must be a day for running late because, that night, Theo and I stumble into Lorelei and Emory's house, out of breath and jumbled.

"Sorry we're late!" we chime at the same time.

We catch each other's eyes, then walk in opposite directions. She sits at the breakfast nook. I lean against the wall, next to Quinn and Landon.

Quinn raises her eyebrows.

"Theo offered to help me wrap up stuff at the bar," I say in explanation. Which is the truth. I wish we had a more fun excuse, but that woman showed up at four o'clock on the dot with her hands on her hips.

"Put me to work, boss," she'd said.

"No."

"Yes."

"No."

But then she wouldn't leave until I threw her an apron and let her work. I have no idea what I'm gonna do with her if she keeps this up.

"Not a problem," Lorelei says from the dining table, her

173

head still tilted down toward the paper. "Bennett isn't even here yet. Oh, but, Orson, the beer? Is that all right?"

"Yep," I say. "Squirreled away for the party. We'll have enough."

"Perfect," she says, making a large, swishing check mark on the paper.

"Oh, I brought a taco spread, guys," Landon says, gesturing to the counter, where a buffet of food is laid out.

Theo lets out a low moan.

That moan.

But when she follows it up with a, "Thank God I'm starving," I have to hold in my laughter.

I dislike that she's so unintentionally funny, but that doesn't seem right. Shouldn't I be happy that my wife is funny? Shouldn't I be happy that we get along so well? Shouldn't I be happy that I got to shower with her this morning?

I'm still repeating the moment in my head—how she ran that loofah over the peak of her breasts, how the suds sluiced down between them, the water glistening on her smooth skin.

Her moving in was an awful idea. That is now, undeniably, a fact.

But the alternative wouldn't have been preferable either.

I look over to the couch, and I see how it could have been instead. She would be on some other person's spare piece of furniture. At least she has a bedroom in my house— even if we have been spending most nights in the same one lately.

So irresponsible.

The front door opens, and Bennett walks in with his fiancée, Jolene. It's been a while since I've seen her, and I'm assuming it's the same for everyone else because the whole room goes silent. But Jolene's arms are full of notebooks and a laptop. She grabs the seat next to Lorelei, letting her armful of materials slide down to the table.

"Hi," Jolene says, putting her hands on her hips. "I have ideas."

Lorelei blinks before nodding. I think she might even steal a look at my cousin, Emory, who seems more impressed with Jolene's forthright nature than offended by it.

"Perfect," Emory says in the silence.

"Yeah," Lorelei echoes. "Absolutely. Let's do this."

I don't have time to watch the side show of Jolene taking over Lorelei's carefully planned party. I'm too busy watching Theo, who looks at the unfolding scenario, slowly crunching on a guacamole-dipped chip as if it were popcorn for this movie.

"Don't stare," I murmur in Theo's ear.

She shivers in response, pushing my arm with a snicker.

And then I proceed to dig my grave deeper and deeper with my wife.

Throughout the evening, we continue our collection of stolen touches. I grip her waist when I need to slide past her in the kitchen. I brush my fingers over hers when I take the salsa spoon from her. I even find myself widening my stance so that our thighs touch when we stand together.

But I'm not the only culprit here. When I finally take a seat, she sits in the same one, scooting me over with a bump of her butt and running a hand down the length of my thigh when she adjusts my leg over.

All it takes is one side-glance from Jolene, her eyes trailing down and back up, to make me stand and choose another chair. To gain some sort of decency as Theo also straightens her spine and realizes we're being too obvious. Crossing too many lines.

When we finally leave, there's a part of me that feels like I should apologize. She doesn't want anything more, and yet here I am, stealing touches when I can. She wants a friend she can shower with in peace. Not a husband who is pawing for a full meal after getting crumbs.

So, when we get home and she starts toward my bedroom with her toothbrush in hand, I stand in the doorway with a hand gripped on the opposite side.

"I've got to get up early tomorrow," I say. "We should ..." I can't finish the sentence, but Theo's eyes widen, and she nods quickly.

"Oh. Right," she says, stopping mid-brush.

She walks back to the bathroom, and my chest tightens. I hear her spit in the sink, and when she emerges, she has a smile on her face.

"Too many slumber parties," she says. "Totally get it."

"I just gotta get up early," I repeat.

"Absolutely," she says.

I hate that it's come to this, but we have to set boundaries. This needs to be nipped in the bud now before either of us gets into more trouble than we already have. First marriage, then a house, and now a bed? What's next? Bonnie and Clyde shenanigans? Or, God forbid, Sid and Nancy? We all know how that ended.

"See you tomorrow," I say, holding out my hand for our secret handshake.

Without hesitation, she meets in the middle, and we end with our usual snaps. Two from me. Three from her. I'm relieved to find there's no awkwardness.

This can work. We can do this.

"G'night," she says. "Don't let the bedbugs bite."

"Don't let Don Corleone get you."

She gasps. "Rude."

I chuckle and close my bedroom door behind me. I slide into my bed, but without Theo there, it's so cold. So empty.

That's fine. It's how it should be.

I lie in the dark, hearing her roam around the house. Rummaging through the bathroom cabinets, turning the sink on and then off, walking back into the kitchen, getting water from the fridge ...

I need to distract myself.

A book. I'll read a book.

I reach into my side table and find only my flashlight.

Fine. No book.

That's perfectly fine.

Her bedroom door shuts. The light clicks off.

Good. We'll both fall asleep now. In our own rooms, as it should be.

I close my eyes, counting down from ten. Then starting over at fifteen. Then thirty. But no amount of sheep or lambs or hogs or even Buzzy the Bears will lull me to sleep.

And then I hear something.

A low buzzing.

My eyes snap open.

Is a fly in my room? A gnat?

I sit up. It sounds like it's coming from right behind me. I turn and only see my headboard. No bugs. Nothing.

But then I hear a low, breathy moan. And that's when it hits me.

Theo is using her vibrator.

Theo is masturbating in the room right behind me.

I swallow.

It's fine. She's an adult. She can do whatever she likes. It is none of my business. My house is her house.

But then it happens again ... a small, whining moan.

My body stiffens. My blood rushes down to my chest, my stomach, and finally further south until my sheets are tented with ache.

The pitch rises. She's increasing the speed.

Does Theo not know how thin these walls are?

Just close your eyes. Don't think about it. Don't think—

"Oh God." Her words float through the wall. Louder this time.

I move my sheets to the side and dip my hand beneath my underwear. I don't need any start-up. I'm already hard as a rock, and even one stroke is enough to send a low, grunting moan leaving my lips before I can silence myself. And it's louder than I would have liked.

I stop.

She must have heard me. There's no way she didn't.

The buzzing pauses. I wait for the embarrassed shuffle, the sound of her moving her toy back to her drawer. But I don't hear her putting the toy away.

Instead, the buzzing starts back up, followed by a very clear, very purposeful, hiss of, "Yes."

Christ.

I lean back, settling my back against the pillows, and I grip myself, taking long strokes. And with every stroke, it's only more agonizing.

Theo moans again. It's unrestrained.

I let out a moan to match hers. It's met with a louder one from her.

Oh God, this is happening.

She wants me to hear her.

I stroke myself faster, closing my eyes and soaking in the sounds of her on the opposite side of the wall. My mind drifts to the shower this morning. What if I'd pressed her against the tiled wall instead? What if I'd sunk my fingers inside her when I had the chance?

I let out an exhale. Her whining breath replies. Like a twisted game of Marco Polo.

But Theo isn't making the noises I know she can make. I remember her catlike yowls. I wish I could be in there, giving her the orgasm I know she deserves. The orgasm that would have her clenching all around my cock, her head whipped back in ecstasy, the faint shimmer of sweat on her long neck that I ache to lick …

I'm pulled back to the present as I hear her voice say, "Orson, I'm gonna …"

My name on her lips is enough to make me grunt back, "Do it, sweetheart."

And then she lets out a cry. She lets go, and I do too. I moan so she hears it. So she hears what she does to me.

My heart pounds. The buzzing stops.

Everything comes back into view. The darkness of the room. The moonlight filtering through the window. And the reality of what we just did.

I don't know how to feel. Ashamed? Embarrassed?

Instead, I reach behind me, knocking two times on the wall.

If she responds, it's okay. If she returns the secret handshake through the wall, then we'll be fine.

After a moment, she knocks back three times.

"That's my girl," I say. And I don't bother to whisper it. Because now, we've crossed a line. And I'm not sure I can go back.

27

Theo

It's been two days since Orson and I ... well ... I don't know what we did exactly.

I genuinely didn't know the bedroom walls were that thin. But when I heard his accompanying moan in tandem with mine, like he'd popped right out of my already-racing fantasy, I let it happen. I let it play out, and, God, I haven't had an orgasm like that in months.

But where do we go from here? We've thankfully been on busy schedules. I've barely had time to wave to him after my morning yoga. Plus, he's been in and out, prepping the final renovations for The Honeycomb.

I want to talk to him, but what do we say?

Hi, buddy. Loved the Jack-and-Jill party! Let's do it in the same room next time, okay?

Except ... that would cross so many boundaries that I don't even know where to start.

It's selfish of me to want to cross anything at all—boundaries, the small space between our rooms ... I remember the look on his face when he said he was falling for me last year.

And I remember how close I was to saying, *Why not try this out for real?*

But *why not* would have been a reckless response to a man saying words akin to *love*. And I worry I'm being reckless again now.

I should hold my ground and be a decent roommate—a decent friend. I shouldn't be instigating masturbating sessions—though he technically started that, right? How was I supposed to know his walls were made of paper?

No. I need to focus on important things. And I definitely shouldn't be imagining him gripping his monster cock as I train the new ride's skippers.

With The Great Forest Journey's channel filled with the water and the boats now installed, we've been cycling through the spiel for hours. The skippers are at the front, reciting the lines, while I sit at the back of the boat, squirting them with a water gun whenever they mess up.

It's all in good fun. If they're struggling enough, I take over and recite it with them—or at least attempt to. And finally, after a few hours, they're starting to get the hang of it. I'm proud of them. Spiel jobs are a tough gig, but there's camaraderie in pain. I even hear talks of buying crew jackets with *Skipper* on the back.

We pull into the loading dock after a perfect run, and with one final squirt, I tell the newbie Ryan to go on break. As he runs off, I lean back in the boat, closing my eyes and soaking in the sun.

It's nice, being in a secluded part of Honeywood while the rest of the park carries on with its usual hum of roller coasters and laughter and screams. This ride feels like my secret, very shaded corner of heaven.

When I first came to Cedar Cliff, I didn't anticipate

falling in love with this theme park. I don't think anyone does, which is why our senior staff is a bunch of thirty-year-olds who have been on the payroll for around ten years. But there are a lot of things in Cedar Cliff I also didn't expect to be interested in. Like a certain bar owner with his massive—

"You look relaxed."

I jump almost five feet in the air.

"Orson." There he is, at the start of the queue line, with his head tipped to the side.

When did he get here? My hot husband. My masturbating mate. My co-sinning collaborator.

I swallow. "You scared me half to death."

"Aren't you supposed to be off work by now?" he asks.

"No," I say, passing a glance over at Quinn, who is speaking with the on-break skippers. "I'm helping them practice this script until they're comfortable."

"You barely know it by heart yourself."

I gasp. "I *do* know it."

"Perform for me then."

He lifts an eyebrow, and my breath catches.

"Hilarious," is all I can get out when he's looking at me like that.

"Oh, hey, Orson." Quinn comes up beside him, arms crossed, looking between us.

I wonder if she can feel the tension—or smell it, like ooey-gooey pheromones in the air.

"Theo said I could watch her do the spiel," Orson says,

Quinn narrows her eyes, and I instantly shake my head with a, "No, I absolutely did not say that."

"I'm just sayin' ... happy to be a guinea pig," Orson says.

"Actually"—Quinn tips her head to the side—"yeah, that's a good idea."

I have about fifty of her secrets I want to let loose in this moment as an act of rebellion, like how she and Landon routinely do the dirty in Honeywood's security offices or the fact that they still argue during sex and they both get off on it. But I would never tell her secrets. Instead, I mirror her crossed-arms pose.

"No," I say, my voice dipping lower. "Seriously, Quinn. Please no."

She shrugs and innocently says, "I wanna know how the script sounds to someone new."

But Quinn couldn't be innocent if she tried. I see her sly, barely hidden smile. She thinks she's being funny, placing me alone on a boat with a guy I've talked about crushing on in the past. She doesn't know the half of our mess.

"Fine." With a heavy sigh and my knees almost buckling beneath me, I climb to the bow of the boat.

Orson grins, taking a seat in the front row. His legs are stretched out, his foot almost touching my own. He looks like dominance personified, and after my recent fantasies, it's enough to make my mouth water.

The boat jolts forward, and off we go. We flow down the makeshift swamp with ease while I clutch the oar in my hands and pretend to paddle. The two of us disappear around the corner and into the tunnel.

Just me and my husband.

Alone.

In a boat.

In the dark.

"Are you really steering this ship?" he asks.

"It's on a track."

"Theme park magic," he says in a mystical, wobbling tone.

I let out an anxious laugh.

Is this what we do now? We joke? We pretend like nothing happened?

"Well?" he asks, raising his eyebrows.

"Right," I say. "The script. Welcome aboard ..." I start, but then he shifts in his seat, his legs spreading more as he gets more comfortable.

My mouth feels like it's filled with cotton. I know what lurks beneath those jeans. It's suddenly far too humid in this ride tunnel.

"Is that a caterpillar?" he asks, pointing overboard to the new animatronics we installed.

"Sir, you're interrupting."

Orson chuckles, holding up his hands. "Oh, sorry. I'm a guest. Go, go. Spiel away."

I start reciting. Tentative at first, but then I relax when I see his lips silently mouthing the words back to me. He's helped me practice so many times that he knows the lines better than I do. When I get them right, he grins at me, like a proud husband should.

No.

Not my husband.

My roommate.

My friend.

I stumble over a line and then apologize. I'm never embarrassed. But he puts me on edge.

"Hey, no worries," he says. "So far, so good."

"How's the ride?" I ask. "Too dark and squishy with fake bugs?"

"Nah, it's fantastic."

"Good, because we can't change it now."

He gives a small smile, and then he shifts in his seat uncomfortably. It's almost as if he's considering saying something. I wonder if now is when we talk about our weird little rendezvous. Do I just blurt out the elephant in the room—the vibrating, purple-colored elephant?

I open my mouth to talk, but then he clicks his tongue.

"The ride is weird though," he says.

"Of course it's weird. It's Honeywood."

"Yeah, but ... I don't know. I guess I kinda imagined you'd be sitting next to me instead."

I laugh. "What are you talking about?"

He pats the seat next to him. "Figured I'd be cozier with the skipper."

"Excuse me, sir. I'm the captain."

"Sorry," he says with a wide grin. "Captain."

His grin is contagious.

"Anyway, I can't sit down," I say. "The rest of the guests wouldn't be able to see me."

"Maybe I'd drag you down," he says. "Grab your hips and pull you to me."

Wait ... I'm sorry ... pardon me?

I freeze on the spot.

What did he just say? Maybe I misheard. No, maybe he's just joking around.

"Hey now," I say with a weak laugh. "You're just trying to get me to mess up."

But then his smile widens as he mutters, "It's working, isn't it? I can't help that your hips are so ... grabbable."

We stare at each other for a moment. The ride music fades to our spookier track with low cello notes and a cawing crow. But we're not paying attention to our surroundings anymore. My hands grip the canoe oar tighter, my rowing gone by the wayside. I can feel a bead of sweat roll down the back of my neck.

"Orson ..."

"Theo."

I'm not sure what is going on, but I have a sneaking suspicion.

"Okay." I say the word slowly. "So, the skipper sits next to the guest. Then what? How do they run the ride exactly?"

"They wouldn't."

"Well, that defeats the purpose of ..."

"You'd be in my lap. Pretty legs spread wide over me."

My mouth goes dry.

If I remember anything about last fall, it's that Orson has a dirty mouth, and he loves to use it. He liked secretly whispering in my ear in public, writing me texts with crafty emojis—the parachute emoji somehow pushed me to an orgasm one time—and grunting sweet yet foul words as he exhaled into me with each thrust. Orson has always been confident, and he's never apologized for it.

I fantasized about his dirty mouth the other night when I got caught through the wall. And now, it's here again, and I want it. I want it so badly that I swear my body aches for it.

I swallow. "Would I?"

"Yeah," he says. "I bet you'd look really nice, straddling me on this seat."

For a second, there's only the sound of the lapping water hitting the boat, the squishes of the animatronic caterpillars, and the crickets over the sound system.

And then he asks, "Would that be ... okay?"

I can feel my heart pounding in my chest at the realization of this moment. Is it greedy for me to want this? Is it reckless? Yes to both. But also ... it's Orson. Capable, smirking Orson. He's all I've thought about in the quiet of my bedroom. Since last year, there's been nobody else haunting my sheets. And I want his words to serenade me.

His head is tilted to the side. He's asking permission. And I grant it to him.

I'm going to hell for this.

I nod. "Yes. That'd be ... really, really hot."

Orson gives a slow smile, placing his hands between his legs, gripping the bench seat as he leans forward and whispers, "I wish I could slide a hand down those cute shorts of yours and feel just how wet you are for me."

The gun has gone off. He's off to the races.

"You'd want me wet for you?" I ask.

"Yes," he says, and the words are like a growl. "Theo, sweetheart, I bet you already are. I bet two fingers would glide in real easy about now, don't you?"

I let out a small whine. I can't even stop it from coming out. I bite my lip to stifle anything more, but it doesn't help.

Orson's smile beams.

"God, you'd feel so good," he continues, the words melting out of him. "And I know you'd take me so well. Because you have before, haven't you? I'd rub that little clit with my thumb, just how I remember you like it. Do you remember the way I used to touch you?"

It's not until he stops talking that I, desperately waiting for him to continue like a dog with a bone, realize he wants me to answer him. I feel the oar slip beneath my now-weak hands.

"Yes," I rasp out. "I remember how you touched me."

"That's my girl."

"What else?" I whisper.

"Well, I wouldn't be able to resist touching all of you. In

fact, I might lay you down on this seat so I can devour you first. I'd rip off your shorts and move those pretty panties to the side just to savor the taste of you. I miss how you taste, sweetheart. I bet you think about that when you play with your little toys, don't you?"

"Yes."

"Good. Because by the time you were all over my tongue, when you were grinding against my palm, begging me to take you, I'd be a respectable husband and oblige. I'd give your delicious pussy everything it deserves. And you'd make those little noises we both love. I didn't hear them the other night, and I was hoping I would, Theo."

"Yeah?"

"Oh, yes. But that's fine. I know how to get those noises out of you. I know exactly"—his hand then reaches out, hovering his palm over my hips—"where"—ghosting over my pelvis—"to"—down to between my thighs—"touch."

I swallow, and my hips tilt forward of their own volition, but he pulls his hand back before our bodies can meet.

"And you'd come for me like the good wife that you are." His voice is now a low hum amid the knocking of the water against the boat. "And when my wife comes, I want to hear her clearly. Understand?"

I can barely breathe.

"Yes?" he prompts.

I get out a very small, shaking, "Yes."

We emerge on the other side of the tunnel, the sunlight filtering in. The ride is somehow over already. My chest is rising and falling. My heart is pounding.

Screw our invisible lines. I need that exact fantasy. As quick as yesterday.

"How'd it go?" Quinn asks.

"Stellar," Orson says. "She's a natural."

He winks, and my knees give out. Literally. They fail beneath me so that I sink to the seat of the boat, letting the water rock me into what I hope is some form of peace.

"Have a great night, ladies."

I won't be getting peace anytime soon.

28

Theo

Turning thirty is a big deal. Or so they say. I've got another year until I hit that milestone. At least, I will if Orson doesn't send me to an early grave.

I look over at my husband, carrying in tin cases of catering to the picnic tables behind Honeywood's amphitheater—his biceps looking far too good in that black T-shirt of his.

Christ Almighty, he will *be the death of me.*

I continue winding the streamer around the railing. Bennett and Ruby's birthday party is tonight, and I can barely concentrate.

"And you'd come for me like the good wife that you are."

That one single sentence has been circling my mind for days now. Thankfully, Orson has been busy prepping for the party, and I've been busy avoiding him. It's like the magnet pulling us together keeps trying to flip. Together, then apart. Together, apart. Our schedules rarely have time to intersect and yet ...

Orson walks back down the midway next to Landon and Fred. Each step has purpose, yet somehow also seems light, like a man walking on air. Like the world is nothing but a playground for him. A dream.

His eyes catch mine mid-conversation with Landon, and he levels a look at me. Raised eyebrows. A tilt at the edge of his mouth. The fire through his eyes razes me. His tongue whips out to lick his lips, like he's anticipating something much more sinister. My face heats.

I fiddle with the streamer, my fingers fumbling over the excess.

I'll have to rethink my efforts at avoidance because it is clearly not working.

But isn't this what I wished for? Marriage without the big to-do? Friends with benefits without the expectations? Isn't this the carefree life I wanted?

"That's my girl."

Aren't words like that all I've ever craved?

I look over at Lorelei, blowing up balloons with Emory. She sucks in the helium and laughs with a chipmunk voice. Then, I glance at Quinn, who Landon is now running over to before picking her up in his arms. He pretends to drop her in the Buzzy the Bear fountain as she yells empty, giggling threats.

I picture Orson and me. How he leans over me when I play the piano. How he adjusted my baseball cap at the stadium with that crooked grin and boyish laugh.

"I see you, Theo."

I smile to myself, tape down the streamer, then move on to the next railing.

"SURPRISE!"

Half of Cedar Cliff jumps out from behind Buzzy the

Bear's fountain, greeting Bennett and Jolene with cheers and congratulations. It's not a surprise at all, and we were very visible, but it does make him laugh.

Jolene hangs on Bennett's arm, rising to her toes to kiss his cheek. Orson immediately places a tumbler of whiskey in Bennett's hand.

"Where's Ruby?" I ask. Jolene side-eyes me when I do, so I add in an extra chipper, "It's her birthday too!"

"She's running late," Jolene says.

"Actually, can we do this again in maybe an hour?" Bennett asks. "I'd love for her to get the full effect too."

"Sure!" Landon's already on the job, telling people they have one hour to mingle before we do this all over again.

He drags Quinn with him, who looks reluctant but still smiling. I bet they're sneaking off to the security offices again.

I linger near Lorelei and Emory, trying to use literally anything and anyone to distract me from the presence of Orson. It's like I can feel his energy across the midway. And I know I'm staring too much because he peers over from his conversation with Bennett's mom and gives me a small wave. I pull my bottom lip under my teeth and return it.

I am so screwed. Literally.

Lorelei rubs my shoulder. "You all right?"

"Hmm? What?"

I look between her and Emory. Emory's thick eyebrows are scrunched together. Then again, they're always scrunched together.

"Yeah," I say. "Good job on the birthday planning, by the way."

Lorelei exhales. "I was hoping it'd turn out okay."

Emory shakes his head and snorts. "I knew it'd be perfect. You worry too much."

"It's what I'm good at."

"Then, find another hobby, beautiful."

Lorelei loops a hand through the crook of his arm and over his biceps. I love the way Lorelei looks at Emory. I love the way he looks at her even more. It's the only time this man looks like he's happy with the world, and Lorelei deserves nothing less.

But that worries me. What if that's the slippery slope Orson and I might fall into?

"How'd you know?" I blurt out.

Emory lifts an eyebrow. I don't think he likes personal questions all that much, but he knows me well enough after one year to know my filter is thin.

"Know what?" Lorelei asks.

"That you liked each other? Was it all fun and then, whoops, love happened or ..."

Lorelei laughs. "He couldn't take his hands off me at first. That's what happened."

Emory shakes his head and points a finger. "That is not true."

She leans in, teasing her face close to his. "Should I remind you about the time the bumblebees—"

"Hey, let's not," he says, kissing her forehead, then muttering against it, "Let's not."

Lorelei's eyes flutter shut like she's lost in a daydream, and then she comes to.

"Yeah, we had fun," she says. "But if we weren't in a lawsuit, we probably wouldn't have gotten as close."

I think I understand. The lawsuit made them fall in love.

Well, hell, I'm not in a lawsuit with Orson.

This is fine. Perfectly fine.

"Thanks," I say. "That helps."

"Helps what?" Emory squints, but it's that knowing look he has. That intense stare of a man that sees through to your soul.

Sheesh, he's hot as hell, but Lorelei took one for the team, didn't she?

I poke his large bicep—okay, so maybe Lorelei got a decent deal—and grin.

"It just helps," I say.

"Theo ..."

"Well," I say with a clap, "I'm gonna get going."

"Wait a sec!" Lorelei says through a laugh. "Are you having fun with someone too?"

"See y'all!" I throw them a wave and run off.

The last thing I see is Lorelei shaking her head and Emory giving the smallest of smirks.

Thankfully, I was telling the truth. I offered to take a shift operating The Beesting for the party, so I get the ride up and running. Plus, it gives me a place to hide out so that I don't stare at Orson like a creep for the rest of the evening.

Operating rides is routine by now. The Beesting rises and falls. I unload, then reload and double-check the safety harnesses. I watch the security panel and send them skyward. Rinse and repeat.

I'm almost through the fourth ride when I hear a knock on the booth door.

"Thought you'd have raided the buffet's fruit bowl by now," Orson says. "There're far too many blueberries left."

He leans against the doorway, hands in pockets, one ankle crossed over the other. He is everything I've been daydreaming about for days. Except now that we're here, sort of alone, my heart thumps into overdrive.

Fun. We can have fun.

"Well, hey," I say. And it sounds ridiculous, like, *Why*

couldn't I come up with anything else? Am I nervous *around Orson?*

He's just my roommate.

My roommate who also says, *That's my girl,* though.

Okay, I'm definitely nervous.

With his hands still dipped in his pockets, he leans out the window to the booth, watching the rows of guests high in the sky.

"When are you gonna drop them?" he asks.

"It's fun to make them wait," I answer. "See them sweat."

His eyebrows rise to me in a curious way. "It is, isn't it?"

I swallow, the small fan in the corner of the booth not pumping nearly enough air in this small, humid room.

I mash the button and drop the guests. The sounds of screams follow as they fall. And once they land, I shimmy past Orson to go help them out. He sidesteps, but it's not enough. We still brush arms, and the feeling zips through me like electricity.

I help the new guests on, double-check their harnesses, then walk back to the booth, where Orson now stands in the opposite corner, watching me work with his hands still in his pockets. I sit in the booth chair, double-check the safety panel, then launch the guests back up.

It's quiet for a moment after that. And when I look over at Orson, his eyebrows are turned in.

"I'm sorry," he says.

"What?" I ask. "What for?"

"Did I make things awkward between us?"

"What?"

"The boat ride. Did I ..."

"No," I say immediately. "Absolutely not."

"No?"

"No."

He pauses, kicking his shoe out and looking at the ground, then peering through hooded eyes back up at me. I haven't stopped looking at him for one moment. And my heart hasn't stopped pounding.

"How about you?" I ask.

"Me?"

"Are you ... is this ..."

"Sweetheart, I'm perfectly happy with whatever this is."

"With just fun?"

"I *live* for just fun."

I give a small smile. He returns the gesture. It only makes me smile wider.

"Do you want me to stop?" he asks, taking a step closer to me.

"With ..."

"With what we've been doing. With the flirting and ... everything. I can stop. If it's too much."

My face feels hot. My toes curl inside my shoes. He takes another step.

He's worried about me?

I could think of a billion reasons why we shouldn't hook up again. But not a single one is more convincing than how turned on I am by his sheer presence.

I shake my head slowly with a smirk.

"No," I say. "Don't stop."

"But it wouldn't be responsible."

"Good thing I'm very irresponsible."

He laughs and then pinches one eye closed, as if pained by his response as he says, "Me too."

My cheeks hurt from how wide I'm smiling.

"How long do you intend to make them wait this time?" he asks, tilting his chin toward the ride above.

"I'm not sure."

He drops down to his knees in front of me in one smooth motion, those hazel-colored eyes never once leaving mine.

"Okay, so let's play a new game," he says, running a hand up my ankle, my calf, and to my thigh.

My breath catches in my throat as I try to say with any form of confidence, "What kind of game?"

His hand twists to my inner thigh, then thumbs the gap between them.

I pull in a sharp gasp and look to the open door. But nobody else is around, except for the hanging hostages in the ride above.

"Keep them up there," he says. "And don't drop them until you come for me."

Orson lifts my skirt and disappears beneath it.

Oh my God.

I feel the scruff of his short stubble scratching the inside of my thighs. The softness of his lips grazing over my skin in long, languid kisses. Then the warm touch of his tongue seeping through my already-wet panties.

I gasp, my head falling back against the chair.

"Understand, wife?" he murmurs against me.

"Yes," I stammer out.

"That's my girl."

He slips the fabric aside. I feel his hot breath against me and then *him*. His tongue. His lips. My stomach drops—no, melts—as he laps me up like I'm his last meal on earth. Every lick of him against me is like a whip against my nerves. And when he groans, it's a rough sound, as if he's enjoying this as much as I am.

It's too much. It's not enough. It's everything all at once.

He dips two fingers into me, curling as he does. I let out a mixture between a moan and a high-pitched whine.

"Yes," he hisses. "There are those noises I missed."

I'd be embarrassed if his response wasn't so hot.

He pumps his fingers faster, and my breath gets more erratic. I can feel myself clenching around him.

"Don't you dare come yet."

My thighs are shaking with need, my palms finding his head beneath my skirt and holding him as close as possible.

"Orson, I ..."

"Be good for me, sweet girl."

I can't hold it. I can't believe how good this feels. I am about to explode.

And, as if reading my mind, he flicks his tongue faster, dips his fingers deeper, and right as I'm on the cusp, as I'm barely able to catch my breath, as the feeling between my thighs spreads up to my stomach, he growls, "Drop them."

I mash the button, and the ride falls. The sound of their screams masks my own as I let myself release. My head knocks backward past the chair and against the booth wall. It stings, but not as much as the absence of Orson as he removes himself from under my skirt. And when I look down, I don't know what to expect. But what I don't expect is the heat in his eyes as he licks the rest of me off his lips.

"I want you," he says.

"I gotta ... the ride ..." I point with a shaking finger.

"Do your job, then come back to me, Theo."

He doesn't have to tell me twice.

I leave, my legs barely functioning as I do. I reset the ride—weakly nodding as I hear Frank say, "The wait was awesome!"—and load in new passengers before sprinting back to the booth, where Orson waits for me in the chair.

I double-check no alerts are signaling safety concerns, then smash my hand on the button to send them soaring up.

I crawl onto Orson's lap. I don't know what he has in mind, but I don't care. As if sensing my eagerness, he laughs, gripping my hips and grinding himself against me.

"So needy," he says through a half-groan.

God, I am.

But right as I reach for his belt, we hear voices outside the booth.

"It's not the same without her," Bennett says.

"It's *never* the same without her," Jolene responds. "We can't do *anything* without her."

Orson's gaze whips to mine, and we both halt our fevered movements.

"Shh," he says softly, placing a finger over my lips.

I lick it from knuckle to tip. I taste a bit of myself on his fingers, but it only turns me on more.

Orson lets out a low groan and shakes his head.

"You'll pay for that later," he whispers.

I wiggle my eyebrows up, then down in a challenge.

"She'd never miss our birthday," Bennett's voice continues from outside the booth.

"*Our?* You know you weren't actually born on the same day, right?"

"Jolene, come on." I've never heard Bennett as irritated as he is now. "Ruby's my best friend."

"Oh, and what does that make me, Ben?"

Then, my phone rings on the control board. The sound echoes throughout the booth. I fumble to grab it as it crashes to the ground, continuing to buzz louder.

Orson covers his mouth as he tries not to laugh.

I leave his lap, crawling under the table and picking up the phone. And when I look at the name, it's as if the universe put me in the middle of something I didn't want any part in. I flash the phone to Orson, whose eyes widen. I bring it to my ear.

"Ruby?" I whisper.

My friend's shaky voice is on the line as she says, "Can you come get me?"

"Where are you?"

I distantly hear the whoosh of what might be a car.

"Um ... side of the road?" Ruby says. "Interstate? I ... there's not a lot of lights."

"What happened?"

"Flat tire." She laughs, but it seems nervous and not at all amused. "Happy birthday to me, right?"

"Okay. Stay there. I'll grab Bennett and ..."

"No," she quickly says. "Please don't tell Bennett. Or his mom. He's been trying to get me to add air pressure for weeks. And to get a spare."

"You don't have a spare?"

"I don't need the lecture," she says with another weak, forced laugh. "I'm sure I'll get one later."

I laugh. "Okay, well, can I tell Orson?"

I wince up at him because, obviously, he already heard all of this anyway.

Thankfully, she says, "Yeah. Of course. Just ... nobody else?"

"Absolutely."

Orson's holds out his hand and crooks a finger to me. I hand the phone over without question because the motion is already enough to send my nerves on edge. I like being demanded by this man.

"Hey, Rubes. It's Orson," he whispers. "We'll come meet you. Don't call the tow company for another ten minutes so we can get halfway there. I don't want you to feel forced to ride with a stranger alone."

Seeing him take control is not good for my own self-control, which I've clearly already lost.

He hangs up and looks at me with a sigh and tilt to his head.

"We'll pick this up later," he says, running his finger over the length of my nose.

"We'd better," I say.

I mash the button on the control board and drop the ride from above.

29

Orson

We find Ruby sitting on the back of her car with her feet dangling over the edge. I inspect the damage, but there's no helping a flat without a spare.

The three of us pile into my car after the tow guy arrives. He says he'll drop it off at the dealership and she can swing by tomorrow. But as we drive back, I can't help but wonder how I would react if this were Theo instead. I know I'd feel the same type of irritation that I felt at the baseball game—the possessiveness for Theo's safety. But I also know I can't always be there for her.

At some point, we'll divorce and go our separate ways when one of us finally comes to our senses. Though I'm kind of liking being senseless right now.

Friends with benefits is doable for us. I know my place. I'm her friend. I like being her friend, and I refuse to mess that up this time.

My hand twitches at my side, desperate to grab Theo's thigh and possess her once more, but that's when I finally tune into her and Ruby's ongoing conversation.

"Are you sure?" Ruby asks.

"Yeah, let's watch anything you want," Theo says.

I look away from the road for two seconds to cut a glance at her.

"I don't know ..." Ruby says.

"Ruby, it's your birthday," Theo continues. "We're going to celebrate even if it's on your couch."

I know what she's doing. Theo is putting a pin in our plans.

It's her friend's birthday. And she's going to spend it with her. But I don't say anything because I'd do the same thing too. Even if it does make the bear inside me thrash around at the idea of not ravaging Theo like I wanted.

Calm down, buddy.

We pull up to Ruby's house. Ruby gets out with her purse strapped over her shoulder, eyes darting between me and Theo. She's a smart girl. She can sense something brewing between us. I know because the moment she meets my gaze, I see her eyebrows tilt inward.

"You know what?" Ruby says. "I'm feeling sleepy. I'm just gonna call it a night."

"No, you're not," Theo says with a laugh. "We're celebrating your birthday, weirdo."

"It's fine! Go back to Honeywood. Have fun."

"Too many people," Theo says. "Blegh. Not my style."

I smile because it's absolutely her style. She's just being nice.

"I want a fun movie night with you instead."

Ruby points to me. "Orson, do you want to ..."

I raise my hands up. "No, no. I'll let you two have a girls' night."

"Ooh, you know what would really hit the spot? *When Harry Met Sally*," Theo says.

I can tell she's trying to keep Ruby on track.

Ruby's face falls. "Maybe something else."

"Well, think on it," she says, then looks at me. "I'll be inside in a second."

Ruby nods, but not before shuffling over to me and pulling me into a tight hug with a muffled, "Thank you for your help, Orson." I hug her back, just barely hearing an additional whisper of, "Sorry for cockblocking you."

I laugh, and then Ruby keys into her house, leaving Theo and me alone.

Theo winds her hands together, looking from the door, then to me. She is always beautiful, but in the burnt-orange glow of Ruby's porch light, Theo's sparkling party dress and inky-black curls look even more breathtaking.

"Sorry," she says. "It's her birthday. I can't let her be alone."

I smile. "I would have done the same thing."

"You're rubbing off on me."

"Not yet, I'm not," I say.

She bites her lower lip with a grin. "Later."

"Yes," I say. "Later. Have fun."

Theo holds out her hand. I smile and do as she's silently asking, maneuvering through our complicated secret hand-shake before ending in our snaps.

We're different now. I'm not the man from months ago, ready to confess my undying love for her. Our situation has changed. I'm now Theo's friend. And that's just fine.

She walks backward toward the door. I give a small wave.

But before I can turn around, she's storming toward me again. She grips a fist in my shirt. We both pull each other in, and our lips collide.

We fall into our kiss like starved animals—lips moving, breaths staggered, hands roughly pulling and tugging at anything we can. Her hand is under my baseball hat, tipping it aside. I hear it hit the concrete. My hands grip her jaw.

I pull away and take a stumbling step back. I blink quickly, shaking my head, as if coming back from a dream. Theo laughs.

Through a ragged breath, I swing down to pick up my hat. I point it at her with a small, "Later."

"Later," she echoes.

Our mantra for the night.

Then, she turns, opens Ruby's door, and disappears on the other side.

Instead of heading back to the park, I go to The Honeycomb instead. The parking lot is still full of the party guest overflow at Honeywood, so I distract myself by slinging drinks for a while, trying to piece together the left-over gossip from the party. How Fred got caught kissing Honey on The Canoodler. How Emory and Landon competed to see who could ride Bumblebee's Flight the most, resulting in Emory getting sick. How Frank lost his shoe on Buzzard of Death.

And finally, once it all dies down, after Frank limps out to the parking lot, holding his one shoe, Bennett swings through the front door.

He slumps into a barstool. He looks ragged. Tired.

"Have a good birthday?" I ask.

Bennett runs a heavy hand through his messy black hair, pulling it off his shoulders and into a bun. He doesn't respond.

I pour him a drink instead and ask, "Where's Jolene?"

He sniffs, leaning back in his chair, hanging an elbow over the back.

"Home," he grunts. "Ruby never showed up. She said she wanted to stay in."

"Makes sense," I say, not revealing that I already knew that anyway. Ruby has a right to her privacy, even from her best friend. "This whole thing wasn't her deal anyway. She probably just wanted a quiet evening, you know?"

"Yeah," Bennett says. Then, he rustles his hair. It loosens from the bun he just put it in. "No, I know. I know that, and I should have said something."

"Hey, it's fine."

"No, it's not," he says. "It's everything *but* fine. I ruined it."

"Ruined?" I say with a cautious laugh. "It's just a birthday."

"No, it's our thirtieth. It was supposed to be ... different. It was supposed to be just us. And now, she's not here. She ... Orson ..." He levels a stare at me. "My best friend missed her own birthday. Because my fiancée didn't want her around."

And there it is.

"She didn't?"

"No. Jolene made that ... quite clear. I think Ruby got the message."

He's hurt. And selfishly, I wonder if this is what being close friends with someone of the opposite gender can do. I wonder if this is what will come from being so close to Theo.

Will I be in Ruby's shoes when Theo decides to marry someone else? When she inevitably asks for a divorce? No, we're different. Our situation isn't even remotely the same.

I feel my hand make its way to my chest, rubbing the

stress out from me. I quickly lower it down—a habit from not wanting Theo to be worried, I guess.

Bennett lowers his head to his hands on the bar top. I turn around, pour a quick shot, and slide it to him. His eyes peek over his hands. He takes the shot like a tentative cat before swallowing it back.

"Sorry, man."

"I don't wanna talk about it anymore," he says, which is definitely par for the course with Bennett. "How are you holding up?"

"Fine," I say. "I've been busy. You know. The usual."

Bennett narrows his eyes. "You okay, man?"

"Yeah. No. I'm fine."

"You don't look fine."

I thought I looked okay, but maybe he's seeing something I'm not.

"Well"—I consider not saying the next thing, but if I can't tell one of my oldest friends how I'm feeling, then who can I tell?—"I've got chest pains, y'know?"

"Chest pains," Bennett echoes. His eyebrows rise with concern.

"It's not a huge deal," I quickly say. "Really. It's not. Just ... the renovations. You know."

"Have you gotten it checked out?" Bennett asks.

"Yeah," I say. "Yeah, I see someone." When he's quiet, I add, "It's fine. Really."

He nods, and then we fall silent.

"Well, if you ever want to talk ... you know ..."

"I know."

"Cool."

"Cool."

He clears his throat, rapping his knuckles on the bar and nods.

"Well, I should get going. Jolene's probably worried."

"Yeah. And, hey."

"Hmm?"

"Happy birthday, man."

"Yeah," he says with a nod. "Best thirtieth ever."

I walk him to the front door and lock up. Then, there's the familiar, reliable pain in my chest again. My hand rises to greet it like an old friend, massaging it as it slowly dissipates. It's tight. It's irritated. But more than that, it's concerning. I work out. I eat mostly okay, aside from bar food. I'm, for all intents and purposes, healthy.

But every time I'm faced with stress, I can't help the burn. The shiver that runs down my spine. How, sometimes, my eyes feel itchy, and I just want to close them to block out the piles of paperwork and the little red notifications on my phone.

I go to my office, but instead of doing work, I find myself staring at the wall. Specifically, at a chipped spot on the wall. I remember when that chip got there. When Theo leaned against it with her heeled boot, causing a crack not only in the wall, but also in my own foundation.

I should have known we'd be back here. With the sly smirks and pulsing hearts.

I absentmindedly sift through paperwork, looking at receipts and audits and ... I'm just not interested.

I love this bar. I love the people. I love it all. So, why am I sitting here, doing nothing?

Why am I sitting here and only thinking about my wife?

30
Theo

"We're coming to Cedar Cliff!"

"Oh my God, why?"

"We want to see you and Orson! Plus, your mother has never been to Honeywood!"

I have the phone pressed to my ear, raising my palm up to shield my eyes from the sun. I've been stuck on The Great Forest Journey all morning, working out the final kinks, training with the last nervous skipper who can't seem to memorize his lines, all while trying my best to process what the hell I'm supposed to do about how badly I want to sleep with my husband.

But, of course, now is the time my father calls.

"Dad, I have to work today," I say.

"We're perfectly fine with roaming on our own. Callie wants to try the drop ride!"

"Wait, Callie? Who all is with you?"

"The whole Poulos fam!"

"Dad, no. Please."

But *no* is not in my dad's vocabulary when it comes to vacations. He's a sightseer at heart. Which is why, one hour later, I'm standing beside the Buzzy the Bear fountain at the front of Honeywood Fun Park, watching my dad shove his hands in the pockets of his khakis, squinting around like he's observing ancient architecture. My mom is beside him with her black sunglasses that look like she stripped them straight off Audrey Hepburn's corpse. Off to the side are Kassandra and David. And finally, there's my little sister, Callie, and her husband, Alex, who look thrilled to even be standing on Honeywood's blacktop.

She runs toward me full tilt, ramming into my chest with a hug and squeezing me. I barely feel it under her toothpick arms.

"Oh my God, how are you? It's been so long! Where's Orson? Is he here? Everyone met him but me, and that's just unfair."

I'd bet a million dollars that's why they're here.

"He's next door," I say, nodding my head in the direction of The Honeycomb, which sits one block down.

Her eyebrows scrunch in, and I realize that, if you're not a Cedar Cliff native, that probably doesn't make much sense.

"So, what do you want to ride first?" I ask.

"Ooh, I saw there's one called Little Pecker's Joyride!"

"Can we even say that?" Alex whispers to her with a conspiratorial grin.

She kisses him on the cheek.

Kass walks past with her nose in her phone, David following behind her with a less than impressed sneer. His nose scrunches more when he passes Buzzy the Bear bounding around in his fluffy suit. My mom asks where she can sit in air-conditioning. I direct her to The Bee-fast Stop, where she says she'll be staying for the remainder of the afternoon.

I grab Callie's hand, showing her, Alex, and my dad around—letting them meet Fred, sneaking them in the back entrance of The Great Forest Journey, where they ooh and aah over the boats as Quinn gives them the grand tour—and then I ferry them over to Lorelei, who is overseeing the final animatronics, and finally to the monitors, where Bennett is installing the preshow movie. It's not a bad day, even with my mom and Kass being sourpusses.

When my shift ends, I corral the gang over to The Honeycomb, where Orson stands behind the bar, taking us in with wide eyes. I texted him we were coming. However, I don't think he realized it was *all* of us dropping by.

It's the first time I've seen him in person since Bennett and Ruby's party. By the time I got home this morning from Ruby's, he had already left for work. But even as he looks overwhelmed by his in-laws, my heart still races at the sight of him.

My nerves alight at the memory of the soft, *"Later,"* that left his lips and how it seems our *later* is now claimed by my family instead.

We settle into a long table. Orson drops off a row of beers, then takes the seat next to me. The moment he sits down, David's phone rings. He picks it up without hesitation, disentangling himself from the table and walking off to the bathroom hallway.

Ass.

"Nice establishment you have here," my dad muses, looking at the walls filled with framed vintage beer posters and Honeywood Fun Park memorabilia, like he's a connoisseur of off-site theme park bars. Typical dad behavior.

"Thank you," Orson says. Under the table, his hand splays over my thigh, and I shiver under its touch. "We're actually expanding out back."

"No kidding?"

"Happy to show you, if you're interested."

"I'd love to. You know, I've done some renovations myself."

"You mean, the safety hazard tree house?" Callie interjects.

My dad laughs. "The wonderful tree house you girls adored."

"Adored," I say. "And feared for our lives in."

We all laugh, but my dad sucks in another breath, as if the first wasn't enough.

Odd.

I narrow my eyes, stealing a glance at Callie, who sits next to him with a mirrored expression to my own. Mom is looking at him funny too. We all see that something is wrong with Dad.

But true to form, my mom gets distracted by my hand on the table instead, leaving the moment of weirdness unanswered.

"Where's your ring?" she asks.

The table grows silent.

"My what?"

"Engagement ring. Wedding ring. Any of it."

Something passes over Orson's face as he looks down to my blank ring finger. His palm squeezes my knee.

"Theo's getting it refitted," he says. "She has my grandmother's old ring actually."

And my memory shifts back to it. The velvet box he held that day on the edge of the bed.

"I'm falling for you."

I wonder if that was his grandmother's ring or if he's just spitballing to make me look better.

"I'm gonna go find David," Kass says, pushing off from the table and walking to the restrooms.

My dad looks between us, a lingering glance kept on Orson. "I'd love to see that side room now."

"Of course," Orson says. "Let me show you."

He and my dad get up from the table. Callie's husband, Alex, follows as well, leaving only me, Callie, and my mom to stare at each other across the table, twiddling our thumbs as I take occasional sips of my beer. My mom doesn't touch her drink even though Orson was thoughtful enough to bring her wine instead.

"So, Orson is nice," Callie finally says, her shoulders rising to her ears with a cheeky smile, as if we were teenagers again, gabbing about boys.

I smile. "He's great."

"You two aren't planning to have a proper wedding?" Mom asks.

"Nope," I say. "Not really on the table. We're both pretty busy."

"Hmm."

I clear my throat. My hands feel clammy. I gotta get out of here.

"You know what? I've gotta use the ... yeah."

The cruddy words spill out of my mouth like spoiled milk, but I just let them do their thing. I exit the non-conversation with a look of *sorry* sent to my sister.

Callie furrows her brow, as if to say, *No, I get it. It's okay.* She's always understood me.

I take the hallway to the restrooms, and at the end of it, I see the backs of Kass and David in the corner next to the fire exit. I catch the tail end of David letting out a groan.

"You don't need to know everything, Kass."

"Okay, but when you're texting secret numbers—"

"You're so paranoid, you know that?" David says with a laugh. It doesn't sound genuine at all. "Secret numbers? Seriously?"

When he turns around to see me waiting behind him, he pulls in a surprised inhale.

"Hey, Theo."

"David," I counter.

He walks past me, a hesitation in his step.

I look over at Kass, her hands down by her sides in fists. Her jaw is grinding while she's still watching the place where David once was. If I were him, I'd be taking a plane a thousand miles away. Anything to avoid that glare.

"Everything all right?" I ask her.

"Yeah," she says, eyes darting to me before she spits out, "Perfect."

"If you ever need anything," I say, "you can always call."

"When do we ever do that?"

She moves with purpose from her corner, nearly shouldering me as she passes.

My sister and I aren't the best of friends, and we never have been. She's five years older than me, and we somehow never closed that age gap. I was never quite the adorable little sister, but also not old enough to share makeup or clothes. She always seemed to have her shit together, and I never did. But for the first time, I'm worried she might be just as lost as me. And I feel sorry for her.

Orson appears at the end of the hallway, the side of his mouth tipping up in that crooked smile of his. When I give a weak smile back, his expression falls.

"Everything all right?"

"I think something's going on with my sister and her husband," I say.

"Yeah?"

"I don't know. I think."

Suddenly, he chuckles, and I snap my head to him.

"What?" I ask.

He shakes his head, tonguing the inside of his cheek.

"You're a good sister."

"No, I'm not."

"It's clear you care."

His hand reaches out, trailing over my waist, taking a fistful of my shirt. My heart pounds as I take a step closer. The energy in the hall changes so fast, but if I could, I'd only pump the heat higher.

He whispers into my ear, "I missed you last night."

I can feel a tingle along my shoulders, trailing over my back, like a raindrop tickling its way down my spine. I lean into his neck, running my nose over him, inhaling his wood and hops scent.

"I missed you too," I murmur back.

Even curled into Ruby's soft blankets, watching movies and having a good time, I still missed our ruddy den couch and Orson's baseball trivia.

"I have to call Mrs. Stanley," I say.

He laughs. "Not the sexiest thing you could have said, but okay."

I nuzzle against him and groan. "My family didn't tell me they were coming until today. I gotta cancel our yoga session."

He pushes my shoulders away and looks me in the eye. "Do you want me to take care of them?"

"Who?"

"Your Poulos party," he says with a chuckle.

"I couldn't ask you to ..."

"You don't have to ask. I'll show them around Cedar Cliff this afternoon. It's no big deal."

I blink at him. "Really?"

"Of course."

I want nothing more than to kiss him, but when I glance over his shoulder, the whole family is staring at us, like we're two animals in a zoo.

Nosy.

"We're being watched, aren't we?" Orson whispers.

"Mmhmm."

"I've got them. Don't worry."

I feel my eyebrows tilt in as my eyes trail down to his lips and back up.

"Thanks."

"If you keep looking at me like that, I'll give everyone a show right here," he says.

"No, really. Thank you."

"Hey," he says, lifting his knuckles to knock them playfully against my chin. "What else are husbands for?"

31

Orson

I show the Poulos family around Main Street, to the pastry shop with sweet bread, through the small park in the middle of downtown with the gazebo and music coursing through the speakers.

They have tons of questions, ranging from, "What do you even do out here?" to, "Is there even a police force in this town?" and, "So, where is Theo's yoga studio?"

"Yes, I'd like to drop by," her mom says.

"Well, she's a bit busy with a client," I say. "We probably shouldn't."

"We can wait in the lobby," her mom says, pausing to blink at me.

"Mom," Callie chastises, tossing me a worried smile.

I can feel the tension between the family, but I cut it with a laugh.

"Actually, Sophia, there's an antique store on the other side of Main. I'd love to show you this beautiful piano they have on display there."

I can see the slight twitch at the edge of her pursed lips.

"All right. I'd love that."

Our small crew cycles through the antique store, breaking away in couples or groups, shimmying through the tall stacks, walking slowly so as not to trip on old trunks or piles of frames or dolls or records. Eventually, after three narrow hallways, it's just me and Theo's mom staring at the old grand in the back.

"Has nobody bought it yet?" she says with a tsk. "Such a shame."

"I think it's waiting for the perfect home," I say. "But this antique shop isn't going anywhere. Been here forever. This might as well be its home."

Her eyes catch mine, and I see so much of Theo in that look. The curiosity.

"I can ask Luke about the price, if you'd like," I offer.

"No," she says quickly. "It seems to like it here." She ghosts her fingers over the dusty keys.

"I think the hardwood has dented around it actually."

I step back, and she does too—a weird contrast of my boots squeaking against the floor versus her small sneakers. We observe the flooring, warped inward near the piano's feet.

I think I hear Sophia laugh, but it's so short and quiet that I might be mistaken.

"It's definitely settled in," she says. "Maybe you're right. Maybe this is its home. Theo seems to like it here well enough."

I halt at the sudden change in conversation.

"Yeah, I think she does."

Her eyes dart over to me. "And you're good to her?"

"I try my best to be."

"And she's good to you?"

I smile. "Your daughter is a wonderful woman."

As if satisfied, Sophia nods. "Good. Now, did you mention ice cream earlier?"

"Have you never been to our downtown shop?"

She shrugs. "Everything is new."

"Everything? Well, don't I have the treat for y'all. Let's go."

I stick out my bent arm. Sophia slides her hand into the crook of it with a smile.

As we make our way through Cedar Cliff, I find it increasingly odd that they've never been here. How long has Theo lived here? Seven years or so? And they've never visited before?

It makes me uncomfortable that she was cast aside like that. And why? Is it because she's the one child who moved away from the city? The one child who didn't follow in the family's footsteps?

"I swear we're not normally this crazy," Callie whispers to me when we're in the bookstore.

"Yes, we are," her husband says with a small laugh.

"Okay, we are. But you get used to it."

I smile, feeling weirdly welcome in their little slice of life. Especially when Callie tosses me a book from the shelf that says *Marriage for Dummies*.

"Kidding."

"See?" Alex adds. "Crazy."

When I finally wave them off in their Suburban—Eli waving back, Sophia giving me a small wink, and Callie tossing an extra air kiss from the backseat—I let out a heavy breath that has felt caught in my throat all afternoon.

Marriage.

Is this all it is? In-laws and mediating and trying to figure out whether they like you, but never being quite sure?

I feel the small ache in my chest, but it isn't the usual pressure. It's something else.

A longing.

I don't mind playing the role of son-in-law or brother-in-law. I like it. I like their eccentricities. But what I don't like are the side comments. The judging looks from her older sister.

Is this normal for Theo?

I hope not. Because she is so much more than that. And it's unfortunate they can't see it.

32

Theo

I haven't seen Orson since I left him with my family. And I already miss him.

When I walk to The Honeycomb from yoga, I'm feeling that annoying nervousness again. It's like a little elf is living in my stomach with gnashing teeth and little growls of, *Mine, mine, mine.*

It's actually kind of terrifying.

I creak open The Honeycomb's wooden door, hoping to catch Orson in his usual spot behind the bar, but I don't see him.

Even when I sit down at our table, surrounded by my closest friends, I can't help the tug at my brain, the curiosity of which Cedar Cliff resident distracted him now, roped him into helping rescue a cat from a tree or something.

"I think he's in the back," Ruby whispers to me.

I glance to her.

"I've only seen him once," she says. "He's been busy. Go. Go."

I rise from the table, patting her red hair with a,

"Thanks, Lassie," before sliding down the hall to the back of the bar.

I make it to Orson's office door and peer in. He's at his desk, his head in his hands.

He looks like a tortured man, but a beautiful one. I wonder how stressed he is, and I wonder how much of it I can take off his plate. I've never wanted someone to look less miserable in my entire life.

"Orson?" I ask.

His head whips up, and when I expect a smile, I don't receive one.

Instead, he's up in one swift movement, walking around the desk, taking my face in his hands, and kissing me. I sigh into it.

Orson is so good at kissing. His lips form to mine—together, apart, together again—like a man desperate for a taste. And with the way his hand slides up my neck to my jaw, how he grips me close, like he doesn't want to let go ... Orson has a way of making you feel like you're the only person in his world. And right now, I'm his sun and stars.

He takes steps forward, walking me backward until I hit the wall. He holds out a hand beside my head, shutting the door in the process.

"Hi."

He laughs. I laugh with him, the energy of his happiness like a balm to my soul.

"How was my family?" I ask.

"Delightful."

I snort. "That sounds like a lie."

"I was too distracted to notice if they were anything but delightful."

"Distracted by what?"

"You."

"Me?"

"Yeah. You. And how much I missed you last night," he says. "Theo, you can't have slumber parties anymore. The house is too quiet without you."

I laugh. "It was probably nice to watch baseball without my stupid questions."

"Your questions aren't stupid."

"Or my face masks."

"They're relaxing."

"Or my smelly candles."

"Stop," he says, closing his eyes. "They smell like home."

He plants another long, slow kiss on my lips that I sink into.

"I also missed these pants," he murmurs against me, running a thumb over the top hem of my yoga pants. "And I want them on our floor as soon as possible."

Our.

I don't want to think about how wrong this might be. How we might be close to crossing that final line—ruining the good thing that we have. Because, while he might be my husband, he's also my friend. And I don't want the same outcome from months ago. I want to keep my friend this time.

"Theo, I'm serious."

Well, if you can't have mind-blowing sex with the person you trust most, then who can you have it with?

"They can be on the floor tonight then," I say.

I turn to open the door, but his hand slams beside my head, keeping it shut.

"If I have to wait a few more hours, I might not make it," he says with a breathy laugh.

"If I go back to the table with sex hair, literally everyone will know."

He lets out a musing noise, a low exhale as he smooths back a curl on my forehead.

"Then, don't go back out there."

"Orson," I say with a laugh, but he shakes his head before I can continue.

"Theo," he echoes, and part of me feels the edge to his tone. "I want to kiss you. I want to taste you. And I want to be so deep inside you that I forget everything *but* you."

His thumb rubs roughly over my cheek as his palm grips my jaw harder. He looks serious. Dead serious. *Here lies a man deader than dead from blue balls* serious.

"Now?" I ask.

"Now," he confirms. "Let's go home *now*."

A thrill zips through me, but I can't muster up any arguments. I don't think my brain would let me anyway.

"Okay," I say before repeating, "Okay."

"Okay?"

"Yes, Orson." I laugh. "Let's get the hell out of here."

I'm going to have sex with my husband. Damn the consequences.

33

Orson

We take separate cars home.

Not that I wanted to, but I knew if she sat next to me, I wouldn't have been able to contain myself. I might have even pulled over and had my way with her, which didn't exactly seem like the best idea, considering there are zero places in this town to be alone in public.

So, I drive like a bat out of hell to my house, screeching as my Jeep nearly topples over when I pull into the driveway. And right behind me is her car, cutting off the moment she stops.

Theo runs toward me, jumping into my arms without abandon, her legs wrapping around my waist.

God, this woman.

I pepper her with kisses on her mouth, in her hair, on her chin, and down to her neck. Her body arches into mine, breathy sighs leaving her mouth. I carry us up the porch steps, pushing her against the exterior of the house as I dig into my pocket to get my keys.

Once they're finally in my hand, she snatches them from me, fumbling the key in the lock as I bury my face in

225

her chest, tugging down her shirt, spilling her breasts out of her bra. I run my tongue over her, tasting the sweet almonds and oat I've missed so much. Inhaling the lotions and perfumes that have been teasing me for weeks.

When I hear the door click open, I shove my boot against it. It flies in, hitting the opposite wall with a bang, but I couldn't care less. I carry my wife into the house and toss her on the couch.

"Go shut the door," she says with a laugh.

"I'm a little distracted here." My hand is in fact dipping into her pants.

"I'm not going anywhere," she says, pushing my chest.

I growl, turning around and closing it. But when I turn back around, her shirt and bra are already removed.

I tilt my head to the side and sigh.

"I was supposed to do that," I say, stalking toward her, gripping her face in my hands again, pulling her lips to mine.

She bites my bottom lip in retaliation. I bite her back, running a thumb over her nipple, eliciting a low whine.

"God, those noises," I groan.

Her head falls back. I take her chin in my hand and pull it back to me, placing another kiss against her lips.

She arches into my hand, allowing me to bend down and pull her nipple into my mouth, flicking my tongue where my thumb once was. Her hands dive around my neck, tugging me closer, exhaling against my head, kissing along my temple.

We both lower over the arm of the couch and down onto the cushions. She wiggles out from under me and turns around, rising to all fours, her ass pushed up in the air.

I run a hand over her shoulders and down her bare spine, in awe of her.

"I missed this," I say, the words more strained than I would have liked.

"You see it every morning when I do yoga," she says, tilting her hips side to side. A taunt.

I exhale out a laugh. "Not like this."

"So, you do watch me," she says.

I walked into that one, but I'm not gonna sugarcoat anything tonight.

"Of course I do," I say. I smack my palm against her ass, and she jumps. "You still like it when I spank you, don't you?"

"What do you think?"

I hook my hands around her front and tug down those tight yoga pants of hers.

"I think I need you," is all I get out before I'm moving her panties to the side and burying my face between her legs.

Her pussy tastes amazing, and she sounds glorious too. She lets out loud, unashamed moans, pushing back against my face and only spreading her legs out more. She is a goddess. Confident. Unbothered by the act of sex. Just the woman I remember from months ago, but somehow better.

I strain against the zipper of my jeans with every subsequent lick, every call of my name from her lips, and right as I feel her knees start to shake, she bucks forward.

"Get back here," I growl, grabbing her hips as she laughs.

"No, I don't want to come yet."

"I promise to give you multiple orgasms."

"Orson ..."

"Have I ever lied to you?"

Slowly, she smiles and says, "No."

"Then, why would I start now, sweetheart?"

I bury myself between her thighs again. It only takes a few more minutes of my tongue whipping over her, a few more minutes of her heavy, breathy moans, to have her rolling into an orgasm and slumping forward onto the couch with my name cursed on her lips.

I stroke a finger over her thigh. She looks over her shoulder at me, ever the look of a sex kitten, batting her eyelashes under hooded eyes. She doesn't say anything, but I can tell she wants to.

"Yes?" I ask, placing a chaste kiss right on the peak of her round cheek.

"I want ..." And Theo hesitates, which isn't like her. Confidence runs through her body as thick as blood.

"What?"

"I want you to show me you want me," she says.

"Show you?" I ask.

And while part of this feels like a test, I know that, with Theo, it isn't.

Prove to me I'm the woman for you, is what she's really saying.

Theo has been told too many times in her life that she's not the smartest or the most successful or the center of anyone's universe. I'm happy to prove that she is the center of my world. I'll prove every belief she's ever had, everything she's ever been told, every single lie that she believes, isn't real.

I'll prove it all wrong.

I glance over to the mirror leaning against the wall opposite the couch. I tilt my chin toward it.

"I'd love to. And I want you to watch me while I prove how much I want you," I say.

Something leaves her lips that's a mix between a desperate whine and a wet moan as her head twists to see the two of us reflected back. She lowers down to her fore-arms and knees, ass poised up to me. My greedy hands palm over her backside.

I unbuckle my belt, clinking the metal against metal as I unhook it from its hold and hiss my zipper down. I pull myself out, and she sucks in a breath, watching me stroke the length of it in the mirror's reflection.

I grab her hips, scooting her back, the backs of her thighs straddling mine. I run the length of me between the cheeks of her exposed ass. I slide along her wetness, teasing up, then down. It's a sight to see, only made better by her lips parting in awe in the mirror.

"We look good, don't we?"

She nods against the cushions.

I need to get a condom before I make a reckless decision though, so I sigh, lean down to kiss her behind, and say, "I'll be back—"

"I'm on birth control," she quickly interrupts. "And I haven't slept with anyone since you."

I pause.

"You haven't?"

"No," she says.

I swallow as the truth of it hits me. The realization that the last person the both of us slept with is each other.

"Me neither," I say. "Just you, sweetheart." I run a hand over her spine. "Just you."

And those are the words lingering between us when I line up my hard cock to her slick center and push in.

She lets out a moan. I pull out a little, then inch my way back in. Out, then back in, and out again until our hips finally touch. The next thrust sends a slap echoing through the living room.

I lean over her back, sliding my hand down to caress her

chin and turning her head to look at the mirror. I meet her eyes in the reflection, and we watch each other, seeing as our bodies slide together, as I give longer and longer thrusts with louder and louder sounds.

"Look at how good you take me," I say, eliciting a small moan from her as her eyes close in ecstasy. "No, Theo. Watch your husband when he fucks you."

Her eyes snap open, and I can see the change. How they transform from longing to passion to the fire that ignites in her at the sound of that sentence.

She grinds herself back against me, pushing against me at the same time I thrust in.

"Christ," I breathe out.

"Do you like your wife on all fours?" she asks.

"I think my wife *likes* being on all fours."

"She *loves* it." And the word is expressive and filled with poison. But if she's poison and I'm the victim, I'll gladly accept my slow, agonizing death.

It's sex like we've never had before. Never, not once in the two months we were messing around, did Theo talk like this. This is different. Like we're on the razor's edge, driven forward by our desperation for this moment. As if we've been waiting for each other all this time.

I snap my hips to her, reveling in the sound.

"You're taking me so well," I breathe. "My good, sweet wife. All mine."

"All yours," she says.

"Say it again for me."

"Yours." She practically hums the word.

"Yes," I hiss through gritted teeth. "That's right. And I want to be the only one who knows how you sound and feel. Do you understand?"

"God, yes."

230

I let out a laugh, which causes her to laugh too. And I'm not surprised. This is so easy with her. Even when I'm pounding into her, even when we're saying the nastiest words with our bodies echoing throughout the living room, we're still laughing together.

It's easy with Theo. It always has been.

With every subsequent thrust, I can feel the pressure build. I watch us in the mirror with her green eyes heated, lips curled into a devilish smile.

"Is this enough evidence?" I ask with a grin. "Does this show you how bad I want you?"

I lean over her, keeping eye contact in the mirror as I whisper against her ear, "I see you, Theo. Now, look me in the eye and come for your husband like my good girl should."

And when I feel her tighten around me, when she calls out my name—*my name*—as she orgasms, I follow closely behind, releasing all of me inside her.

We lie for a moment, heavy breaths passing between us in the silence of the house. I run a hand over her back, placing kiss after kiss along her shaking spine, her body spent from me.

Me.

"Thank you," she whispers, almost so quiet that I don't hear it.

I plant a kiss right between her shoulder blades. "You never have to thank me. Now, turn over. I want to make my wife come again."

I see her smile in the mirror, but she's not looking at me. It's like the smile of satisfaction is only for herself.

"Yes, husband."

34

Theo

I wake up the next morning to an empty bed. None of Orson's breathing. No arm slung over my waist. No knees pressed into mine, fitted like a cozy puzzle piece.

I reach my arm out to nothing.

My heart—and the piece that I set aside for Orson last night—sinks into my chest. Deeper and deeper into dread.

Oh my God, what did I do? Hell, what did I say?

"I want you to show me you want me."

I've had worse things come out of my mouth while on the precipice of an orgasm, but nothing that needy or insistent.

And what a ridiculous thing to say. No, what a stupid, selfish thing to say to a man who spilled his heart for me months ago. But last night, everything in me ached for him to want *me*. This man, who gives everything to everyone else ... I wanted him only for *me*.

I sigh, slamming my head back against the pillow.

I deserve to be in this bed alone after that stellar performance.

This is fine. This is perfectly fine.

I close my eyes and take a deep inhale, but then I hear the clanking of plates coming from the kitchen.

I shoot up, listening closer. More faint clattering. The moving of drawers. I climb out of bed in only the baseball jersey he bought me and my underwear—definitely not dressed appropriately if there's an intruder—before opening the bedroom door.

Except it's no intruder. It's Orson. He's over in the kitchen with his back turned to me, messing with something on the counter. The smell of coffee is already permeating in the air. Everything about the scene reminds me of mornings at my parents' house. They were always awake before us kids with coffee brewing and waffles being prepared. It's a sign of home.

Home.

I walk slowly across the living room, pausing at the brick column in the center of the house. He must hear me because he turns on the spot in his checkered pajama pants, wired glasses, and bare chest on display as much as my bare legs. And then Orson smiles, and right where my heart sank, it's like he reached his hand in and plucked it back out.

"Good morning, sweetheart."

"You're ... still here," I say. "I mean, you live here, so of course you would be, but ..."

I can't find the words.

"Of course I am," he says. "Eat with me?"

"You made breakfast?"

He tosses his head side to side and squints. "Sure. Let's call it that."

I walk into the kitchen, peering around him, seeing a plate of blueberries and yogurt. And beside that, a sheet of stars. Stickers in a rainbow of colors.

He follows my line of sight and grins. "Would you like a gold star?"

I laugh. "What?"

"For last night."

He thumbs through the sheet, peels off a gold star, and walks over to smack it against my forehead.

I blink. "You ..."

"Got up early to get you *good job* stickers and breakfast?" he finishes. "Yes. I would ask if it's weird, but ..." He pops a blueberry in his mouth and grins. His eyebrows lift, then fall in a tauntingly gorgeous gesture. "I know it is."

And then he winks, and my knees buckle under the weight of it. No, under the weight of all this. Orson remembered. He's *here*, and he remembered my stickers and my blueberries and *me*.

He pulls me into his chest. I place a hand over it, running along the roughness of him, the stray curls of dark brown hair littering across its hard surface. He places a kiss on my forehead—on the single gold star.

I reach around him, grab the sheet of stickers, and take a purple one. I push it into his cheek, pressing my thumb around for good measure.

"I think you deserve the star this time," I say.

"So, last night was okay?" he murmurs.

"I was gonna ask you the same thing."

"It was perfect."

The last breathy word almost echoes in the space between us. I inhale every piece of it. Every syllable.

"It was," I say. "Perfect."

And after a few more silent moments, he finally reaches around, smacking my ass. It hurts, but in a *I can't get enough* kind of way. In a *please give me more* type of way.

"Good." It's a conclusion to this moment—whatever this

is. This intimacy that permeated into my chest and down to my soul. "Now, go do yoga or something. Before I demand round two."

I arch into him, causing him to take a sharp inhale. "But I like round twos."

He teases his face closer with a grin. "And I like watching your ass in the air while you salute the sun or whatever it's called."

I pull away, laughing. "My sun salutation?"

"Right. That."

"Would you want to join me?"

His eyes widen.

"Really?" he asks.

"Yeah," I say. "It'll be good for you. You never relax."

"But that's your private time."

"Is it?"

I guess, to a degree, it is. But another glance at the purple star on his cheek and the blueberries and coffee and all of this ... why wouldn't I share a piece of myself with him?

"Well," I say, "who cares? I like time with you more."

The look on his face that smiles back is filled with something else. A giddiness almost. I want him to make that face as often as possible.

"Okay. I'll join you," he says. "It's probably for the best I can't watch anyway."

"For the best?"

"Well, if I watch you, I won't be able to keep my hands off of you," he says, promptly pawing again at my nearly bare ass. My thong leaves nothing to the imagination.

I tilt my head to the side. "Think of it like foreplay."

"Oh, sweetheart, you already instigated foreplay when you came out in that."

He looks me up and down, his eyes roving every inch of my figure and my baseball jersey. I trail my hand down his forearm and entwine my fingers in his.

"I'll make it even better. I'll do yoga in *only* this."

With a gnash of his teeth and more laughter from me, we do exactly that. Coffee, blueberries, then yoga. As promised, in only my baseball jersey. And after fifteen minutes, when I lift myself to a final downward dog, he's already behind me, running a hand along the curve of my ass and shifting my thong aside.

I look over my shoulder.

"No, no, don't let me stop you," he says with a grin before pressing two fingers inside.

We're just lucky his backyard has tall fences.

35

Orson

I've been at The Honeycomb for the past ten hours, and it isn't until I am pushed out the back door by my employee, with the door locked behind me, that finally I decide to leave.

Yep. Totally my decision.

But instead of driving home, my steering wheel directs me elsewhere. I pull onto Main Street and parallel park in front of Yogi Bare.

Leaning over the center console, I peer into the lobby and see Theo. She's sitting behind the reception desk, scribbling on a sheet of paper. I can't help but smile.

The past week has been a surreal dream. Mornings full of yoga, blueberries, and sex. Nights, exhausted in the den, watching baseball, playing piano, and then having sex again. On the couch. On the stairs. On the piano itself with the discordant rings echoing through the house.

But between every breathy sigh and desperate bites against skin, I try to shut out the thoughts tapping at the back of my mind like an unwelcome neighbor.

Julie Olivia

When do you fall for her again? When do you get your heart broken again?

I have to shake it out, flexing the muscles in my hand as I take deep breaths in and out to steady my heart. My chest twinges in a weird way when I think about that—stiff like a muscle I've contracted too long, an exhale just waiting to let loose but unable to.

But I won't ruin this. Not this time.

The bell above the door rings when I walk into Yogi Bare. The lobby smells like patchouli, and the only sound is the running water of the small fountain on the reception desk.

Theo looks up at me and smiles, a sliver of her white teeth shining through the deep shade of maroon on her lips.

"Done with work today?" I ask. "I'm about to head home if you want a ride."

"Yes!"

She rises to her feet, running off down the hallway beside the front desk, her butt looking amazing in those tight orange pants. I love the wacky colors she chooses, like she's perpetually stuck in '70s shag carpet fashion.

Then, she suddenly comes back to the lobby, smacks a quick kiss on my cheek, and disappears down the hallway again. I laugh, and my heart fills to the brim.

The curtain to the main studio shifts to the side. I turn to wave at who is coming out, and all those good feelings fade when I see an all-too-familiar face.

My ex-girlfriend, if she could be called that, looks at me from the open curtain like she's seen a ghost. And in some way, I suppose she has. It's been months since I've seen Meghan. Though I'm not counting the time I saw her at the end of the produce aisle and wheeled my cart in the oppo-

238

site direction, almost running into the display of stacked soup. Not my best moment.

"Meghan, hi."

"Orson," she says. "Good to see you."

It's not. Her face betrays her with her clenched jaw and twitching eyebrow.

"You haven't been to The Honeycomb in a while," I say, which is a ridiculous thing to say because, of course, she hasn't. Why would she? I own the place.

"No." She pauses to probably swallow back whatever other words she wanted to add like *you idiot* or *pig*. Instead, she politely continues, "I haven't."

I'll give her credit for that.

I wonder how it feels to avoid Cedar Cliff's watering hole for seven months. No, I rather wonder how it feels to be told by the man you're seeing that he doesn't want commitment, only for him to get married one month after that. Not that anyone knows that's what happened, but the guilt glints in my soul like a stuck shard of glass.

"Heard you own the place now," I say, looking around the studio.

"Yep," she says.

"Looking to expand?"

"Not really. Looking to ... leave actually."

"What? Why?"

"I wanna get my master's degree. Maybe go overseas. I don't know. I'm done with small-town life. I haven't told Theo yet, but I'm selling the building to Frank. He can keep this place running if he wants, I guess. He's always looking to blow all his retirement money."

"No kidding, huh? That man and his real estate, I swear."

"I told him not to spend all his retirement in one place."

"Me too."

She smiles. I forgot how funny Meghan is. And whoever ends up with her will be a lucky man. I didn't do right by her.

"Hey, I'm ... sorry," I say.

"No, don't even apologize," she says, holding up a hand. I nod, opening my mouth to continue, but she says, "Why are you here, Orson?"

And there it is. The truth hanging right between us like a dangling fruit, ripe for taking. I told her I didn't want marriage, and yet the woman whose name is next to mine on a piece of legal paper saying otherwise is right down that hallway.

My mouth hangs open like a fish, on the edge of another apology.

She sighs.

"You're not as sneaky as you think, Orson," she says. "It's Theo. I know you're here for Theo."

Women. How do they know everything?

I don't deny it.

"How'd you know?"

"She talks about you a lot," Meghan says. "She tries not to, but ..." Her words fade off before she shakes her head. "I don't mind. Really. It's a small town. Not dating other people's exes would be impossible. I told her it was fine months ago. Didn't think she'd actually get you to commit, but ..."

I let out a small laugh. "I do feel bad, y'know."

"I know you do. You're Orson Mackenzie. You always worry about whether people are mad at you."

Well, I don't know about that ...

But she's smiling, and I'll take that as a good sign.

Meghan leans back, as if seeing whether Theo is in the hallway before whispering to me, "She's been happy."

"Is she normally not?"

"Well, of course she is. She's Theo. She's always happy, but ... it's different. It's good. She needs someone like you."

I feel that familiar twinge. The restlessness in my knees and heels that makes me want to bounce on the spot.

The words from a week ago course through me.

"I want you to show me you want me."

"She puts on a nice front with her friends," Meghan continues. "But she needs someone there for her. Only her. And even if it's you—you jerk—I'm happy. As long as she has someone."

I nod, more to myself than anyone else.

"I can be that person," I say.

And I can. Because I know Theo needs someone. And if all I am is her friend, then that's all I'll be. I can do that.

"So," I say, changing the subject, "how have you been?"

"We don't need to be cordial, Orson," Meghan says with a laugh.

My head juts back in surprise. But something about the reaction feels nice. For once, someone isn't asking for me to help them clean their garage or move their stuff or give them anything. I stick out my bottom lip in a weird type of unspoken satisfaction.

"Fair enough," I say.

After another minute, Theo emerges at the mouth of the hall, her duffel bag slung over her shoulder. She halts in place, looking between us, her eyes wide and eyebrows slowly tilting in. Something is passing over her face. Her cheeks burn red.

Meghan is right. Theo needs someone. A long-term

friend who won't fall in love with her. Someone to prove to her that she isn't a vacation friend.

Plus, we're really good at being best friends. It just needs to stay that way this time around. Then, nobody can get hurt.

Not Theo.

And not my aching heart.

36

Theo

"I didn't break it."

"We'll need Bennett to take a look."

"But it wasn't me. For the record."

"Nobody is taking notes, Ryan."

The teenage skipper eyes the canoe's oar on the ride boat's floor. It's lying like a sad piece of driftwood, and some of the water on it might actually be Ryan's tears. Still unsure.

The Great Forest Journey had been running smoothly, but right as we turned the corner to the ride's final scene with the new Queen Bee and Ranger Randy animatronics, Ryan's hand slipped, and the paddle knocked aside a control panel beneath the lip of the boat. Some of the interior paneling swung down. The ride came to a halt.

Since Bennett is our head of maintenance, I radioed him as soon as possible.

Bennett arrives with Quinn in tow, taking a large step from the animatronics' platform and onto the boat. Bennett, glancing from the panel and back to Ryan, puts his hands on his hips and glares.

"So, you're the one who broke it?"

"I didn't ... I ..." Ryan sputters, whipping his head to me desperately.

"I know; I know," I say, patting him on the shoulder because, sometimes, you gotta sooth the trainees' little puppy souls. "Take ten, Ryan. Get a pancake. Get some tea. Just relax."

He nods to himself, stepping off the boat, giving a wide berth to the new animatronic, as if he might break that too, then power-walks away. He only glances back once. I wonder if he's paranoid Bennett will chase after him with his toolbox.

I twist toward Bennett. "That wasn't very nice."

Quinn smirks. "But it was hilarious."

I'm still getting used to the sight of her in a manager polo. After she shifted away from the Queen Bee acting role, her Honeywood attire now looks weirdly normal. But everything does in comparison to the poofy pink dress and shiny crown.

Bennett bends to one knee, observing the panel.

"Theo, it looks fine," he says. "You just need to go to the control booth and signal it's good to go."

"I know," I say with a shrug. "But the screw holding it closed fell in the water. I didn't have another one handy."

"Is this what my job has boiled down to?" Bennett says with a sigh, cracking open his toolbox. "Screws?"

"Don't tell Jolene that," I joke with a wink.

But instead of barking out a laugh like he normally would, head back and delightful grin on display, Bennett deflates. And it feels wrong, seeing a man of his size shrink that fast.

I wince. "Oops, are we not joking around anymore?"

I glance to Quinn, who has her arms crossed.

"Everything all right, Bennett?" she asks him.

"Yeah," Bennett says, but it's slow and almost haunting. "It's just ... wedding stuff. You know."

"Oh, well, if it's just that," Quinn says with a joking laugh.

But when Bennett, once again, doesn't laugh back, we exchange a secret look.

"Hey, we're just kidding," I say.

Bennett shakes his head. "Yeah, I know. Sorry. I feel like I haven't been fun to be around lately."

"Oh, everyone is a little stressed right now," I say quickly with a dismissive wave of my hand. "I mean, look at this place!" Then, I gesture to the open air, as if signaling to Honeywood Fun Park as a whole. "With this ride opening in a week and then The Grizzly reopening soon too, we're all feeling the pressure."

"Exactly," Quinn says with a nod. "It's going around for everyone. Lorelei is working longer hours."

"Isn't Landon too?" I add in.

"Oh, definitely. And Emory is working hard on the Grizzly. He's so stressed."

I laugh. "Seriously! Heck, even Orson is a bit stressed."

Cue the record scratch.

Nothing follows that statement.

Zip. Nada. Silence.

Quinn squints at me right at the same time Bennett's hand halts mid-screw.

"How do you know that?" Quinn asks.

And that's when I realize my mistake. How *would* I know that? Are Orson and I suddenly BFFs?

I catch myself smiling.

Well, Orson *is* kinda my best friend, isn't he? My best friend forever, if you want to get technical. The thought

245

almost makes me laugh a little. It's so childish, yet also ... I kinda like it.

I like us.

"We're ... friends," is all I say.

"Are you ..." I can tell Quinn is trying to avoid an accusation, so I let her slowly work into the next sentence. "Wait, no, isn't Orson still with Meghan?" Quinn turns to Bennett. "He is, right?"

Bennett shrugs. "Don't ask me."

"I could have sworn he was just talking about someone last week," she says. "I bet it was her."

But when Quinn looks satisfied with the answer she supplied herself, probably happy she didn't accuse one of her closest friends of lying—even though I definitely have been—the whole thing doesn't sit right with me. In fact, the thought of Orson and Meghan together again makes me feel itchy inside, the same way it did when I saw them together yesterday. How they looked like a perfect little couple. And maybe that's how everyone else sees them too.

"Seven," I blurt out.

Quinn blinks. "What?"

"He and Meghan have been broken up seven months," I say. "I just ... she tells me. Yoga buddies, you know."

"Oh, huh, okay," Quinn says. But she lingers, and something tells me she feels an inkling of a lie within those little knowing bones of hers. "Must be why he looks stressed lately. He's not getting laid."

I let out a laugh that is far too forced. "What do you mean?"

"He just seems ... tense," she says. "I don't know."

Then, Bennett chimes in, "He told me the other night he's been getting chest pains."

Quinn and I whip our heads over to him.

"Like ... heart issues or something?" she asks.

"No," Bennett says, leaning back on his heels. "I don't know."

Quinn twists her lips to the side. "Wonder if he has anxiety."

"Anxiety?" I ask, blinking at her words. "He's never mentioned that before."

Quinn shrugs. "It's not like it has a start and end point. Maybe it's popping up now. With the amount of stuff he does around town? I wouldn't doubt it."

It's quiet while this settles over us. I know I'm not the only person considering the obvious—Orson gives too much of himself to Cedar Cliff. And nobody is giving back to him like he deserves.

And I feel so silly now. So ignorant of the thing staring me right in the face.

Anxiety.

The thing is, he's been seeing doctors—I know he has—but maybe it's something more than they're currently treating him for. Or worse than that, is he even telling his doctor the truth? Does he talk about his chest pains? He won't even talk to me about it.

Anxiety.

Another thing Orson might be shouldering alone.

Oh, Orson.

"Anyway," Quinn says, "I should go."

I blink back, trying to not think too hard about Orson. But I have to see him. I have to talk to him about it.

"Wait, why did you follow me here to begin with?" Bennett asks.

Quinn nods to the platform.

"I heard the new Queen Bee animatronic is working," she says. "I wanted to see how dumb I looked."

I glance from her to the animatronic. It was modeled after her likeness. But it's also more cartoony. Bigger eyes and wider hips.

"And?" I ask her. "What do you think?"

She sputters out a laugh. "I look ridiculous."

The two of us burst into laughter. Even Bennett lets out a low laugh.

"Landon looks worse though." She snorts.

We all look over to the Ranger Randy animatronic Queen Bee is hand in hand with. His slightly wonky eye malfunctioning. His beard that looks almost *too* well groomed.

It sends us toppling into laughter once more.

Quinn leaves with a wave of her hand, and then it's only me and Bennett. He wastes no time swiveling his head toward me with a single lifted eyebrow.

"What?" I ask.

"They're gonna know eventually," he says. "About you and Orson."

I laugh. "How would they know?"

"Because you looked like you got hit by a truck when she mentioned Meghan."

I can feel my face heat. "No, I didn't."

"Sure you didn't. But it's going well?"

"Yeah," I say. And then I settle into the word. It feels nice, so I repeat it. "Yeah."

Everything about this seems so ... easy.

But it can't possibly be this simple, right? If relationships were this easy, then Kass and David wouldn't argue all the time. If it were this easy, then Bennett and Jolene wouldn't be struggling with wedding planning. Because if it is this easy for us—the two people who didn't want it in the first place—then why is it hard for everyone else?

"Is it fixed?"

I look over and see Ryan with a honey iced tea in his hand and a worried expression across his brow. His hand is shaking, like a squirrel entering a room with a big pit bull.

"Nope," Bennett says, standing up with his toolbox. "You broke it forever. We can't run the ride now."

Ryan slumps down on the spot, and I laugh, saying, "He's joking! Ryan, he's just joking."

"Oh." The teen quickly nods with a weak laugh, blending into a stuttering, "G-good one, Bennett!"

And in that moment, as I sense the relief flow through Ryan with every subsequent nod of his head, I suddenly wish someone would tell me my current issues were all a joke too.

I'm way too concerned about my fake husband. And that, in itself, is concerning as well.

37

Orson

Paint is slapped on the bridge of my nose faster than I can anticipate it. But I should have known that involving Theo in painting The Honeycomb's new rec room would be a disaster.

"If you keep stalling, I'm gonna be late," I say.

"But I don't want you to leave just yet."

"Mrs. Stanley isn't gonna clean her living room without me," I say with a laugh. "I can guarantee it."

Theo slumps down, but I hold her tighter. She's sitting in my lap on the lone folding chair in the corner.

"Come on. Don't leave." Her hand goes to my chest, running the heel of her palm over it.

I close my eyes at the motion. It admittedly soothes the pain that lurks there sometimes—the tugging of a string around my heart. But why she started doing what I'd already been doing for months, I don't know.

"Well, I can't," I say. "Your wall is still blank."

"Isn't it supposed to be?" she counters, following my eyesight to the off-white eggshell color of plain drywall liberally dappled with spackle.

She makes a fair point. But considering our mural artist will be here in a couple of days and our only job was to ensure it's a smooth, evenly prepared white wall, we're a little bit behind.

"It's fine. I can finish it later," I say.

"No, I've got it," Theo says quickly. "Seriously. Don't. Worry. About. A. Thing."

There's a pause between each word as she inches closer with a paintbrush before putting another dot on the tip of my nose.

I grin. "We've been entirely unproductive."

"Sometimes, it's okay to be unproductive," she says. "Breathe in, breathe out."

"Nuh-uh. None of those breathing exercises for me."

Her shoulders fall, and she gives me a look that says, *Party pooper*. I don't know what party I'm crapping on though because it sure isn't ours. I haven't kept my hands off her since she got here, and she's done the same. With us, I think it's impossible.

"Thanks for helping out," I say.

"Yeah, well, it's either spend time with you or train the newbies," she says. "And I have more than enough time to do that."

"You don't have more than enough time to spend with me?"

She grins, but the words still settle between us. Something unspoken we don't dare touch. The question of, *How much time do we have?*

We never settled on an end date or a solid timeline or any type of parameters that would be the cause for our divorce. We just agreed to let this go into eternity. It was irresponsible then, and we're still being irresponsible now—her on my lap, the walls that should be painted left untouched, and my never-ending ache to be inside her.

"You're thinking about being inside me, aren't you?" she asks.

"How'd you guess?"

"You get that twitch at the edge of your mouth," she says, poking me with the brush again. "It's very sinister."

I lean in, teasing my lips over hers.

"Sinister, am I?"

"Maybe," she says, drawing out the word before placing a kiss on my lips. Slow. Hard. Followed by a sharp inhale from both of us, as if we're breathing in the other at the same time.

My hands grip for purchase on any part of her, finding their home in the bunch of her jeans.

I don't want to let her go. I want everything about her to stay. I want her laughter, her creativity, and her spirit to inhabit these four walls. Which is why I don't plan on letting her leave.

"So, I've been thinking," I say.

"Uh-oh." I grip her thighs harder, and she laughs. "Okay, what?"

"I think we need more variety here."

Her eyebrows rise. "Cuffs?"

"What? Oh." I feel my face redden, quickly followed by blood rushing south, which only makes her grin wider once she feels it against her. "No, you minx," I say, biting at the tip of her nose. "Though your little toy is still unused, and that bothers me."

"Ahem, you were saying?"

"Right. Well, we need more variety in the bar," I say. "Different events to take advantage of this new room. And I think it would be awesome to host a yoga session once a week or something. And I'd like you to lead it."

Her head pulls back. "Whoa, seriously?"

"Yeah," I say with a laugh. "We've got tons of people who would love that. It'd bring in visitors, and we could pair it with a Sunday morning brunch."

Her face starts to fall, and part of me wonders if I did something wrong. But it's not disappointment on her face. It's disbelief.

Theo lifts her knees up, twisting in my lap to straddle either side of my hips. She extends her legs out and tightens them around both my waist and the back of the chair. Her arms wrap around my shoulders.

I settle into the tight, awkward koala hug.

"You'd do that for me?" she mutters against me, the words a bit wobbly.

"Yeah," I say, dipping a hand into her hair. "I like to invest in good decisions, and you're a solid investment, sweetheart."

Then, her head lowers down, her ear resting against my beating heart. The small tension of a tug settles right behind it. An itch I can't scratch.

"Thank you," she murmurs.

"Thank you," I reply. And what I'm thanking her for, I don't even know.

For being her.

For being here.

There's a knock on the door, and we both jolt up. I stand to my feet, sending Theo flying off my lap. I reach out to grab her right before she hits the floor, and thankfully, Theo folds in half really well—thank you, yoga stretches. But this is how my cousin finds us: my hands under Theo's arms and my crotch positioned in front of her mouth.

"Good Lord," Emory says.

"Not what it looks like," I say.

He gives a heavy sigh. "This town stresses me out."

"I know it does."

I look down to Theo, who is holding back what I know will be one of her snort laughs.

Emory throws a thumb over his shoulder. "You asked for a stack of wood," he says. "And I brought it."

"Oh my God, this is the start of a porno," Theo breathes.

I lower her to the ground and pat my jeans off, as if removing dust from them when, really, it's the scent of her. All of Theo that is slowly seeping into my clothes and into my soul day by day, minute by minute. I'll soon be consumed by her.

"Thanks," I tell Emory. "I'll meet you out back to carry it in."

His eyes dart from me to Theo, and he shakes his head. Once he leaves, Theo uncovers her mouth and bursts out into laughter.

"Oh no, Mr. Roller Coaster is angry."

"He'll be angrier if he hears you calling him that nickname."

"Hey, why do you need wood?"

"I'm building the cabinets in here myself."

"Wait, why?"

"The contractor bailed," I say. "It's fine. I can figure it out."

Her face falls, and I think I see her eyes twitch to my chest, then back again.

"Orson, you can't do everything. Ask Emory for help or something or—"

"Hush, you," I respond, reaching down to wrap my

hands around her thighs, where I pick her up and throw her over my shoulder.

She instantly laughs. "Oh my God, Orson! Put me down!"

But I can't. I can't fathom not having her in my arms. In this bar. In my life. And that's going to be a problem.

38

Theo

The morning of The Great Forest Journey's opening, I wake up to a note on the kitchen counter.

Wife,

Sorry I missed yoga this morning. Had to leave early and meet the muralist at the bar. I would have woken you up, but you seemed like you were in a deep sleep. Didn't want to interrupt in case you were fighting Don Corleone. Made you a pot of coffee. Restocked blueberries.

Good luck today, Captain! See you tonight for board game night!

—Your Husband

A tiny gold star glitters in the corner. I tap a finger on the last two words.
Your Husband.
I smile, but it fades just as fast as it came.

Orson has been working more lately. Too much. And though I keep trying to help at the bar when I can, it's never enough. He still looks stressed.

I hoped the small chest rubs, the extra affection, all of it … it might change things for the better. But to be honest, I don't know a single thing about anxiety, if that's even what's happening to him. I don't know how to help.

During my morning yoga routine, I keep thinking about it. The note on the counter. The *Your Husband*. The fact that he bought me more blueberries and star stickers. That he made coffee—and I love the way he makes coffee.

Love.

I pause in place, mid-headstand, and that word hangs there, dangling in front of me like an unwanted guest. In fact, the word lets itself in my house without knocking or even ringing the doorbell, like it's expecting a well-balanced meal and a foot rub in return for its long journey to me.

I topple, lose balance, and fall.

Love.

Did you hear me the first time? it sneakily asks.

No. Absolutely not. And I refuse to hear it at all.

I get up and run to the back door.

Love, love, love.

It's following me like some serial killer. No, like Don Corleone, mumbling sweet nothings.

I give the door a tug. It doesn't budge.

Love, love, love.

I locked myself out. And now, I'm stuck out here with that darn word.

I can't call Orson to key me in. Though it's not like he would be mad. In fact, he'd probably find it funny with his low, rumbling laugh and goofy grin.

I adore that goofy grin.

Adore.

That's a word I can use.

Yes, I *adore* his grin.

Not love.

But either way, I know Orson is busy at the bar. So, instead, I call Ruby, who says she'll be here in five minutes, and when she shows up, Emory climbs out after her.

"You brought reinforcements?" I ask.

"I don't know how to get back into a house," Ruby says with a shrug. "So, I called Emory."

Makes sense, considering he's an engineer. Or does it? Do roller coaster engineers know how to break into houses? I don't know.

Then, Lorelei hops out from the passenger side. And Quinn follows from the back seat. It's like a freaking clown car.

"Well, howdy there, lady," Quinn says in a faux accent. She's trying her cop routine, I'm sure. "What's going on here, hmm?"

"We were all at breakfast together," Lorelei says with a wince.

"Sorry," Ruby says too.

"Any reason you're at Orson's?" Quinn asks.

"You don't have to answer that," Lorelei says quickly.

Quinn exchanges a glance with Lorelei and then looks back at me. I swear they have some type of best-friend telepathy.

"I don't want to know why you're at Orson's," Emory says bluntly. "I'm just here to lock-pick in."

He rolls out a small kit that does, in fact, have tiny tools that look like they might belong to a thief.

"You know, you scare me sometimes," I say.

I think I see the edge of Emory's mouth tip up into a smile.

"Well, *I* want to know why you're at Orson's," Quinn says, crossing her arms, like we're playing some game of whodunit.

I shrug while Ruby lets out an anxious giggle.

"Knew it," is all Quinn says. "I freaking knew it. You're sleeping with him."

"It's ... complicated," I say.

Love.

I growl at the invisible word.

Quinn lifts an eyebrow. Emory grunts. But I'd need Lorelei as an interpreter to tell me what that sound even means. As it is, she stays quiet, looking between me and the house, as if we were the ones in an illicit affair.

The back door finally cracks open, and Emory rises to his feet.

"All done."

"Oh my God. Thank you so, so much," I say, running over to pull him into a hug.

He's stiff against me and only gives two pats of acknowledgment.

"Do y'all want coffee or something?"

Emory shakes his head, holding out his palm. "We shouldn't ..."

"I'd love some," Quinn says, waltzing into the house before the rest of us. "And I expect you to spill your secrets ASAP."

She says all this while glancing into the living room, peering around the corner, and peeking over the spiral staircase into the basement den, as if she expects to find Orson hiding in his underwear. But it's Emory who finds the sweet note on the counter. And suddenly, I hate it. I hate it all.

259

Emory raises his eyebrows.

"Wife?" Emory asks.

"It's a joke."

Quinn gasps when she spots it too.

"If it's a joke, what's the punch line?" she asks.

When I don't answer, both of them cross their arms. They're looking at me like it's some *good cop, bad cop* scenario. Except they're both the bad cop.

"It's nothing," I say.

Nothing.

Even the thought of having nothing with Orson tugs at my stomach in an odd way.

Love.

No. Stop it. Stop it.

I inhale and shake my head. "Coffee is on the counter. I'm gonna get the spare key to put outside."

I go to our junk drawer. It's packed full of our stuff—takeout menus, old notes left for each other, tic-tac-toe sheets on the weeks when we're ships passing in the night. Every little *you win, sweetheart* and *suck it, loser* set in ink and shoved in here like a memento drawer.

I smile to myself.

Love.

I dig below them, feeling around for a key but then feel something entirely different. Something square. I pull it out and slowly uncover beneath piles of paper, like a gem at the bottom of a treasure chest, a small black velvet box.

My whole body freezes at the sight of it.

I know that box.

I toss it across the counter like a cursed hot potato, and in the process, it pops open.

Inside is a ring. Gold with ornate, curved decoration along the sides, twisting up to an emerald gem. It's beautiful. It's classic. It looks like an heirloom engagement ring. Orson's grandmother's heirloom engagement ring.

Ruby's hand flies to her mouth when she sees it.

"Oh my God," Lorelei whispers.

I turn to look at Quinn, who, mid–coffee pour, gasps.

"Holy—"

I have enough sense to take the pot from her and place it back.

"You'll burn yourself," I say quickly.

"What's that?" Quinn asks, not acknowledging my life-saving maneuver.

"That," I say, twisting on the spot, staring at the glinting ring in the corner, "is not for me."

Emory snorts. I shoot him a glare.

But something in me, not that far down in my soul, like a tiny prick of a needle on the skin, knows I must be wrong. Because why else would he have an engagement ring?

"What the hell is going on in this house?" Quinn asks.

And I'm not sure how to answer that.

Why *is* that ring in the house? And, out of all places, in a junk drawer?

"It's complicated," I say, repeating the same excuse from earlier.

But complicated doesn't even begin to cover it.

"Theo ..."

"Theo's business is Theo's business," Lorelei says. "If she doesn't wanna talk about it yet, then she doesn't have to."

I give Lorelei a small nod. She smiles back. More than everybody here, she's had enough drama in her own love life to know the importance of secrecy. But that's what happens when you fall for the guy you're suing.

Behind her, Quinn's brow is still furrowed. And Ruby is

261

winding her hands together. I wonder if she's mentally beating herself up about letting our secret out. It's fine. It was bound to come out eventually, especially with how much time we had been spending in public together.

Despite that though, I do feel bad for putting her in this position. I feel even worse about keeping such a huge secret from my closest friends.

"You said you had coffee?" Emory asks.

Well, at least I can count on Emory to be nonplussed.

I nod.

"Good," he says. He grabs a cup and the pot and starts to pour. "Now, if anyone talks about anything except coffee —and that includes you, beautiful"—he tosses a look at Lorelei, who returns a small, blushing grin—"then we're leaving."

And just like that, the rest of the morning is silent. Even if Quinn does cross her arms the entire time.

39
Theo

It's a sunny day when The Great Forest Journey opens to the public. The ride's staff did end up buying jackets for the event, complete with *Skipper* written on the back. They even gave a special one to me with *Captain* written on it instead.

But I have a hard time enjoying the day and being the supervisor I need to be when all I can focus on is that ring from this morning.

The gleam of gold.

The ornate floral.

The emerald.

I sit in the back row of the first few boats as they take their inaugural ride, watching the guests' heads turn to see every new installment and watching the skippers perform their spiel with over-the-top delivery. I can already tell it'll be an instant hit.

But when we pass the final wedding scene with animatronic Queen Bee and Ranger Randy holding hands and staring at each other with uncanny, dazed electronic eyes, it stirs something in me.

Marriage.

Love.

The ring.

I can't watch that final scene anymore.

I hop off the boat and exit through the queue line.

Honeywood's walkways are humming with crowds as they bustle to the back corner of the park, desperate to see the new ride. The character actors for Queen Bee and Ranger Randy stand outside the front, waving and signing autographs. There's the familiar smell of the park's syrupy pancakes, the rumble of roller coasters nearby, and the squeal of toddlers' laughter at the sight of Buzzy the Bear. It's another day at Honeywood Fun Park. And for once, I feel overwhelmed by it all.

I go against the crowd, walking to The Grizzly's fenced-off construction area, pausing at the roped-off queue.

The new roller coaster—the love child of Lorelei and Emory—is opening next. It is cycling through its final stages of testing, and I can already tell it will be everything they imagined. You can see their labor of love in every section of the track, how the harsh turns come from Emory's rougher approach and the thrilling launches stem from Lorelei's bubbly energy.

Are Orson and I like that? A perfect mix? Do I want us to be? Does he?

He must though. He has a *ring*.

But is that ring still for me? And if it's not, how would I feel about it?

I already know how I'd feel.

I'd be devastated.

God, how *ridiculous*.

Me, the woman who left him sitting on the edge of that bed months ago with his hands tossing that small box back and forth, the words *falling for you* lingering in the air.

For months, I relived that moment over and over—the way Orson's face looked as he glanced over to me, drained of color, like the admission had stolen every bit of energy from him. How my own heart leaked of all feeling, a slow drip into my stomach that churned at the thought of *forever*. That, even though he was the last person I saw at the end of every day and the first person I thought of in the morning, the words *falling for you* implied so much more at that time.

I didn't want anything to do with it. But now, I'm on the other side of the equation.

I might just be falling for Orson. I'm falling for my husband. Could I ever ask him to reconsider?

No. He already has too much on his plate. I cannot complicate things for him. So, that means I need to think. What do I do now? I'll have to move out. I'll sleep on Ruby's floor if I have to, just while I apartment-hunt again. It'll be even longer until I can buy my own studio.

But I have to do it. Because I can't break Orson's heart again. And I can't break my own either.

"Hey, lady."

I look to my left and see Quinn walking toward me, chin dipped low. For once, her arms aren't crossed. She's winding her hands in front her.

"Hey," I say. "Why are you walking toward me like you're about to say Journey isn't working?"

"No, no. It's working. But ..."

It's silent for a moment before I let out a laugh—a sound to break the awkward silence that never usually exists between me and Quinn. Nor me and anyone else for that matter.

"Okay, yeah, I'm living with Orson."

She exhales. "Why didn't you tell us?"

Us. The core group of friends that are held together like glue. Me, Quinn, Lorelei, Bennett, and Ruby. The fearsome fivesome.

"I don't know," I say. "Didn't think anyone cared, I guess."

"That's ridiculous," she scoffs. "You know that's ridiculous, right?"

I laugh. "I don't know. Y'all are busy."

"We're never *that* busy."

"Okay, Miss I Kissed My Best Friend's Brother."

Quinn snorts. "Touché. But you know we're never too busy for you. We've all got to stick together. Nobody gets left behind."

"Nobody gets left behind."

I think of all the times that's been true. All the Trivia Nights, the birthdays, the hospital visits from various mishaps, and the way they barged into my apartment as a group when, last winter, for some inexplicable reason they couldn't figure out, I had a broken heart.

"I always assume you're an open book," Quinn continues. "But you really do keep things to yourself."

"What are you talking about? I'm still an open book."

"I asked about Orson. And you still haven't told me. I don't know why either. We all like Orson."

I laugh. "Yeah, he's pretty great."

"Yeah?" she asks. "Well, I want to hear more."

"Do you?" I ask.

"Of course I do. Sure, I'm not gonna gush for hours over boys like Lorelei or Ruby might. You know me. But I care about you. We all do. And we want to be happy for you. I know what it's like to pull away and be lonely. You don't want that, I promise."

Maybe I have been unfair. These four have been my best friends for years. Ever since I moved to Cedar Cliff, they've accepted me with open arms. We're a team. And yet I've forced them into the dark throughout my whole relationship with Orson. I haven't given them the chance to show they care. I assumed they wouldn't want to know.

That I'm just me.

The vacation friend.

But Orson doesn't think that. Maybe they don't either.

"See? You're smiling," Quinn says. "He does mean something, doesn't he?"

I didn't realize I had been, but I am. Just the thought of my husband makes me smile.

My husband.

"Yeah," I admit, and then it comes at me full force. The overwhelming feelings I have for Orson. For my best friend. "God, he really does."

I see a slow smile creep along her face, transforming into a proud grin.

"He's a lucky guy," she says.

"Him?"

"Yeah, *him*. You're a catch, lady. Who would know you and not love you?"

There's the word again. *Love.*

And her words permeate through me. Because, while I'm not sure about me, I know about Orson. And to know Orson is to love him as well. To know him is to realize that he's the most generous person I know, who gives way more than he should—more than some people deserve.

But Orson deserves the world. He deserves it all.

"Does he know?" she asks. "Are you gonna tell him?"

"I wasn't going to."

"Why not?"

"I don't wanna stress him out more."

"Well ... have you considered that maybe this would make him a little less stressed? Shouldn't he have a say? He deserves a shot at happiness with you."

Orson deserves happiness more than anyone.

But how do you tell a man you've rejected before that you've now changed your mind?

If he turns me down the same way I did to him, I don't think I'll be able to handle it. And what's worse is, I'm not sure I'll survive the cuts of a broken heart if my best friend isn't there to stitch me back together.

40

Orson

The rec room is starting to come together in little swathes of yellow and pink and purple. Renderings of Cedar Cliff's historic downtown in the glow of a sunset. Tiny bumblebees that float over light switches. The arch of The Grizzly's first hill silhouetted in the background.

"It's wonderful," I say to the muralist, tracing a finger along the dried brushstrokes of Queen Bee's crown.

"I'm leaving room for the cabinets on the other side," she says.

I look to the pile of wood still in the corner. Just another project looming over my head.

"Thanks," I murmur.

But I won't worry about that now. For now, I leave the bar to enjoy an evening with my wife.

Theo and I invited Bennett and Jolene over for a game night, and everything about it feels so domestic. But lately, everything has been. The struggle over bedsheets every night, followed by laughter, the frozen pizzas we make because neither of us is very good at cooking, and those sacred kisses we give whenever one of us walks through the front door after a long day—like it's a landing strip for home.

Now, we're a couple hosting another couple.

It feels so real.

It's too real.

But despite that, I open the front door anyway. To happiness.

Theo is in the kitchen with a smile on her face. Jolene is sitting in the corner with her arms crossed. Bennett is next to her, his palms pressed together in concentration, as if he's trying to read her mind but struggling.

Okay, so Theo is the only happy one here. Ah well.

I walk up to her, placing a hand on her lower back and sliding it under the ridiculous apron she's put on. And I feel relief. I feel the stress of the day washing off, sloughing down to my ankles like a second skin.

"Hey, wife," I whisper.

"Hey, husband," she murmurs back, the heat of her lips on mine sending waves of energy coursing through my body.

When I look to Bennett, he's looking away. Jolene's jaw is clenched.

I help Theo prepare dinner—both of us awkwardly placing vegetables on a cookie sheet like we might actually know what we're doing—and I try to make small talk with Jolene. But all her responses are short. It's Bennett who mostly carries the conversation. It makes me wonder if they had a fight on the way here. And why does it feel like they're *always* fighting?

We laugh over a board game after dinner, one that Jolene keeps saying she doesn't get and lazily lays her cards to the side when it's her turn.

But Theo and I make jokes. I slap her cards out of her

hand, she tells me I'm being dumb when I can't pick up her hints, and when we don't win, I'm convinced it's only because we didn't play with the military precision of Bennett and Jolene.

By the time they leave and we're waving from the doorway like parents sending their kids off to college with Bennett giving a wince of *sorry* under the porch lights, I suddenly feel wrong.

I feel like what Theo and I have shouldn't be allowed. Because how dare we be more functional than a couple about to get married? Us and our faux marriage?

"Nope, don't play the *Jaws* theme," I say.

"Why not?" Theo asks, playing the two dreaded notes again with a teasing giggle.

I knew I shouldn't have taught her that.

"I'm about to take a shower," I say. "I don't want to picture him coming out of the drain or something."

"Sharks can't come out of the drain."

I snort. "Well, how would I know? I'm blind as a bat in the shower."

"Sounds like you need assistance then," she says.

I growl, nipping at her ear and lifting her off the piano seat. I hoist her over my shoulder, tromping upstairs with her bouncing giggles following me the whole way.

"So, what do we do about their wedding?" she asks, continuing our conversation that prompted the *Jaws* theme.

"I don't know. Nothing?" I say, but it's more a question than a definitive statement. "Bennett and Jolene are who they are, and if they're getting married, then there's something there that we can't see."

"Think they're having crazy sex behind closed doors?"

"Wouldn't be far-fetched, would it? We're having unstoppable, mind-bending, world-changing sex behind closed doors."

Theo doesn't respond. And her giggles are gone.

"Oh no, am I wrong?" I ask with a laugh. "Is it just stoppable, mind-numbing, world-keeps-turning sex?"

"No, it's just not behind closed doors anymore."

"People can see us? Hot."

"No," she says with a laugh. "Quinn knows. Emory probably does too."

I pause, swallowing back the feelings that start to float up from my chest to my throat.

"Did you tell them?" I ask, trying to laugh the feelings away instead.

"Well, I locked myself out of the house this morning actually."

I halt before dropping her backward onto the couch. "You what?"

"Emory, Quinn, Lorelei, and Ruby came over to help get me in," she says. "By the way, did you know Emory can pick locks?"

"And you told them?"

"Well, they saw your note. And Quinn talked to me about it. I wouldn't be surprised if Landon knows too. She tells him everything."

I let out a small laugh. I understand the impulse. And it almost feels wrong that I do know the feeling so intimately well—that urge to tell Theo every detail of my day and every stupid thought in my head feels like something I should reserve for someone else.

A girlfriend.

A wife.

"Is that bad?" she asks.

I blink down to her, to this beautiful woman splayed out on my couch with her wild inky-black curls framing her face. The face that is normally happy and grinning, now concerned.

"No," I say, tracing a thumb over her jaw. "No, it's fine." But the words feel harsher than I intended them to, so I laugh. "Better than fine. Amazing. I'm gonna go put the spare key outside because *someone* can't stay out of trouble," I say, pointing a finger at her as I walk into the kitchen, ripping open our junk drawer.

"Oh, I already did," she says quickly.

The junk drawer has been junkified to an extreme—her morning notes pushed every which way with the key missing and the box sitting there right on top ...

The box.

I snap the drawer shut.

A haunting of a past dream. The ring I got from my mom last fall when I wasn't sure whether Theo would want to actually wear one. The ring that burned a hole in my hand the day I told her I was falling for her. The ring I buried in the back of the junk drawer that night. Because that was all the box was.

Junk.

Because if it wasn't for Theo, then my grandmother's ring wouldn't be for anyone.

Except now, it's staring me right in the face, like an old friend saying, *Yes. She is the one, isn't she?* A raspy, twisted, one-ring-to-rule-them-all, Gollum-esque groan of, *My precious.*

I turn on the spot to look at Theo, now standing in the empty living room.

There's no way she didn't see the box.

She bites her plump lower lip and reaches to the bottom hem of her shirt, tugging it over her head, leaving her topless in front of me.

A defense tactic. But I'll take it.

She steps backward into the bathroom, and I follow her. I catch her in my arms, pinning her wrists above her head, running my tongue over her nipples. She moans low and needy and loud. Louder than usual, as if showing me just how much she enjoys this.

I know we won't be talking about that velvet box. We'll be melting into each other, as we always do, with our claims of, "Mine," and, "Yours," bouncing off the shower walls.

But we both know what she saw.

And that scares me more than anything. I can't have her thinking I want something more. That ring was for her months ago.

But now?

My heart can't take the disappointment again.

41

Theo

Today, I'm going to tell Orson that I'm falling for him. Today, I'm going to be the woman sitting there, begging for a second chance.

Me.

I walk through the back door of The Honeycomb, past someone prepping for tonight's menu, past the slightly constructed cabinets on the floor, and right to the boss's office.

My husband's office.

I halt right before I turn the corner. I almost consider turning around.

No. I need to bite the bullet. I need to put on my big-girl panties and admit my feelings. If I embarrass myself, then I embarrass myself. If I lose everything—a place to live, a silly little tax break, and everything that comes with the piece of paper we so flippantly signed—then so be it.

But if I lose him?

If I lose him ...

God, is this how he felt last time?

No, this will be easy. So easy. Like ripping off a Band-Aid.

Just do it.

Do it.

I knock on the doorframe.

Orson's head pops up from his papers. A slow grin spreads over his face. The lazy, crooked thing that tugs at my heart, like a cowboy lassoing me in.

"Hi, sweetheart," he says. "What are you doing here?"

Sweetheart.

"Just thought I'd drop by."

"Lucky me," he says. And he sounds like he means it. He's happy to see me.

I let out a weak laugh and murmur more to myself, "Yeah. Lucky you."

Do it, Theo. Do it. Tell him.

"Can I ask you something?" I ask.

"Anything."

He slides his papers away. All of it. Even the pens. Like he's making space for me and only me.

I close the door behind me. It snicks shut.

It's not the right time. He's at work.

No, it's now or never.

I take a seat, place my phone on his desk, and tuck my hands under my thighs.

"I feel like I'm in the principal's office," I say, leaning forward like it's a secret between us.

He pumps his eyebrows. "Why? Did you do something naughty?"

I try to laugh, but the sound almost comes out like a cough.

"You're funny," I say.

He chuckles. "I promise I'm not."

"Right."

"So," he says slowly, "you wanted to ask me something?"

I nod, thinking of all the words I practiced throughout my shift at work. All the *I'm falling for you*s and *I want to wake up to you everyday*s, but they fall short.

Instead, I find myself asking, "Would you put me down as your emergency contact?"

I don't know why it's the first sentence that pops up. But for some reason, it does. And it's important.

He smiles. "I already did."

"Right. I forgot. Because I'm your wife."

"Well," he says, tipping his head to the side, "I would anyway."

"Why?"

"Because you're my best friend."

My heart leaps into my throat.

I blink at him. "I am?"

He smiles, folding his arms across his chest and leaning back in the chair. He doesn't answer my question.

"What's going on, Theo?"

I swallow. "You know you're my favorite person, right?"

And the second the words leave my mouth, I know they're true.

Orson's face falls. He uncrosses his arms, and they land on the chair. I see his hands clutch the ends, wrinkling the cracked leather beneath.

"Is that right?" he says.

He's trying to be charming, but I see the twitch of his hands. More than that though, I see his sudden lack of a smile.

I bet he knows what I'm about to say. And he's not happy about it.

I wonder how bad he wants to rub his chest. I wonder

how much his heart hurts. Because he's going to tell me no. He's going to give me the same hard truth I gave him months ago. I think about our so-called junk drawer full of anything but junk. Full of our saved notes that maybe never explicitly say the word *love*, but say everything around it. And the ring on top of it all. The ring I've missed out on.

My phone buzzes on the desk between us.

We both jump.

I instantly send the call to voice mail. I don't even think about who it is. Orson is more important. He's the most important person to me.

"Should you take that?" he asks. "It said it was Callie."

"No. I want to be here."

He squints. "And why's that?"

But then my phone rings again, almost as quickly as I hung up.

It's my mom.

My heart tenses. Doesn't my family understand I'm trying to bare my heart here? That I'm trying to convince my husband to love me?

I mute it again.

Orson breathes out a small laugh. "I really think you should take that."

"I can't," I say. "Not now."

His smile disappears, and he sighs.

"What do you want to tell me, Theo?"

He knows.

He knows.

He knows.

But then my phone buzzes again, the harsh, thumping clatter against the desk. Like it's screaming at me.

And when I look to see who is calling this time, my heart sinks.

It's Kassandra.
Kass, who never calls.
I pick up the phone.

42

Orson

Theo places the phone to her ear and stands.

The moment she does, I lean back in my chair.

Theo was about to tell me something big. I could feel it in my bones. And now, I'm left with nothing but the suspense held in the air like a noose over my neck.

I wonder if she was going to break up with me. Or ask for a divorce.

My chest can't get any tighter. There's a fist holding me in a death grip, squeezing the life right out of me. I try to clear my throat, but the lump inside my throat doesn't budge. I lean forward, folding in half and rubbing my chest.

Theo is ... everything to me.

There's no denying it.

I'd be stupid to think otherwise.

But we agreed. We had an understanding. This is fun. This is a no-strings marriage. We're just playing house. If she wants to leave, she can leave.

But my body knows the lie I tell myself. I roll my shoulders, but it only feels like I'm knocking at a closed door, tugging at the knob that won't twist open. I'm so tense.

Theo twists on the spot, and I muster a smile at her across the room. She smiles back. Her smile is like a thousand suns, bright and warm and beautiful. The weight of it presses me back against the leather seat.

I know she's the one for me. I've known it for months, like an itch lying dormant under my skin. But if this is really happening ... if she actually wants to leave ... I can't say no. She's my bird that I promised to let soar.

Theo's smile slowly falls along with the rest of her. She stumbles her way back to her chair, slumping in it, like her muscles lost the function to stand.

"But he's fine, right?" she asks, and something in me tilts. The thought of our situation skitters away.

Something is wrong.

"Okay," she says. "I'll leave for their house right now."

I get up, walk around the desk, and squat next to her chair.

I hear sentences like, "And it's scheduled for tomorrow?" and, "He was out of breath from mowing the lawn? Christ," and, "Yeah, he kept telling me he was gonna quit too."

Eventually, I hear her say, "I love you"—a very soft, wary sentence—and then, "Good-bye."

And then she places the phone back on my desk.

I don't ask what's going on. I don't demand anything of her. I just run a hand over her knee, silently telling her I'm here.

"Dad went in for a heart checkup," she finally says. "Mom thought he'd just a get a stint at most. Turns out, he needs a bypass. Like, yesterday."

She follows it with a laugh. I laugh with her to keep the spirits up. But both are forced, and we know it.

"He's fine though?" I ask.

"Yeah," she says. "Just nervous."

"Well, I can pack my bags and go with you ..."

Her face falls, and she pulls away, leveling me with a look.

"No. Don't."

She might want to leave, but damn it, she's still my best friend.

"Sweetheart ..."

"No," she repeats. Her tone is firm. "You have so many things ... the muralist is here. You need to build those shelves. You're still helping Mrs. Stanley, and you're so close to being done. The Grizzly's grand opening is soon. You have to prepare for that. This place is so busy, and you've got so much going on. You don't have time."

"Slow down," I say. I stand and take her face between my hands. "I don't care about all that."

And I mean it. The words are pushed from my mouth, breaking through the heavy weight of cobwebs and pain in my chest. I don't know what she was about to say to me before that phone call. And I don't care. Because at the end of the day, wife or not, she's my favorite person in the world, and I'd do anything for her.

"No," she says. "I'm not worth the worry. Take care of yourself first, okay?"

"Don't you dare say that."

"What?"

"That you're not worth the worry. You're worth all my worries. You're my best friend, Theo."

Her head tilts to the side with a small smile.

"And you're my best friend too," she says. "My very best friend."

I slide a piece of hair behind her ear, and she nods. A knowing nod. One that solidifies the conversation. Like we've just taken a gavel to our friendship and made it law. And that feels more real than our marriage ever has.

But she still surprises me when she says, "Stay here."

And my impulse is to say no. To demand that I come with her, but her pleading eyes have me instead nodding in agreement. She knows what is best for her family, and I need to respect that.

"Okay," I say. "Whatever you want. I'll do that."

"Thank you."

She reaches out her hand and nudges her knuckles against mine. I say nothing in response as we cycle through the motions of our secret handshake. But this time, it's slow and meaningful, like every move means more than just the silly interpretations we originally came up with.

"Send your family my love," I say. Because in this moment, while her mind is one thousand miles away, I can't say what I really want.

I love you.

43

Theo

I blink up at the stars. Plastic yellow ones that glow in the dark above me. But they don't burn nearly as bright as the stars in Orson's backyard.

I miss our backyard.

I pull the sheets up to my chin. Aside from the ceiling, my old childhood bedroom is very different. The carpet has been changed to hardwood, built-in bookshelves have been installed with texts on astronomy and astrology, and a telescope is in the corner beside a recliner and a deep purple blanket.

My dad once told me this is his star guest room, inspired by the star who grew up inside it.

I smile to myself, taking in a heaving breath and letting it settle in my chest.

He's fine. Everything is fine.

My dad is just waiting for surgery. My mom is at the hospital. And I'm here because the nurse said too many visitors is overwhelming for him. And I get it. I do. But the waiting is the hard part.

"Get some rest," the nurse said.

But I'm not getting any sleep anytime soon. Not when my dad is at the hospital. And not when my husband is more than an hour away, likely working himself to the bone. And I'm here, fretting over our unspoken words.

It's like a piece of me, a string that connects us, is tugged taut, like if we were only a few minutes farther away, it might snap under the tension of our distance.

I'm falling for you, Orson.

I should have said that before I left. I should have told him. But it wasn't the time. And, sure, there will never be a perfect situation. But I know when a time is bad. And me leaving to be with my family was a bad time.

I hear a bed squeak in the room across from mine, and I know I'm not the only one awake. Callie and Kass are in their respective childhood rooms, also renovated into guest rooms or libraries or gyms—all with an uncomfortable blowup mattress.

I crawl out of bed and creep across the hall to Callie's room. When I creak open her door, I can hear her small giggle.

"I was wondering when you'd come over," she whispers in the dark.

"I'm not used to sleeping alone now," I admit.

"Me neither."

I close the door and crawl under her covers, the mattress ballooning beneath the weight of me. We lie next to each other, staring at her starless ceiling.

After a few silent seconds, she asks, "What do you think Dad is doing right now?"

I snort. "Counting down the minutes until he can paint models again."

We both sputter out laughter. It feels good, like it's

relieving the stress in my soul. But eventually, the sound fades to silence once more.

"How's married life?" I ask her.

"Perfect. Wonderful," she answers.

I can hear the wistfulness in her voice, like even the thought of her husband is a dream.

"Yeah," I say. "I can tell."

"I mean, he farts more than I thought was even possible for one person, but ..."

Then, we're laughing again, clutching our stomachs, the sound echoing through the room, like happiness keeping the darkness at bay, even as it tries so hard to suffocate us.

The door creaks open, and a small beam of light floods in. We both lift our heads to see Kass standing in the doorway, silhouetted by the nightlight in the hall. I freeze. I wonder if she's coming to tell us to keep it down.

"Not used to sleeping alone?" Callie asks. It's not tentative. She's never been scared of Kass.

"No," Kass says. "I actually wanted to be next to someone for once."

Oh.

Kass closes the door behind her, and I scoot over. The mattress sinks beside me. My legs shiver as Kass fluffs the covers, letting the outside air in. And in our lingering silence, she sighs.

"David and I are getting a divorce."

"What?" Callie and I say simultaneously.

"Shh," Kass hisses even though the three of us are the only people in the house.

"What happened?" Callie asks.

It takes Kass some time to answer. I almost wonder if she even heard the question. But then she says, "We happened. Us and our shitty personalities."

"Oh, Kass, don't say ..."

"No. It's true," she says, and there's not one single slice of emotion. It's like she's presenting an argument to a jury—just the facts. "We never stopped fighting. Ever. If it wasn't one thing, it was another. And when we finally went to couples therapy and the therapist asked if either of us was willing to change, he said no. Turns out, he was already looking at houses. He was already planning to leave me."

Callie lets out a small breath of air. "I knew I didn't like him."

"But you know what finally did us in?" Kass says.

"What?" I ask.

"You and Orson."

My breath catches in my throat, and I repeat, "What?"

"David didn't look at me the way Orson looks at you," Kass says. "And I didn't look at him like that either."

"It's fake," I blurt out. "Our marriage. It's not ... it's not real."

"Yes, it is."

"No, really, we're married, but ... it's only because he needed insurance."

"Shut up," Kass says.

"Come again?"

I can feel Callie freeze beside me.

"Shut up, Theo," Kass continues. "Shut up with your stupid lies you tell yourself. Okay, sure, I'll buy that it started with some fake marriage sham or whatever. You always wanted to get out of whatever responsibility you could. I know that. And, God, sometimes, I hate you for that."

"Okay ..."

"But anyone can see how much he loves you in less than two seconds of being around you," she continues. "He loves you. He's so desperately in love with you that it's sickening. You're a lucky bitch, and you don't even know it."

I don't know why I do it, but something in me causes me to turn on my side, wrap my arms around my big sister, and pull her into a tight hug. For a moment, she stiffens under my touch, but then she relaxes into me, wrapping her arms around me and holding me closer.

"David is a fucking idiot," I murmur.

"Thank you," Kass whispers.

Callie curls into me from the opposite side. Kass reaches around and holds her too. And then we've somehow ended up in some odd group hug. It's weird. But it's nice.

"Safety fort makes a comeback," Callie says.

The three of us laugh. And it feels right, like a piece of me that's been missing all this time. My family.

"You're doing great, by the way," Kass says. "Orson showed us your yoga studio. It's beautiful."

I laugh. "It's not my studio. But thanks."

"Then, get one."

"You make it sound so easy."

"If anyone can make it work, it's you."

I smile and close my eyes. But the subject is dropped. And we're quiet.

I think of the stars in Orson's backyard, of the memories of home. Of Orson's wood and hops scent. Of the whir of the fan in our bedroom. Of his rough hands that hold me close, tightening around my waist at night like he's afraid he'll lose me.

And right when the world starts to feel light and I am slowly drifting off, one of our phones buzzes us awake once more.

44

Orson

I miss my wife.

Bennett sits in the corner of the room, clicking through his laptop as I call out numbers for the Wi-Fi router password. When he repeats it back wrong, I almost slip out a small, *No, sweetheart*, but I have to stop myself mid-sentence because I remember he is Bennett and not Theo.

God, I miss my wife.

I haven't spoken to her since yesterday afternoon. But I can't stop thinking about how she's doing. Whether her dad is okay. I hold my phone up in the air to get a signal I know I already have. But there are no new texts.

"Any updates?" Bennett asks.

"No. I think it's fine though," I say placing my phone down, but part of me doesn't believe that. Something in my gut—some disturbance in the force, if you will—says otherwise. "Bypasses are rough, but they're done all the time, right?"

Bennett shrugs. "I think so. I don't know, man."

That doesn't make me feel better, but I force a smile anyway.

Bennett sighs. "You look tired. You should get some sleep."

I should, but I haven't. I didn't even go home last night. I couldn't stand being in the house without her. It was too empty. Too creepy almost. Like the Godfather was gonna jump out at me any second.

The thought makes me laugh.

Damn those Don Corleone jowls.

"What?" Bennett asks.

"Nothing," I say. "It's just ... she's funny. I miss Theo's humor already."

He smiles. "I get that. It's easy to take it for granted, isn't it?"

"Yeah."

Bennett nods, but then his face falls. Mine does too.

"Yeah," he muses. "I take her laughter for granted a lot."

He's been sad a lot more lately. I think about how Jolene looked the other night. Her arms crossed. A consistent scowl adorning her features.

"Everything okay?" I ask. "Y'all looked distant the other day."

His head swivels to me. "We did?"

"Yeah, at dinner. She was ..." I laugh. "Well, not really into it, I guess."

"Oh," he says, and it's like his whole demeanor changes. He fumbles with the charging cord plugged into his laptop, his thumb rolling over the end of it. "Oh."

I let out a laugh. "What?"

"No, no, you're right. She was. Jolene was distant."

But his words drift off, and it doesn't sit right. Maybe it's the yoga Theo and I have been doing that makes me feel in tune with other people's emotions or whatever, or maybe it's just the fact that I've known this man for most of my adult life, but I realize that he's talking about someone else instead. And it's not his fiancée.

"We *were* talking about Jolene, right?" I ask.

"Yes," he says, but it's too quick. Sudden. "Of course."

I swallow and inhale, testing the waters with Bennett, my friend who doesn't reveal much of himself to anyone, including me.

"No," I say. "I don't think we were."

"Yes, we were." His tone is irritated, but I don't stop.

"No. You were talking about …"

The side door from the kitchen bursts open, almost slamming into the wall before Bennett catches it with the palm of his hand.

"Ruby," Bennett finishes.

Bennett's best friend stands there, ginger hair askew, partially tucked behind her ears, but mostly falling flat on either side of her shoulders. She looks like she rushed back here, out of breath and panicked.

"What's wrong?" Bennett grunts out.

"Her dad," she says. "Theo texted me and said her dad had a heart attack in the hospital while waiting for surgery."

The world stops. My heart races, every muscle within me catching like a trail of dominoes—one right after the other—falling piece by piece at the sentence. And I can't parse through my thoughts fast enough.

I rush out of the room and back into the main part of bar. The tables are full; the bar is buzzing with life. But I don't care. I need to leave. I grab my jacket from behind the counter. I turn to go out the back, but Bennett and Ruby follow me, blocking my way.

All I can think is, *Elias Poulos had a heart attack.*

"I've got to go," I say. "I have to be with her."

The words rush out before I can stop them. But I look out at the packed bar and slouch. People need me here too. And all at once, I feel overwhelmed and exhausted, but all of it also seems so irrelevant and unnecessary.

I shake my head, biting back chest pain, letting my palm roam over my chest, massaging over my heart.

I agreed not to go with her when her dad needed surgery, but a heart attack? Theo needs me now, whether she'll admit it or not. She'd never ask, but she doesn't have to.

"I have to go," I repeat.

"Then, tell us what to do," Bennett says.

"What?"

"We can hold down the fort."

Ruby's worried expression changes instantly to determination.

"Bennett's right," she says. "We'll run the bar while you're gone. Don't worry about a thing."

And when I look out, I notice almost everyone else has been listening too—everyone in our nosy small town. Not just the people at the bar, like Bill, who is nodding determinedly, but the rest of The Honeycomb—every person in Cedar Cliff who shows up week after week.

Then, they all get up and start to do things. Emory and Lorelei walk behind the bar next to Bennett. Landon sidesteps me with a clap on the shoulder, walking back into the kitchen. Quinn grabs a broom. I even see Frank wiping down a table in the corner even though it doesn't really need it and it's hours until we close anyway.

"Y'all would really do this?" I ask.

"Orson, you do so much for everyone else," Bennett says. "Let's return the favor."

"Yeah. Go be with your wife and family," Ruby finishes with a small smile.

"Wait, *wife*?" Quinn and Lorelei chorus together.

But I'm already disappearing through the kitchen and out the back door.

45
Theo

I've never been more scared than I am when Kass's phone rang with the too-calm voice of my mom saying Dad had a heart attack. It is the same smooth-as-water voice as when she told us our yia-yia passed a few years prior. The *don't freak out, but* ... tone. Except I know she's internally losing it this time around.

Kass, Callie, and I pile into Kass's Audi—Callie irresponsibly curled onto my lap—and we barrel down the back roads to the hospital in our pajamas and house shoes.

As Kass drives with red eyes and fists clenched on the wheel like Cruella de Vil, off to steal some puppies, I pull out my phone. My fingers hover over the keys. I want to text Orson, but I can't. Not with something like this. Not when he's already overwhelmed.

But ... but I need him.

Doesn't he know that? Can't he sense a disturbance in the force or something?

He's my best friend.

I text Ruby instead. Something short. Just so the group knows.

We park in the deck, then run in, crowding the lobby's front desk before being sent back to the family waiting room.

It's quiet when we get there, save for the low hum of the television playing a rerun of some sitcom show. And my mom sits there, hands in her lap, alone.

"Girls," she says, the word flowing out as we melt into the seats next to her. "He's in surgery now."

"He's fine?"

"They say he is." Then, she scoffs. "Honestly, leave it to your father to find a way to get into surgery quicker."

We all laugh right as the waiting room door opens, and David stands in the doorway, his jaw tense. When he sees Kass, she stands and walks to him. He clears his throat and wraps her in an awkward hug. It doesn't look natural, like a *distant stepcousin, third removed, who lives across the country* type of hug. Not the hug from a husband.

I miss Orson.

We all sit in the waiting area with Mom reading magazines or Callie on her Kindle or Kass and David on their laptops. I zone out, watching the show on the television, but also not really watching it at the same time.

After a couple of hours, I get up, offering to get stuff from the vending machines. Nobody notices me asking. I walk off. I pass the vending machine closest to our room and instead opt for one farther down. I want to go for a walk anyway.

But before I can turn the corner, I hear a distant, "Wait!"

I turn and see my mom walking over, her purse clutched on her shoulder.

"You walk too fast," she says.

I smile. "You walk too slow."

"Oh, hush, Theodora. Let's get some food."

We turn the corner to the vending machine near the lobby, and my eyes catch on the mini peanut butter cookies Orson loves so much. I put in quarters and select those. My mom gets chips.

We take two uncomfortable seats across from the machine, eating in silence. It's just us and the crunch of our snacks.

Eventually, she clears her throat, like a drumroll to her next words.

"I know it wasn't the cigarettes that did him in," she says. "But I think I can use this as leverage for him to quit, don't you?"

I snort out a laugh. "You knew?"

"Oh, psht." She waves a hand at me, scrunching her nose up. "Of course I knew. Our backyard reeks of it."

I smile. "Yeah. We could blackmail him. I don't see why not."

"Perfect," she says.

Then, it's quiet once more. There's distant murmuring from other hospital rooms. Squeaky footsteps. Random beeps or keyboards clacking from the nurses' station.

"So ..." Her word is slow as she straightens the folds of the chip bag. "How is everything?"

"Fine," I say. "It's all fine."

"And Orson?"

"He's fine."

She sighs. "I do like him, you know. You don't have to just answer *fine*."

I let out a small laugh. "You like him?"

"Yes. He's an excellent piano player."

"I'm glad that's the qualification that matters most."

"He showed us your yoga studio," she continues.

296

"Not my studio," I correct.

"Well, he said it was."

"I'm working on getting one. But it's not mine."

"Then, get one."

"Kass said the same thing. It's not that easy. I gotta save, and the town is only big enough for ..."

"Take out a loan. Or your father and I will help you out for a bit. I don't care. I want you to achieve your dream. Whatever it takes."

"Why the change of heart?"

"Oh, because life is short. We're in a hospital, for Christ's sake. And you're my daughter. You're incorrigible, but you're my daughter. My little tomato."

I can tell she's starting to tear up, so I smile and lean on her shoulder. "Your capacity for holding grudges doesn't even remotely match your capacity to love."

She nods against me. More silence.

As she stares off in the distance, I can see the haunted look on her face reflected back at me in the vending machine's glass. And despite everything I've seen my whole life, despite the ball-and-chain jokes and the *yes, dear*s and the complaining, I know Mom really does love Dad. The thing is, no love looks the same. Theirs is different, but it's still there.

"I'm sorry I didn't tell you about Orson," I say. "For what it's worth, we only married because he needed my insurance, and ... well, I was just kinda being a snot, honestly. Not sure if that makes it better or worse."

I wait for the blowup, but maybe she's too exhausted because she just sighs.

"I know," she says. "Your father told me. He suspected at least."

"Smart man."

"He really is." My mom's face falls.

I toy with the crinkling snack wrapper. "It's scary, isn't it? Marriage?"

She sighs. "Scary. But worth it."

"I'm sorry for the past few months," I say.

"No, I am. I should have reached out."

"I don't blame you. I didn't have the big wedding with the dress and the ..."

"If you found the right person, then that's all that matters." She pats my leg. "That's it."

Her posture is straighter. Her face more determined. There's a weird type of strength in her that I'm not sure I'll ever understand. A formidability, a totem of strength for her family. But I know, if given the chance, I could be that for Orson. Because I know he'd do the same for me.

Then, I hear that familiar, low Southern voice.

"I'm here to see Elias Poulos. I don't know the room number, but ..."

"Are you family?"

It can't be. I want to see Orson so bad that I'm imagining his voice.

"My wife is back there."

I scramble to stand up.

With an exchanged look with my mom and a jerk of her chin, as if to say, *Go,* I rush around the corner, finding my way back to the lobby. I feel my heart in my ears as I stumble down the hall. I'm holding my loose pajama pants in my fist as they start to slip. My house shoes smack on the vinyl flooring. I look like a mess, but I don't care.

Not when I finally see my husband.

Orson is leaning forward on the nurses' station. His baseball cap is turned backward, like a man who means business. His hand is clutching a fistful of tulips.

"Sir, we can't just—"

"Please. I have to see my wife," he repeats.

And when I let out a laugh at that, Orson's head swivels to me.

There's no *hi*.

No *how did you know I was here?*

None of that.

I simply run to him. My chest beats a million miles an hour as I jump into his arms. Orson stumbles backward when I land, but he holds his ground, clutching my thighs to keep me from falling, crinkling the flower's paper beneath me. I nuzzle into his neck. He smells like wood and hops. He smells like home.

"Hi, sweetheart."

"You're here," I murmur against his neck.

"Of course I am," he says before repeating, "Of course."

He kisses my cheek, but I turn just in time to meet his lips instead. I swing my arms around his neck as he grabs my face between his palms, holding me there, as if afraid I'll let go.

I wouldn't dare.

46

Orson

Theo and I camp out at her parents' house for three days, and we fall into the same rhythm we have at home. In the morning, we cycle through yoga under the backyard pergola; we make coffee and eat blueberries for breakfast; we watch TV and joke and play her parents' piano; and then we visit Elias.

Elias Poulos, soldier that he is, is already walking slow laps around the hospital floor with his IV clutched in one hand and his mouth in a straight, defiant line.

"Another lap," he insists when the nurse's face screws up in worry.

"Mr. Poulos ..."

He's only completed one lap so far, but he's determined to get in two.

At the same time, both Theo and I stand up.

"I'll walk with him this time," I offer to Theo's mother, who has spent the last few walking sessions by his side with the nurse.

"You can come with us," she says, tipping her chin up. "But I'm not leaving him."

I glance to Theo, who nudges me on.

A lot of things have changed in the past few months, but my feelings for Theo haven't shifted one bit. If anything, they've grown deeper, and this time, I'm prepared to do things the right way. Which is why, once we turn the corner, I blurt out, "I'd like to marry your daughter."

To his credit, Eli does not stop walking. Neither does Sophia. Though the nurse has wide eyes, as if excited she's getting hot gossip.

"Son, you already asked me for my blessing," Eli grunts out with a wet laugh.

"I wanted to ask both of you this time."

Eli seems more focused on staying upright, so he just lets out a small grunt, but Sophia is staring at me.

"You love her?" she asks.

And I don't need to think before answering, "I do."

The words I should have said with meaning almost a year ago. The words I should have announced in front of our friends and family with my hands in hers and rings on our fingers. But I mean them now. I mean every single letter, and if there were more scattered in, I would mean those too.

"That's all I ask," her mom finally says. "Love her. With everything you have."

"Walk laps with her at the hospital," Eli mutters out with a crooked smile, looking over to Sophia.

His wife smiles. "I'd walk a billion laps for you, Elias."

Elias leans over and kisses her on the cheek. Sophia's face flushes red, and her shoulders slouch in place.

"Me too, dear," he says with a soft smile.

We round the final corner. Theo stands at the end of the hallway beside the door to her father's room. Her full bottom lip is pulled in, and she gives a small wave beside her waist.

I think of everything that's back in Cedar Cliff. I think of all the responsibilities that await me. The new rec room at The Honeycomb. The mounting to-do list for people around town. The plethora of tasks building in my mind, pulling from the center of me like a sick game of Jenga.

But as Theo waves, I realize she's filling my gaps with her own wooden blocks—with little pieces of herself. She's giving me these slices of life with her parents, with yoga, with Honeywood. She's giving me her support.

That night, as we drift off to sleep on the air mattress with the plastic stars glowing from above, I kiss the top of her head and murmur, "I'd walk a billion laps for you."

And without context, my wife still whispers back, "I would for you too."

47

Theo

I'm sitting in the large hospital room with my dad when I get a text from Meghan, saying she sold Yogi Bare to Frank.

Poof. Just like that.

The hospital has already been exhausting me, and I've been trying to stay strong for Dad. But this is enough to finally have me slouching in my seat.

I stare at my and Meghan's text thread. It sounds like she's been planning this for a while. But with me being in the dark for so long, I can't help but feel like it's an afterthought that leaves the yoga studio high and dry. She says Frank will let me use the empty space for my side business until he figures out what to do with it.

I guess there's that silver lining.

Yogi Bare was my peaceful sanctuary for years. Outside of Orson offering me a co-op role at The Honeycomb, I'm not sure what I'll do with my side business now. I definitely don't have the funds saved up to buy the building yet. Do I set up something temporary in my backyard? Except it's not even my backyard—it's Orson's. And I won't ask that of him.

I'm done inconveniencing my husband. I want to ask for a relationship with him, whenever we eventually get the chance to talk post-hospital madness. But no more transactions between us. No more deals.

"What's wrong, Tomato?"

I look over at my dad. He's sitting up in his bed, hands in his lap, eyes turned away from some golf tournament on television. It only took him five minutes to seek out the golf channel in the hospital, and his eyes have been stuck there since. Except now.

It feels selfish to bring up my issues to him. He winces every time he sits up and gets poked and prodded with needles or other gadgets every couple of hours. He had a life-threatening event, and yet I'm over here, worried about a studio I didn't even own.

I shake my head. "It's nothing."

He narrows his eyes. "You know, your mother isn't here to make sarcastic comments, so this is your only chance to vent without judgment."

My lips tip up in a smile. Mom and Orson went down to the cafeteria for lunch, and it's admittedly been very quiet since she left. Less questions for the nurses. Less huffing about my dad's health. This hospital must be sending her nerves into overdrive.

"We normally have serious conversations while you're smoking," I say. "Think you can handle all these emotions without waving something around in your hand?"

"If it gets to be too much, I'll just call your mom back," he says with a small smile.

"Okay. Well, the yoga studio I work at got sold. And I'm not entirely sure where that leaves me."

"Buy it."

My head jerks back at how quickly he responded. It

popped out like gunfire, leaving me to choke on the powder.

"Buy it?" I laugh. "It's not that simple."

"Yeah, it is. Let your mother and I loan you the money."

"I absolutely could not—"

"You could, and you will. What? You think we didn't loan start-up money to your sisters?"

I think about my mom's similar offer earlier. I've been so naive about their marriage. They seemed so different, but they've always had an underlying united front to do what is best for us kids. This is why they're together. Because they love hard.

I swallow. "I can't accept that. I'm not sure how fast I can pay y'all back."

"It's fine," he says. "We know where you live now. If we don't get a return on our investment, we'll put a severed horse head on your pillow. Don Corleone–style."

"Dad."

"Hey, if you can't use your kid's fear against them, then what was the point of showing them a movie that young?"

"That's diabolical."

"My evil mustache should have tipped you off to that a long time ago, Tomato."

He winks at me. Something so subtle that I'm almost not even sure he did it.

"We want you to succeed," he says. "We're rooting for you. Think on it."

"Last time I was told to consider something serious, I moved in with my husband."

"Perfect. Then, you're prone to making decisions that are good for you without even trying. What a talent."

"You deserve a hug for that one."

"No, I deserve a cigarette."

We both laugh. He stops short to hold the heart-shaped

pillow the nurses gave him for healing against his chest. Laughing probably isn't the best idea. But with the two of us, it feels impossible not to. My mom's eye rolls at the golf channel will heal him faster than me being here.

"No more smoking," I say. "You know that, right?"

"I know," he says. "I'm gonna try."

"Good."

He smiles and turns back to the golf channel.

"All we can do in this life is try, Theo."

It's funny how your home's true scent seems to show up once you've been away for a while. And when I walk through the doors of Orson's house, it's not just his woodsy smell that hits me, but my almond conditioner as well. It's a mix of both of us.

Home.

Orson carries both our bags into his bedroom. Our bedroom.

We haven't talked about our relationship yet, and I wonder if now is the time. The moment isn't perfect, but it's close enough. Yet when Orson emerges from the bedroom, he's already checking his phone's messages with one hand over his chest.

Okay, so now is maybe not *the right time.*

We're home, but that also means the return of Orson's stress. Of people who tug him in every which direction. It's odd; after some time away from Cedar Cliff, I expected Orson to come back rejuvenated. But I think it might have only stressed him out more.

He sighs, looking up from his phone with weary eyes and a weak smile.

"Who is texting you?" I ask.

"Mrs. Stanley. Frank. Emory. Bennett," he says. "It's fine. I've been gone three days. I just need to knock some stuff out and ..."

He walks past me, but I grab his hand.

"Orson."

He stops, running a thumb over the back of my palm.

"I'll be home tonight. We'll watch baseball and ..."

"Orson," I repeat. "No."

And maybe it's demanding. Maybe it's unfair. But he doesn't need people who will take, take, take without giving back. He needs someone to take care of him for once. To pay attention to him.

He blinks. "No?"

"Stay," I say, tugging on his hand. "Stay with me. Just for tonight."

His eyes dart between mine, and his smile slowly fades. He knows I'm serious.

"Stay," I repeat.

I step closer, taking his face in my hands, like he always does to me. I catch his lips in mine, wind my hands around his neck, and knock off his baseball cap.

"Please," I murmur against his lips.

And within seconds, Orson is kissing me back, his palms raising up to capture my jaw in that possessive gesture he's made since day one. Since the very first time we were together. He doesn't want to let go. And for once, I won't let him. I'm here. To stay. Just like he is.

We're a mess of mouths and moans and clothes getting ripped off piece by piece, thrown on the living room floor, my bra unlatched through one snap of his fingers, as I walk us backward toward his—no, our—bedroom. I start to fall backward, but I miss the bed, and we stumble.

Then, we're on the floor, laughing, kissing, him jerking my pants down. Me fumbling for his belt, unfurling it from its hold, ripping down his zipper as his own hands grip the top of his jeans and push them down the rest of the way.

He's naked in front of me, hovering over me with his broad chest with brown hair and strong arms, kissing down my stomach, between my thighs, moving two fingers along my slick center, dipping them in, curling them up. My back arches into the motion. My moans follow.

But before I can fall prey to his touch and forget my own name, I instead rise up to my elbows and push against his shoulders.

"On your back," I say.

He chuckles but does what I said. And when I reposition myself between his legs, poised on my knees, I lick a line down his stomach and pull him into my mouth. I take all of him that I can, the thick head, the thicker length, stopping only when I reach the tuft of hair at his base.

He hisses in air, bucking into me, and I continue licking and sucking—the room filled with his groans.

But after a few moments, he pushes me off.

"Hang tight," he says, getting to his feet. "I have an idea."

I watch his tight ass walk off, go into the guest room, then return with my purple vibrator in his fist.

I burst into a laugh. "Orson, you don't need that."

A lazy grin tugs up his face.

"Oh, sweetheart," he says, almost in a mocking gesture as he falls to his knees before me. "It's going to only make things that much sweeter. Now, I want you to keep sucking me. But face the opposite direction."

I raise my eyebrows. "I like where your mind is at."

And then I'm crawling over him as he lies on the floor,

his head between my legs and my face over his cock. I lick from base to tip before dipping my head lower and taking all of him once more.

"That's my girl. Such a good, sweet wife."

Orson's warm mouth exhales against me before I feel his tongue. His eager licks stroking over me.

Then, the buzzing sound starts.

I feel the toy's vibrations coast along my lower stomach, causing me to jump.

Orson chuckles, and a simple laugh has never been hotter or more intoxicating.

He moves it closer, down my pelvis, along my sensitive inner thigh, then between my legs.

My head jerks back. The combination of the vibrations and his tongue is unreal.

"How's that feel, sweetheart?" he murmurs against me, giving another flick of his tongue.

Sweetheart. It's better than anything he says. Better than any bit of praise. Because it's just him. It's Orson.

"Amazing," I breathe, taking him into my mouth once more, giving him everything I have. Taking as much as is possible.

It's a fury of moans and buzzing and bucking I can't control as he devours me, and I do the same.

And just when the both of us are saying, "That feels too good," Orson grabs my hips, flips us over so we're back face-to-face, and places his palms on either side of my head.

I feel the length of him running between my legs as he slowly thrusts his hips along my slick center. He tucks a curl behind my ear, kisses my apple of my cheek, and then pushes himself into me, snapping his hips to mine in one fell swoop.

I let out an ungodly moan. Normally, I would love to

turn over, get on all fours, feel him pound into me, take me, own me ... but not today. Today, I hold the back of his neck and watch as he thrusts into me. Appearing and disappearing, wetter and wetter each time, slick with me all over him.

"Oh, Theo. Look how good you take me."

And then buzzing starts again, the sound echoing through the room as Orson picks up the vibrator and places it right where it needs to go—between us. Vibrating against my clit and rumbling beside his cock. We both let out a low moan.

"Oh my God."

"Yes," he hisses out. "God, I can feel it too."

His voice, the toy, the sight of him—my *husband*—jerking into me—no, *making love* to me—exhaling my name against my lips, letting out a choking moan ...

"I love this," I find myself saying.

Love.

And he answers, "I love us, sweetheart."

The words tremble through me. Every little syllable sweeter than the last.

"I can't hold it in," I say.

"Let go. Come for me."

My orgasm barrels through me, wiping any thought from my mind, sending me soaring with my eyes closed and stars pouring over my vision into little constellations.

Orson pumps into me, pressing the vibrator closer to him, sending himself reeling within moments. Grunting, groaning, and leaning in to place a kiss against my chest.

I kiss into his sex-heavy hair, his flushed cheeks, and when I nuzzle against him, I mouth silent words against his neck. I try them out just for me.

I love you.

And it feels right. It feels perfect.

48
Theo

"So ... husband?" Lorelei stretches out her elbow to nudge mine across the table.

"It's complicated," I say with a grin.

My friends and I sit at a long picnic table in Honeywood. It's a few days before The Grizzly's reopening, and half the town is in the park to celebrate a quick preview. But it's just my group of friends at this table.

"Please tell me you're ready to talk about it," Lorelei says.

"Nosy," Landon says.

Lorelei nudges her brother with a small *hmph*.

I glance over at Quinn, who tosses me a knowing smile.

"I don't know what we are yet," I say.

"You don't know?" Landon asks with a laugh.

Lorelei sticks out her tongue. "Who's nosy now?"

I open my mouth, then shut it again. But I can't find the words to say how I feel. Plus, Orson and I haven't had a conversation yet. It feels wrong to classify it to them before we have the chance.

"Boyfriend. Husband," Quinn interjects, tilting her

head side to side. "Theo will have it be whatever it needs to be. Whatever makes the most sense. And that's what we'll call it."

She tips her beer toward me in a *cheers* motion, and I smile.

"I still can't believe I didn't know," Lorelei says.

"Nobody knew," I say.

"Ruby and Bennett knew," Quinn says with crossed arms and an accusatory eyebrow. But I can tell it's just a joke.

"Well, technically, only I was supposed to know," Ruby says.

"But you tell me everything so ..." Bennett finishes.

But Ruby smiles only for a few seconds before it fades away.

"Yeah," she says, her voice quiet before she smiles at me again. "I knew y'all were meant to be. You and Orson."

I laugh, not because I don't believe her, but because I do. I think Ruby has known since day one that this was the only way it could have ended. With me falling deeply in love with the one man I didn't want to love.

I lean over and see Orson talking to Mrs. Stanley on a bench. He's leaning forward, resting on his forearms with a smile on his face. He sees me looking—maybe he can feel me looking—and tosses me a wink. My knees buckle. Is this how it's supposed to be? Butterflies and childlike glances and a blush that can't seem to disappear?

I distantly hear him laugh. That low, gorgeous, genuine laugh of his. People know how special Orson is, but sometimes, I wonder if they understand just how much.

Then, I see Frank walking with Fred, glancing at the new Grizzly build.

"I'll be right back, guys."

I walk over to Frank with purpose. With determination. Because today is my day. Today is the day I take what I want. This first, then maybe Orson next.

But for now, I've got to find my own future.

Frank and Fred stop talking when I come up.

"Hey," I say, glancing at Frank. "Mind if I talk to you for a second?"

"Of course."

We walk a few steps away, and Frank is already saying, "Hey, if this is about my gas during the last class ..."

"I'd like to buy Yogi Bare's building," I interrupt. I say it quickly before I can convince myself not to, before my thoughts resist the roots clutching to the fertile ground. The idea of doing something so permanent as buying property feels like the wildest decision I've ever made, but Cedar Cliff has held my roots for years now. And with Orson, my roots are now planted so deep that there's no digging them out again.

I want to be here. I want to grow here.

"Oh," Frank says. His face falls. "I already sold it."

"Oh," I echo. "You sold the studio."

"Sorry, Theo."

"No, it's ..." I smile. "Don't worry about it. It's fine."

And I smile because it *is* fine. Sometimes, things don't work out the way you want them to. I knew there was a possibility it would get snatched up, and that's okay. Something else will open up, or maybe I'll just host at The Honeycomb, like Orson wants me to. Maybe, maybe, maybe. There're a thousand different outcomes. But sometimes, the things you expect the least turn out to be the best.

I glance over at Orson, still talking to Mrs. Stanley, and now his employee Kailey.

Just like him. The least expected outcome.

Orson's hand rises, absentmindedly rubbing over his chest with the heel of his hand. My face falls. I immediately walk over.

"You all right?" I ask him.

"Yeah," he says, managing a smile. But it's weak. It's not him. "It's fine."

"Try again," I say with a little laugh.

"I gotta miss my shift again," Kailey says, connecting my loose dots.

"Oh. Well, that's not a problem," I say. "Wife on duty."

He laughs. "Absolutely not. Go hang out with your friends."

"No, I wanna help."

Orson tugs me into his waist with a smile. But he doesn't say yes.

I roll my eyes. "I'm helping. Don't argue."

He leans in to kiss me, but then another person walks up. This time, it's Emory, arms crossed. Mr. Grump, who looks like he's here to deliver bad news.

"We've got a problem," he says.

"Is now really the time?" I ask with a laugh, but I can feel Orson already on edge beside me.

Uh-oh.

"What's wrong?" Orson asks.

"They don't fit," Emory says, giving a small shrug.

"What?"

"The cabinets don't fit," he says.

"What are you talking about? I measured a thousand times."

"I tried to push them in, but it's not gonna work out," Emory says. "Things like this happen in renovations. I can help rebuild, but ... Orson?"

Emory's thick eyebrows furrow in. And we both see Orson's face turn white.

"It's fine, see?" I say quickly. "We can redo it. It's not ... it's fine."

I want to make it better. I want to ease his worries, but I can see it all catching up. The renovation that was supposed to be finished and now isn't. The fact that if he had had those three extra days—no, even the extra one I selfishly stole—he might have had time to finish.

Maybe it hits him, too, because he says, "I gotta ... I'll be ..."

And when he disappears, walking away from our crowd and to an alley, I follow.

49

Orson

My body is so tight.

It's like I'm being lassoed, being dragged down, down, down, hurled toward the ground.

I land against the brick wall of some building in Honeywood. I don't know. I don't care. I'm inhaling, exhaling, trying to catch a breath that won't come. Trying to steady my pounding heart.

Theo rushes to me right as my hand lands on my chest. But no amount of massaging is making the tightness go away. No amount of inhaling is giving me the air I need. I let one out. I choke on the next.

Her eyebrows are pulled in as her eyes scan over me. Her lips are parted, like she can't find the words to say. I think I see Emory in the background. She waves him away.

"I'm fine," I find myself saying. It's a lie.

"That's right," Theo says. "You're fine." But her words are coming out quickly too.

She has no idea what's happening. And though it's happened to me before, this is worse. This is different.

My chest hurts—the tension is hard as a rock—and then

my eyes burn. I cough, and tears come with it. Tears. I'm crying. I'm fucking crying.

"I can't stop," I say. My heart races more. "It won't stop."

I'm crying in front of Theo.

"I know," Theo says. "I know. We can ..." But then her jaw sets, and she nods, as if she's just made a decision in her mind. "We're gonna figure it out, okay? Come on. Let's breathe. Close your eyes."

I choke out another breath. More wet tears.

I'm losing it.

"Orson," she says. Her palms go to my cheeks, and she holds my face. "Close your eyes, sweetheart."

She's using the name I gave her. My chest loosens just a little—a tiny crack in the glass.

So, I do what she said. I close my eyes.

"Now, breathe," Theo says. She inhales three breaths and exhales three breaths. One right after the other. "With me. Come on."

Every subsequent breath she takes, I follow with it. And then her hand is on my chest, massaging into me, unfurling the tension bit by bit, circle by circle.

Breathe in three, breathe out three.

Waves in, waves out.

Slowly, my mind clears. It might be five minutes or twenty. I don't know. I just focus on the tide leaving. And up ahead, there's a life jacket—Theo. I'm swimming toward her. The current of my heart nudging me to her direction.

Her hands press into my chest until I feel still. Until my ragged breaths finally release. Until I've reached her in the ocean of my thoughts.

I swallow.

In through the nose. Out through the mouth.

While the pain in my chest hasn't fully gone away, I can finally breathe. Like a tiny hole is poked through my ballooned heart. And when I open my eyes, she's staring back.

"I'm so embarrassed," I whisper.

"Not around me, you're not," Theo says. Her thumb swipes over my cheek.

I laugh. She laughs. It makes me laugh harder. And it hurts at first, and I can't tell if I'm laughing or crying or everything in between. Maybe I look ridiculous, maybe I look like I'm transforming into a werewolf with how contorted my face gets, but it doesn't matter.

Not with Theo.

She grips my palms.

"Is this okay?" she asks.

"It's perfect," I say, letting her pull them closer to her chest, where I can feel her rapid heartbeat against the backs of our conjoined hands.

She's nervous, but she's been holding it together for me. My hands twist in her tightly curled fists, and I unfurl them finger by finger.

"Has this happened before?" she asks.

"Yes," I admit. "When I called you earlier this summer. That's why I was at Judy's."

"Why didn't you tell me?"

"And admit this? That ... I was freaking out?" I say it with a laugh, but Theo doesn't join me.

"We should call her."

I swallow. I don't want to. I don't want to admit I'm weak, that maybe the stress is too much. That I just sat, crying in an alley behind the theme park's pancake place.

But I know Theo is right.

I nod. "Okay. I'll call Judy."

I pull out my phone, but Theo touches my elbow. I still with my phone halfway to my ear.

"Hey. It's gonna be fine," she says. "You know that, right?"

And after a few seconds of staring at her eyes—those beautiful green eyes—I give a small nod.

"Yes," I say. "I know it will be."

She smiles.

One look at her, and I know it will all be perfectly fine.

50

Orson

It's the second time I've had something like that happen. I wasn't sure what it was before, but now, I am. When we visit Judy that night, she tells us it was anxiety. Likely an anxiety attack, to be more specific.

And hand in hand with Theo, I say, "Yeah, I think that's right."

Judy says it's because I overwork myself, and I, for once, agree. I'm giving all the remaining pieces I don't have left to give. And I can't keep that up.

I do what Judy said, and I call my psychiatrist in the morning.

The first thing I do is rehash the events in the alley. Theo sits next to me with her knees pulled up to her chin, holding my hand next to the speakerphone. For the first time, I feel like it's gonna be fine. Or at least okay. Better.

We discuss changing medications. I feel vulnerable and weird as he tells me it'll be a journey of trial and error to find the right one. That I should have expressed my concerns about my current medication earlier. I'm embarrassed, but Theo nudges me with a frown when I say that

320

out loud. My psychiatrist relays the same expression but through words.

"This is normal. It'll all be fine, Mr. Mackenzie."

Bit by bit, we work through my life and try to lessen my stress levels any way that we can. That afternoon, when I go to Mrs. Stanley's house, Theo joins me.

We stack as many boxes as we can into my Jeep and Theo's trunk. And when we're done, Theo says she'll be back the next day with reinforcements. Bennett, Ruby, Emory, Landon, Lorelei, and Quinn—the whole gang— agreed to take over clearing out Mrs. Stanley's house for the next week.

"And when it's done," Theo says, "it'd better stay that way, you hear?"

I love it when Theo gets all demanding.

Mrs. Stanley gives me a big hug, lets us play with her dog in the backyard, and even makes us a ziplock bag full of homemade cookies. We don't tell her why I am stepping back from this project, but we don't have to. I think part of her just knows, especially with the little squeeze she gives my hand before we leave.

The next stop on our list is Emory's workshop. The next morning, our shoes crunch over sticks and leaves as we walk down the long trail from my cousin's cozy house on the edge of town to the large shed on his acreage. His yard is a mix of sparse grass and gravel, surrounded by pipes and steel and constant whirring coming from who knows where? We step around a roller coaster track and other things with functions I'll never understand.

Theo places her hands on her hips. "All right, Mr. Roller Coaster, let's build some cabinets."

With a sure nod and a clap on my back, Emory walks over to a new stack of mismatched wood, and we spend the afternoon doing exactly that. When we finish by nightfall, Emory loads the pieces into his truck and drives them over to The Honeycomb. We install the cabinets into the rec room, and the finished product is better than I could have imagined. The reclaimed wood gives it character that fits The Honeycomb just right. The room is ready for a crowd.

But the following morning, I am not there to see the reactions of our guests. I instead take the day off and go to Honeywood Fun Park with my wife and friends for The Grizzly's grand opening. We even stop by the front offices to get me a new vendor ID picture—complete with a big, laughing smile, courtesy of my wife giving Holly bunny ears behind the camera.

Theo doesn't let go of my hand for a single moment as we navigate through the crowded park. It reminds me of how children hold hands and form a chain when they don't want to lose their best friend. I have no intention of losing mine.

Theo bounces around in a cheap Buzzy the Bear costume. It's nothing official, just some homemade costume she created for this opening day. The quality reflects that too, as the parachute material billows out behind her, squeaking when she shimmies through the herds of park guests, dancing like she's the official mascot himself.

Fred, Lorelei, and Emory stand near the front of the line, like proud parents admiring the fruit of their labors. They've been working on reopening this ride for a year now, and I can't imagine the excitement they must feel.

Well, maybe I can.

Because when I smile at my wife, waving her hands in the air like the spark of electricity that is her and her alone, I shake my head and mouth, *You're ridiculous*.

As if to prove a point, she runs to me, her costume

bouncing with each step. She leaps at the last minute, landing in my arms with an *oomph* as she wraps her legs, adorned with brown leggings, tight around my waist.

I carry her off to the side, stopping at the bushes next to the relatively empty queue for the Bumblebee Greenhouse. I place her down on the railing, look her in the eye, and trail a palm over her cheek and into her hair.

"Don't tell me I exhaust you, husband," she jokes.

In that moment, with her grinning at me, her curls bouncing every which direction through my fingers, I've never been happier. Never felt more alive.

"Exhaust me forever, wife."

And I mean it. I mean it so much that it hurts, but not in the ache of anxiety. But in the ache of need, of want.

Her face falls the longer we're both silent, and right as I open my mouth to say exactly how I feel, that I can't imagine a single minute more without her sunshine lighting the way, she says, "I love you."

The words shoot through to my heart, right to the other side of me.

"You ..."

"Love you," she repeats, nodding. "Love. You. Orson."

Her Buzzy outfit squishes under my touch, ballooning out over the top and below from where I wrap my arms around her.

"You love me," I say.

"So much. Too much, honestly."

"No such thing as too much. Tell me again."

She smiles. "I love you."

I grab both her cheeks and pull her toward me. I kiss her like my life depends on it. And considering she's the reason I'm getting help to begin with, I wonder if maybe I do owe her that. She's been my life jacket from the start.

We pull away, my hand smoothing over her hair, tangling in her curls.

"I love you too," I say. "I have for so long."

"I think I knew you were different when you could guess my favorite color."

"It wasn't a guess, sweetheart. I was so beyond into you."

She smiles. "You saw me when nobody else really did, didn't you?"

"You demanded it. How could someone not see you, Poulos?"

She sighs into me, leaning her head against my palm.

"I was never over you," I say. "Not really. You know that, right?"

"I wish I'd known sooner. But maybe if I did, we wouldn't be here."

"I'd do it all over again if I had to."

"Me too. And, hey, if I say I'll love you forever, would that make it up to you?"

I squeeze her hips. Her silly little costume squeaks as my hand roams over her waist.

"I have a better idea," I say.

"Better than forever?"

"Well ... something for now."

"Oh?"

I lean in and murmur, "How fast do you think you can get out of this costume?" against her lips, tugging at the parachute fabric.

She smirks. "Who says I want to take it off at all?"

I laugh and plant kiss after kiss along the column of her neck, up to her chin, cheeks, and eyelids.

"I love you so much," I whisper.

Marriage isn't what I thought it'd be. Heck, I didn't

think it'd exist for me at all. But if this is what marriage is, laughing and enjoying each other's company, if it's sneaking into Honeywood's dressing room and locking the door, if it's cutting through my wife's parachute fabric with my pocketknife and sliding into her as her hands leave palm prints on the mirror, if it's watching us make love with our smiles reflected back to us ... then this is the marriage I want.

51

Theo

I walk into our house with bags full of face masks and Orson's favorite peanut butter snacks as I toss my keys into the bowl by the door.

I know he's home, and I can tell he's been working. The kitchen table is full of résumés and notepads with his chicken-scratch writing—remnants of our hunt for a new manager to take over The Honeycomb. He agreed to take a step back and relax, which I commend him for, but sifting through applications, even though I told him to chill for the night, is the opposite of relaxation.

I sigh, set the grocery bag down on top of the counter, and head for the den.

But that's when I notice it.

A candle near the spiral staircase.

Oh God, he's gonna burn the house down.

I lean down, but it turns out to be a little electric tea light instead. And then on the step below is another. And another. A line of them leading down the spiral staircase.

Taking the stairs step by step, I descend into our den

until I can finally see beneath the drop ceiling. And when I do, my hand claps to my mouth.

Fitted around the TV, made of cardboard and spelled out in markers, is a sign that reads KISS CAM. And on the TV is me.

I wave my hand. TV Theo waves back.

I look around and spot a camera in the corner, lit in blue, capturing me live. But then I look ahead, and coming around the couch is my husband.

"Hi, sweetheart."

I choke out a laugh. "Hi."

He walks closer, and TV Orson appears in front of TV Theo as well. Then, both Orsons lower onto one knee, holding the small velvet box I've seen before.

I have to look away to gather myself. To stop the shaking in my lip and the wet laugh begging to come out of me. But when I finally look back, the lid is open, and there it is. The emerald gem. The ornate, classic filigree running around the edges. The timeless gold.

"It's for me," is all I can find myself saying.

"Yes, it's for you," Orson says with a chuckle. He's grinning, and I think his hands might be shaking. "It's always been for you."

"But we're already married," I say. "I proposed and told you I love you. Isn't that it?"

"You always deserve more," he says.

My head tilts to the side because, God, it's Orson. Sweet, wonderful Orson. And he's staring at up at me like I'm the only woman on Earth. Front and center. Seen. Unforgotten.

"I love you," he says. "I love you so much. You are ... everything I've ever wanted. Everything I'll ever ..."

And I can see he's struggling, so I laugh and fall in front

of him, placing a hand on his knee, running a palm up his arm.

"You're sure?"

"Am I ..." He laughs. "Theo. Please."

"I just ... I'm not too much for you?"

"You're just the right amount for me." He places down the ring box and holds out his hand. "Come here."

Slowly, we move through the motions of our secret best-friend handshake, our eyes darting between each other's, taking in the movements like they're second nature.

"I love you," he says.

Love.

The word isn't enough, but it doesn't matter. We'll find other words, other handshakes, other ways to express what this really is.

But for now, I settle for, "I love you too."

We exchange smiles, slow and assured, and finally, we're on the same page. We were always in the same book, on the same chapter, but maybe the sentences were a little jumbled along the way. But right now, we're finally reading the same story, word for word.

"I want it all with you," he says. "Marriage. Partnership. Whatever you want to call it, I want it with you."

"I want forever with you," I say.

He smiles. "Forever."

Maybe marriage isn't about who does the dishes or the laundry or why he leaves his socks under the bedsheets even after he makes the bed—bless his heart—or who took out the trash last. But it's about how you feel. It's about who is there when you need someone most. And I want Orson there for every single moment.

"One more thing," he says.

"There's another?" I ask. "Are we pregnant?"

He laughs. "I have a gift for you."

"Another?"

Orson reaches in his pocket and takes out a crumpled piece of paper.

"What's this?" I ask.

"Be my business partner."

"Business partner?"

"To your yoga business. Your studio."

"Oh," I say with a small laugh. "Frank sold the studio though."

"To me," Orson says. "He sold it to me. To us."

My mouth opens, then shuts as he hands me a piece of paper. It's the deed for Yogi Bare's studio.

"What? I can't believe ..." But I can. Because he's Orson. And that's just what he does.

"So, is it a yes?" he asks.

Yes wouldn't be enough. It seems just as small as the word *love*. Nothing will ever be good enough for my best friend, my husband who deserves the world.

"Of course," I say.

Orson picks up the ring box from beside him. And when my husband slips my engagement ring on my finger, over the knuckle and down to rest where it's always belonged, I pull my lips in and smile.

He grabs the sides of my face in his palms and pulls me in for that kiss I love so much—the one that says I'm his.

Our marriage isn't traditional. It maybe isn't what I imagined a marriage should be. It's not saying our vows in front of family. It's not wearing a white dress. It's not *yes, dear* or *honey do* or *the ol' ball and chain*. It's us.

It's been a wild ride to get to our forever, but I wouldn't trade it for the world.

Epilogue
Theo

Two Months Later

"Don't touch the flowers."

"Wait, why not?" I ask, pulling my hand back and looking to Orson.

"Trust me," Orson says with wide eyes.

On a table, placed next to the open double doors leading to the chapel, is a slew of white roses. Beside that is a framed picture of Bennett and Jolene in an open field. She's in a white dress. He's wearing a white button-up. It is so *not* Bennett, but along with the plethora of white flowers, there's a lot of this that is more Jolene than Bennett.

"Can I at least touch these?"

Programs are scattered on the table so artfully that I wonder if I'm even allowed to take one, but I reach out anyway.

Orson rolls his eyes with a grin and extends his elbow. "Let me just walk you down the aisle, sweetheart."

I loop my arm in his, and Orson places his hand over mine. I can't help but admire the gold ring on his fourth finger. I probably stare at it more than I should, but Orson's hotness level exploded through the roof the second he put that ring on for the first time. There's something about a man with a wedding ring. No, something about *my* man with a wedding ring.

We pass through the double doors to a church adorned in all white. I walk slowly. Not because it's demure, but because if I trip and bleed over all this beautiful white decor, I think Jolene might pop out of the corner, knife in hand, to finish the job.

"How's Bennett?" I whisper.

Orson inhales sharply, tightening his hold on my hand.

"Truth?" he asks.

"Always."

"He's ... nervous." The words drag out a bit. I can tell he's trying to find the right ones.

"Yikes," I say. "Wedding day jitters, you think?"

Orson slowly nods, but when his eyes catch with mine, I know there's more to it.

"Something like that," he says.

The last month hasn't exactly been great for Bennett.

The drama started when Jolene forced him to cut his long hair for the wedding. He walked into The Honeycomb with a buzzed head, and I swear you could hear Mrs. Stanley and Honey crying into their drinks, mourning over his lost locks.

Then, it was one thing after another. Catering plans. Invitations. Last-minute things that I didn't even know went into planning a wedding. Eventually, Bennett stopped coming to Trivia Night altogether. I've barely seen him in the last couple of weeks, in comparison to seeing him multiple times a week. The dynamic in our group has been a little off-kilter with one of our missing pieces. Not to mention, Ruby is quieter without her best friend there.

After a couple of beats, I finally ask the obvious question. "And how's Ruby? Jitters too?"

Orson nods slowly and whispers, "Something like that."

We don't say the other unspoken thing. That we all thought maybe it would have been Bennett and Ruby at the end of the aisle rather than Bennett and Jolene. Even after he proposed. Even after he cut his hair. Even up to last month. But life doesn't always work the way we think it will. I know that firsthand, being arm in arm with my accidental husband.

I look around the church. The stand holding two candles. The roses at the end of each pew. The piano playing a rendition of a popular song I only vaguely place.

"Is this weird?" I ask him. "Does it feel like we should have done this whole big wedding thing the first time?"

"Nah," he says. "I liked our vows on the mountain."

I smile, kissing him on his smooth, freshly shaven cheek. "Me too."

Orson once said I deserved vows on a mountaintop, and he stood by that.

We celebrated our one-year wedding anniversary on the top of a mountain—well, a lovely grassy hill—somewhere in Scotland. I was proud of Orson for taking a couple of weeks away from The Honeycomb, and, sure, he called every two days to ensure everything was operating okay. But other than that, he was fine. Dare I say, he was relaxed.

When we got back and it spread around Cedar Cliff that we were married, you could say it caused an uproar. It is a small town after all. But the town wasn't angry. No, Cedar Cliff came through with so much kindness. I don't know why I expected anything less. There was a reason I'd moved here and stayed so many years ago.

Lorelei set up an impromptu event at Honeywood and invited everyone with a Cedar Cliff home address, giving free admission to all attendees. Orson and I posted up in The Bee-fast Stop, shoving our faces full of their signature bumblebee pancakes—mine topped with special blueberries just for me and a side of peanut butter snacks for him. It was perfect.

And then, just for my parents, we had an intimate chapel ceremony with immediate family and our small friend group, complete with our crowns, Father Peter, and Kass walking with us as our Koumbara. She came to our wedding without David, and I don't think I've ever seen her smile more.

Three small ceremonies—well, four if you count last year's courthouse fiasco—might seem like too much for one couple. But for Orson, I will never be able to profess my love enough times. And I'd take four ceremonies unique to us over one big, clichéd wedding blowout.

Orson walks me to the pew with Emory, Lorelei, and Quinn. I give Orson one final kiss because he's just that dang handsome in his tux, then sit down next to them.

Quinn's arms are crossed as she glances around the church. Emory sits the same way, occasionally looking down at his watch, as if hoping one of the hands has suddenly jumped ahead.

"Ten bucks one of them cries," I whisper.

"Nah," Quinn says, shaking her head side to side. "Jolene wouldn't ruin her makeup like that."

All three of us inhale and exhale slowly in unison.

"Gonna be weird, having Jolene at trivia," Lorelei says.

"You know she still won't come," Quinn says.

Emory snorts.

"Quinn!" Lorelei says.

"What? Come on," Quinn says. "She won't. She's not a trivia person, just like he's not a country club person."

"Hey, don't hate on golf," I say.

"Oh, sorry, forgot you're a golf pro now," Quinn says, nudging me with her elbow and a smile.

"The absolute best," I joke.

Orson and I have been visiting my dad more, joining him on the golf course as he slowly recovers from surgery. And while my husband might prefer something more like pool, he's surprisingly not bad. At least, he's now decent enough to where my dad lightens up on the jokes.

Emory looks at his watch again.

"How much time do we have?" Lorelei asks.

"Five minutes," he says.

We look at the pews around us. There aren't many people on the groom's side. It's mostly Cedar Cliff locals. Fred and Honey sit a couple of rows back, his arm slung over the back of her bench. And there's Mrs. Stanley with Frank—the two people who are already recruiting new members for the geriatric classes in my yoga studio.

The town seems to be excited about Yogi Bare's new ownership, even going so far as to put the grand opening in *Cedar Cliff Chatter* for a solid week. It only took a couple of Sundays of free yoga at The Honeycomb to gain some new regulars. We're still finishing our rebrand, but I did make sure to get sexy Yogi Bare–branded tops just for Mrs. Stanley. The minx.

I glance around for more familiar faces. Bennett's side might be scarce, but the bride's side is overflowing.

"I bet she'll keep her maiden name," Lorelei whispers.

"Definitely," Emory grunts.

"I didn't," I say with a grin.

"Oh my God, what?" Lorelei asks.

"Yep. It's actually Mrs. Poulos-Mackenzie now," I say. "Had to keep some of my originality in there."

Lorelei and Quinn both move to the edge of their seat.

"Get out!" Lorelei says. "When did this happen?"

"When we got back from Europe," I say, unable to contain the red on my cheeks that is out of pure excitement rather than embarrassment. I could never be embarrassed by Orson.

Lorelei wraps her long arms around me, letting out a small squeal. "Oh my goodness! That's a huge step."

"I mean, getting married already was, but ..."

I inhale, about to say more, but then I look over her shoulder to see Orson walking down the aisle, hands clenched by his sides.

Something immediately stirs in me. And it's not because that tux is seriously super gorgeous on him—though it is. No, it's because he looks like he's about to give an obituary. He's even rubbing his chest, which, though it's less and less nowadays, still indicates something is stressing him out.

He stops at the end of our pew.

"What's wrong?" I whisper.

"Well ... uhh ..." He looks from side to side and nods. "Well, we've kind of ... lost Bennett."

My smile is gone.

"What?" Emory says at the other end. His voice is low, almost demanding. It sends shivers down my spine. "You groomsmen had one job."

"Technically, it is the best man's job," Orson says. "Uh, best maiden's. Whatever Ruby's title is. Anyway, she and Landon are looking for him. Anyone have stalling tactics?"

He gives a weak, halfhearted smile, and I pat his hand.

But then we see Landon cross through the double doors, adjusting the lapels of his tux, nervously tugging at his bow tie as he takes long strides down the aisle. He stops next to Orson, who moves to the side, making room for Landon in our small huddle.

Whereas Orson's face looked worried, Landon's face looks downright pale.

"Any luck?" Orson whispers.

"Uh, no."

"That's not a good look," Quinn says. "What's wrong? Did you find Bennett?"

"No, and there's something else." Landon looks to the back of the church, then the altar, and finally to us.

He leans in, and the rest of us crowd in closer.

Then, he swallows, exhales, and says, "I can't find Ruby either."

THE END

Honeywood Fun Park continues with Bennett and Ruby's story, *Their Freefall At Last*!

Also by Julie Olivia

INTO YOU SERIES

Romantic Comedy

In Too Deep (Cameron & Grace)

In His Eyes (Ian & Nia)

In The Wild (Harry & Saria)

—

FOXE HILL SERIES

Contemporary Romance

Match Cut (Keaton & Violet)

Present Perfect (Asher & Delaney)

—

STANDALONES

Romantic Comedy

Fake Santa Apology Tour (Nicholas & Birdie Mae)

Across the Night (Aiden & Sadie)

Thick As Thieves (Owen & Fran)

Thanks, Etc.

I hinted at Theo and Orson the least throughout this series, so I had one goal in mind while writing their book: To make it the book you didn't know you wanted. As it turns out, I convinced myself along the way too. Theo and Orson slowly but surely–similar to falling in love–became one of my favorite couples I've ever written.

But this book couldn't have been written without an army of support. And I've got the best support network out there.

First, thank YOU! Yes, you! Thank you for reading. Thank you for letting me be me by enjoying these silly little theme park books. I still can't believe I get to wake up and write every day and that's all thanks to you.

To my sister-in-law and best friend, Jenny Bailey. My favorite day of the week is Thursday when you let me loiter at your house, eat all of your cookie dough, and gab about whatever we're both reading. You're the greatest friend a woman could ask for.

My editor, Jovana. You are a dream to work with, and if I could horde you for myself to edit every word that comes out of my mouth, I would.

My dad. I'm only able to do this because you raised me to believe I could do whatever I wanted as long as I put in the hard work. Turns out you were right.

My brother who still binges every book on release day. I

hope Orson is the type of down-to-Earth hero you prefer! (I also hope you cry with this one.)

Allie G. You live too many states away, but I can't imagine going a single day without hearing your voice. I love our sleep-drunk morning messages and our three-minute non-stop rants and all the "we are the same person" moments. You're the reason I believe in this book.

My beta team!! Y'all are always the first people to read these books besides myself, and you're the reason they turn out so much better afterward! Thank you to Jenny, Allie, Emily, Angie (my PT Queen strikes again!), Carrie, Kolin, and Lila Dawes. Special shout-out to my sensitivity beta reader, Georgea Polizos! The Poulos family appreciates you.

All the love for my reader group, the Feisty Firecrackers! Y'all are a beacon of light every day with your endless support for not only me, but each other. I can't imagine a better group to be in.

To every fellow romance book lover I've met through Instagram and TikTok. Thank you for reading my books, for shouting about them from the rooftops, and for all the kind words. You've made Honeywood into something so much more than I could have imagined.

And finally, to my husband. This book wouldn't be possible without you. Not only because you're the most supportive person in my life (which you are) and not because you inspire every single hero I write (which you do). It's because you taught me what love really is. It's thinking about the other person first and talking things out until well past midnight and taking risks hand-in-hand. Without you, I wouldn't be able to write love stories like this one. I'd walk a billion laps for you. I love you.

About the Author

Julie Olivia writes spicy romantic comedies. Her stories are filled with tight friend groups, saucy bedroom scenes, and nose-snort laughs that will give you warm fuzzies in your soul. Her phone's wallpaper is a picture of the Veloci-Coaster. Her husband has come to terms with this roller coaster obsession.

They live in Atlanta, Georgia with their cat, Tina, who does not pay rent.

Sign-up for the newsletter for book updates, special offers, and VIP exclusives!: julieoliviaauthor.com/newsletter

facebook.com/julieoliviaauthor

instagram.com/julieoliviaauthor

amazon.com/author/julieoliviaauthor

bookbub.com/authors/julie-olivia

Printed in Great Britain
by Amazon

19025945R00200